Lightfoot Rising

Mike Demilio

Copyright © 2020 Mike Demilio

All rights reserved.

ISBN: 9798580992914

For my family

This book is dedicated to
David Kendall Rose
February 6, 1967 - November 21, 2020

A brother.
A co-conspirator.
A man of sincere faith.
A friend, always.

Chapter 1

Sunrise

Gordon hunches in a halo of light at his work table, forgotten cigarette in his left hand as his right sketches another line across the page. Through the windows at the end of the loft, the Georgia sky lightens with a winter's dawn. His forearm tenses and relaxes as he works the pencil. Around him on the table are sheets filled with equations, angles and curves generated in three dimensions with a precision that might challenge even the fastest computer. The glow comes from a cellphone resting on top of a whiskey tumbler, casting its tiny flashlight down onto the drawing.

   A woman lies in his bed, mounded in comforters and sleeping amid a tangle of golden hair. Just past the bed, a potbelly stove squats next to one of the upright girders that march across the loft space and support its ceiling. He glances back at the woman and returns to his work. After a few more strokes, he sets down his pencil, moves his phone and drains the rest of the whiskey, then takes one final drag and drops the cigarette into the glass. He lifts the sheet and studies it closely. Smoothing it back onto the table, he opens a phone app and photographs the drawing. He taps an icon on the screen and begins to work the digitized image with his fingertips, smoothing lines and tapping in numbers from his pages of mathematical notes. At last, he puts on a pair of tinted safety glasses and stands holding the phone in front of his face. Ceremoniously, he presses his thumb to the screen.

A deep hum rumbles below the floor, and bluish light begins to rise. Gordon can picture the machinery that lives in the graffiti-covered shipping container outside in the alley, an intricate array that generates blast-furnace temperatures and turns ingots of metal into liquid. The molten material will course up through electromagnetic veins within the two massive pipes that rise from floor to ceiling along the brick wall. The blue light grows, emanating from gaps in a metal sphere held in place by four articulating arms that connect to the pipes. The arms slowly begin to move, separating four rounded plates that form the sphere as a higher-pitched note rises behind the bricks. He closes his eyes and sees the injection mechanism that will deliver the stream of steel to the fingers of light within the sphere. The arms move wider, the plates flexing and spreading to hold the curve of a growing ball of electricity against which Gordon stands in silhouette. He is tall and lean, his hair wild and unkempt. There is a word tattooed on the inside of his right forearm: 'facio.'

He watches as a web of tiny lightning bolts forms within the sphere and sounds cycle up behind the wall like suppressed screams. The arms extend even further. A mist of silvery metal begins to stream from each plate along precise lines toward the center of the glowing orb and take the shape of the drawing on Gordon's paper, its outline coalescing in pulsing bolts of light that draw the mercurial liquid to them. Roughly three feet long, the object oscillates as it grows, rapidly solidifying as the arms twitch back and forth to add material. Within seconds, the arms stop moving and the finished piece hovers within its electromagnetic cocoon.

The whine cycles down. From the surface of a steel shelf below the light sphere, thin rods telescope upward to align perfectly with the shape of the object just millimeters from its surface. He smiles with pride at the word etched into the edge of the shelf: "Shiva." The light grows white, then yellow, orange and red as it fades and the metal form settles gently onto the rods. Gordon lifts it and runs his fingers around its curves, then holds it up to the sunrise and inspects it more closely. He lifts a set of calipers and begins to measure its dimensions, checking their precision against his scribbled calculations.

"Ain't you cold?"

Confused, he turns to see the woman smiling at him from her pillow, and he realizes that he is only wearing shorts and that the fire in the stove has long since died out.

"You didn't look right at the light, did you?" he asks.

"At the what?" She stares at the object in his hands.

"'Cause without safety glasses..."

"Oh. No, I didn't." She brushes her hair away from her face. "Listen, sorry I passed out before we..."

He shakes his head and mumbles, "No big deal. Show ended late anyway."

"Y'all were really good. My ears are still ringin'."

He sets the piece down on the table and steps through the clothes strewn on the floor, past an empty whiskey bottle and an acoustic guitar, slumps onto the bed and gathers his tangle of black hair. His face is angular, with eyes the hazel of old bronze. Around his neck is a leather thong attached to an almond of polished granite. Reaching, he gently moves her hair out of the way and cups the side of her face in his palm.

"What was your name again?"

She laughs and pushes him away. "Least you're honest. I don't know yours either."

Still wearing her t-shirt and underwear, she slides out the other side of the bed and pulls on her jeans.

"Listen," she says, "you're real dreamy and all, but let's just say, no harm, no foul. I generally don't hook up, anyway. Especially with rock stars."

"How about auto mechanics?"

"Them neither."

Gordon smiles back at her and accepts a kiss on the cheek as she leaves. Shouldering into his thermal hoodie, he steps into jeans and a pair of motorcycle boots and clambers down the metal stairway at the far corner of the room. As he walks through the auto shop, he sees his old Yamaha and smiles. Soon, it will be riding season again. The garage sits a hundred feet or so back from the street at the end of an alley slick with melting frost. He walks to the street with his hands jammed in his pockets, his breath fogging as he studies the ground.

Small bells jingle when he pulls the door to Martín's bar. The sun is beginning to stream through the large front windows, playing across the mahogany to a shelf where bottles of brown liquor shine with false innocence. A Georgia Bulldogs decal peeks out from the mirror. Behind the bar, a wiry man grins at Gordon through a grizzled beard, his salt and pepper hair cropped short, deep crows' feet etched into skin like saddle leather. He holds out a fist. Gordon slides onto a barstool with a wince and bumps knuckles in greeting.

"Little brown demons dancing on your head again?" Martín nods back at the bourbon.

"Didn't sleep, is all. But I finished my last test, Tío. Shiva is ready."

Stunned, Martín stares at him for a moment. With a whoop, he vaults over the bar and hugs him, then dances around with his arms in the air. Gordon laughs as Martín sings "Ai yi yi!" so loudly that the families eating breakfast in the back look up. He hugs Gordon again and sits down next to him as Julia, Martín's wife, opens the kitchen door with a look of concern. Martín speaks to her rapidly in Spanish, and her worry vanishes. She rushes around the bar and hugs Gordon's neck. When she finally lets go, Martín beams at him.

"You been working on that machine since I known you, G. Since high school."

"Not that long, but yeah, a long time."

"Vato, we gotta celebrate! Your mother would be so proud of you. She's the only one besides you who ever understood the physics of that thing."

"Tonight, maybe. Now, I have to go see the Stainfields."

Martín's face clouds over, but brightens again with a new

thought.

"Hey, I forgot to tell you! I seen Caroline. She's back here, in Athens."

Gordon's expression freezes. Slowly, he stands and takes a few steps away from the bar. Rubbing his forehead, he walks back to Martín and studies his face as if the answer to something much deeper might be hiding behind his eyes.

"You sure?"

"Yeah man," Martín whispers. "I seen her."

"Where?"

"Walking past the bar." He points. "Right out there. Yesterday."

Gordon stares at the spot outside as if Caroline might materialize at any moment. He looks at the ceiling. The pain on his face prompts Julia to touch him gently on the chest.

"That ain't a good thing?" Martín wonders out loud.

Abruptly, Gordon turns and strides to the door. It tinkles and bangs closed behind him.

"¿Que demonios?" Julia asks.

Martín shakes his head. "Caroline makes him loco. Always has."

There is a grinding roar and Gordon flashes by on the Yamaha, hair whipped back by the wind.

"He may be a genius," Julia says, "but he's always been crazy. She just makes it easier for everyone to see it."

Searing cold blasts Gordon's face and scathes his knuckles. His right elbow dips to roll more throttle as tears stream into his hair, gathering and freezing it into long shafts. He gulps air in spasms. Downtown Athens yields to smaller houses and empty fields as the road cuts like wet obsidian through the gray-brown heartland. His mind empties, yielding to the ferocity of sensation, the pounding of iron and hard rubber and tarmac, the violence of machine and man connected by the thinnest overlap of purpose, a truce struck at the ragged edge of control. Death trails inches from his heels and taunts from beyond his handlebars. In the blur, he can barely see.

A face, then another; father, mother. He wants to close his eyes and see them clearly, but if he does he knows he will join them. He will end. His wrist begins to relax before he is aware that he wants to slow down. The thought forms as the pitch of the motor deepens, the ends of his hair lower and his tears thin enough for him to blink them away. He recognizes the intersection, the angled signpost without a sign, the rotted fence. Downshift, lean. His tires claw into the turn at first, but halfway through the arc they let go. Sudden terror, almost free fall. The motorcycle skitters away and the pavement, no longer an abstraction but a reality against which he must gather and slide, threatens deliverance to a God that he has never understood, as much as he has tried.

Motion ends with the bike slicing into the mud and Gordon's bent knees crashing into its seat, the side of his ribcage bashing the handlebars, his arms wrapping around his bare head and bouncing against the front tire. He bites his own lip. Then he lays still, listening to the idling Yamaha pant beside him like a deranged lover. Scanning his body, he senses the laceration in his side, notes his bruised but unbroken forearms, his raw thigh and hip. The taste of blood. His head, undamaged. Slowly, he rolls to all fours, crouches and stands, reaches down and kills the engine then lifts the bike and sets it on its main stand. It is filthy and scraped and the end of one hand grip is shorn off. When he restored it, he stripped it of things like fenders and mirrors and added the fiber-wrapped pipes and knobby tires, matte paint and wires buried inside the frame tubes, all of which look even better with their new bruises and stains. The steel handlebar mount for his phone protected that device as planned. Under his hoodie, the long slash oozes red across his pale ribs. He lifts a leg over the seat, kicks the engine back to life, toes first gear and rolls on.

The tired ranch cowers on a bare patch of earth, flinching at the judgments of the elite and refined. A mildewed tractor guards an outbuilding with a bowed spine and failing shingles, before a wealth of neglected land that sprawls beyond the small fenced plot. Gordon feels the weight of the place. He knows the trails of habit walked by those who long ago stopped questioning their melancholy routines. Absently, he notes that the sun is climbing in the sky and this makes him think of his town waking up, of people meeting for coffee and shops opening and friends beginning their Saturday routine. He doesn't think of Caroline, but then he doesn't have to, just as he doesn't have to think of the blood in his heart, the bones holding him upright. She is there, always. Her exposure is never a comfortable thing; more, it is an evisceration.

He feels under the tank for the flask his father left when he deployed for his third -- his final -- tour in Iraq and is relieved it's still there. He brushes mud and grit from his torn jeans, from sleeves shiny with the friction of the slide and blackened by tire grime. Blood on his lip tastes like metal. He sweeps hair out of his eyes, inhales and exhales, squares himself to the door, to Wendell Stainfield's father. He wonders why the man is so angry all the time. Tire ruts from the family's gator lead from the garage through a break in the fence and into the fields beyond where, when food money gets short, they take the occasional out-of-season deer to get by. The tracks look fresh. Earlier in March, Gordon replaced the rear differential in the small four-wheeler, and he thinks about that bill now, relieved that he never collected on it, as he steps past the debris in the yard and mounts the concrete stoop.

Inside, a television blares faux-patriotic blather, all split-screen chatterboxes and alarmist chyrons. The usual breathless consensus about 'threats' and 'emergencies' will have Wendell's father worked up if he hasn't already drunk himself to sleep. Gordon knocks and the sound cuts off. The door opens a few inches for a florid face, a vertical line deep and permanent between the man's eyes.

"I ain't got it yet."

Stainfield keeps his left hand hidden behind the door.

"Sir, I'm not here about the bill. No rush on that."

"What is it then?"

In the room behind Wendell's father, Gordon sees a woman

slumped in an armchair, head lolling, semi-conscious. He has met Wendell's mother before. The ridges in her gapped teeth and her blotchy, leathered skin told him she was smoking more than menthols.

"Mr. Stainfield, Wendell has not been to the Lab in a couple of weeks. I wanted to make sure he's okay."

"He's fine."

Gordon hears the thud-clank-clank of a baseball bat dropped on linoleum. Stainfield opens the door wider.

"Been workin' for me since the car broke down. He ain't got no way to get to Athens without it."

"Mind if I take a look at it?"

"We can't pay for the one, much less the other."

"No, don't worry about that. No charge for Wendell's car."

"Ain't *Wendell's* car."

"All the same. Can I take a look?"

"Suit yourself."

The door slams, and the television volume rises again.

Gordon walks to the garage. As expected, there is deer blood on the gator. Next to it sits an old Ford sedan, its vinyl roof shredded to expose metal hoary and red with rust. Gordon slips behind the wheel. Seeing no key in the ignition, he lowers the sun visor, catches the keys and turns it over, the engine screaming urgently but not catching. He climbs out and clocks Wendell ducking behind a corner.

"Hey, bud," Gordon calls to him.

The boy steps out into the open, seventeen, bone thin and hesitant to peek out from under his shaggy ginger bangs.

"I can fix that, no problem," Gordon says. "How you been?"

"Fine."

"Missed you in the Lab."

"Yeah."

"Tell your Pop I'll get Henry out here with the wrecker soon as I can. Meantime, I'll pick you up for class Monday morning."

Wendell brightens. "On the bike?"

"No man, not on the bike. Damn near killed myself on that just now."

Gordon lifts the hoodie to show the four-inch gash, which has bled all the way down to his waistband and soaked into his jeans. Wendell follows and watches Gordon kick the starter and rev it. The curtain inside the front window moves slightly.

"Monday," Gordon says firmly.

He shakes Wendell's hand with mock solemnity, clunks the bike into gear and roars off down the rutted driveway. Wendell watches him go.

Caroline. Here, again.

Gordon rides slowly, as if the limbo of the road could forestall the reality of her. Steam rises from the pavement but the air still holds an edge. Of course she has not left the palm trees and power plays of Silicon Valley for him. Rolling back into their sleepy hometown, he wonders what she might think of it now, and of him. She probably has not thought of him at all. In the alley next to Martín's bar, he looks up at the weathered sign: "G.L. Auto Repair." He taps an icon on his phone to open the door and lets his head hang down.

Chapter 2

Lightning

Church bells ring in Sunday morning, distant and muffled by snow as Gordon puts on his backpack and ducks into the weather. On the bus to the Lab, he scrolls through pictures of Friday night's show posted on social media with the hashtag '#Martins.' The bar has become an institution at the university, music at night and breakfast tacos all day. His screen flashes the usual group selfies, drunken toasts and one or two random views of him playing his hollow-bodied electric guitar and bellowing into the microphone. He is about to close the app when one photo catches his eye: in the background of a group shot, a striking woman with streaky blonde hair leans against the wall and sips a glass of bourbon. Her blue eyes are locked on the stage; amused, intense, almost predatory. If not for the camera flash, she would have remained shrouded in shadows, which is why Gordon did not see her from up there. His skin tingles as he zooms in. Long silver earrings shine against her glowing cheekbones. Gordon looks out the bus window and sees snow on the red tables in front of the burger joint where a little less than five years earlier and not ten feet from that very spot, everything changed. He leans back and closes his eyes.

The doors open, and pinpricks of ice blow in to wake him.

Disoriented, he looks around and realizes where he is, then stands and follows a few students down the stairs. He flips up his hood and trudges past several institutional facades to a two-story steel and glass building. It occurs to him that he may have dreamed the picture of Caroline at the show so his hand closes around the phone in his pocket to check again, but he reconsiders and leaves it there. Turning around to let his backpack touch the security card reader, he bodies the revolving door and steps into the lobby.

"G, how you doin'?"

Gordon smiles at the white-haired African-American man at the desk.

"Mr. Williams, good to see you."

"Snowing, man. Believe this shit? Whole damn town is shut down."

"Except us," Gordon winks.

As he walks past the desk, Mr. Williams leans close.

"He's in there."

Gordon scowls. He lifts his pack to the reader on the interior door, waits for the beep and pulls it open. Inside is a workshop the size of a small basketball court. Across the twenty-foot ceiling are two rows of skylights, dimmed with a rime of snow. Around the perimeter is a series of drill presses, lathes, table saws and other machines, and across the middle of the floor rows of worktables are interspersed with seating areas and whiteboards. On the far wall is a Shiva device identical to the one in Gordon's apartment.

Two middle-aged white men sit over a folder of papers, one well-groomed and hair-dyed in rimless glasses and an executive suit and the other wearing a Purdue University t-shirt. Down the second man's arms, a series of tattoos have melded to form greenish-blue sleeves. His gray hair and beard are trimmed tight and his brow is furrowed behind dark-rimmed glasses. He slaps the table and shakes his head and the executive sits back in his chair. They do not notice Gordon until he drops his backpack.

"G, hey." The tattooed man barely looks up.

The executive turns to Gordon, who extends his hand. The

man considers Gordon's callused palm and clasps it reluctantly.

"Mr. Longmeier," he says solemnly.

"Dr. Carson."

Gordon elbows the other man's arm.

"Stan, 'sup?"

"Money shit." Stan's accent is clipped, Chicago.

"Is the military industrial complex offering us thirty pieces of silver again?"

Stan nods.

"What do we need with all of that?" Gordon asks Carson.

"Well, your 'Maker's Lab' may not need it, but it could help the rest of the university to do a lot of good." Carson patronizes the words 'Maker's Lab.'

"Like what," Gordon challenges, "buy more flatscreens for the locker room?"

"We were thinking of scholarships, Mr. Longmeier."

"For linebackers?"

"For gifted, at-risk students."

Stan puts a hand on Gordon's arm to silence him and addresses Carson.

"You do know the mission of the Lab -- the Lab that I founded with my own funding -- is to serve exactly those at-risk students. People like him." Stan points at Gordon. "Creators, inventors. He was sixteen when he came here. Now he's your cash cow. And we got another one coming back tomorrow. You remember Wendell Stainfield?"

"I'm sorry, I don't."

"He lives way out on the county road. He's seventeen, doing a dual-enrollment here with his high school. His family is... challenging."

"Mom's a tweaker," Gordon interjects.

Carson purses his lips and raises his eyebrows.

"Methamphetamine addict," Stan clarifies. "Perhaps we could offer Wendell a full scholarship. His designs show tremendous commercial potential."

"Professor Malkovich, the board has not yet decided exactly how to allocate the funds."

"So, not scholarships?" Stan challenges.

"As I said, we are considering that. There are many areas of need on campus."

"Do these papers shed any more light on your 'areas of need?'" Gordon pats the folder.

Carson closes the folder and tucks it under his arm.

"These have to do with a confidential proposal from North Industries. We appreciate your, er, 'help' with the Lab, Mr. Longmeier, but this really is a matter for university administrators."

Carson offers each man a handshake. As he walks out, he wipes his hand on his pants leg.

"He's always trying to pimp us out to those goddamn defense contractors," Gordon complains. "What have they ever made except more dead people?"

"Screw it, let's work."

Gordon brightens. "Hey, check this out."

He walks over to the four-armed machine on the wall. A tablet computer is mounted next to it and when he boots it up the splash screen bears a single word, "SHIVA." He scrolls to the drawing he created on Saturday morning and taps it. Slipping on tinted safety glasses, he taps the screen once more and steps back. Behind the wall, the same deep humming cycles up, along with the higher-pitched tone over it. The blue light rises, and soon the finished piece floats above the shelf. Stan peers at it through his own tinted glasses.

"Jesus Christ," he whispers, turning to stare at Gordon. "That looks perfect. You solved it?"

"That was the last hurdle, yeah."

Stan puts an arm around Gordon's shoulders and appraises the gleaming metal shape resting below Shiva's folded arms.

"You know," he says quietly, "this patent is gonna change everything."

Gordon nods but does not smile.

"And that's a good thing." Stan looks to see if Gordon understands.

"Everything..." Gordon whispers.

"You did it, son. It was a helluva long fight but you did it."

Gordon lifts the piece and walks to his station. Hours later, a pang of hunger tells him it is well past dinner time. His plastic cup is choked with cigarette butts and a pile of drawings and documents lays in a semicircle around his laptop. He still wears the safety glasses. Stan is long gone. Gordon sits back, pushes the glasses up to hold his hair back and rubs his eyes. The skylights are black and he needs to eat so he piles the papers onto his laptop and shoves it all into his pack. Outside, he waves good night to Mr. Williams and shuffles through the gloaming to the bus stop where he digs out his phone and scrolls… And there she is.

Damn. It wasn't a dream.

The bus crunches to a stop and hisses its brakes. Gordon flops into a seat, bone tired, his head lolling forward as his eyes close. The motion is soothing. His breathing slows to a sleeping rhythm until suddenly his skin flashes with an electric charge, like a net of thin wires was laid on his body and touched with a battery. It's been nearly five years since he felt this sensation. He looks down the aisle and sees dirty blonde hair, a flash of silver. His stomach flips.

Christ, it's her.

His first instinct is to run.

His second is to wonder why Caroline is on the bus at all. In high school, she hated buses and would walk or ride her bike to Clarke Central every day. He always thought she got her disdain of public transportation from her father, who had inherited one car dealership and built it into a chain across rural Georgia. His shameless self-promotion made Caroline blush, but when it resulted in a successful run for Congress even she had to admit that she had underestimated him.

Gordon and Caroline had been teenage townies, running through the outskirt neighborhood where their two bungalows sat catercorner from one another. Two families, glued by proximity and station and common cause. Gordon's mother, Emily, professor of physics at the university. Gordon's father, George, auto mechanic and national guardsman. George was called to serve ride-along duty -- convoy support -- on supply runs from Baghdad to Fallujah to Ramadi and back. One night, two soldiers knocked and whispered to Gordon and Emily and left. Sixteen and fatherless, he learned for the first time what an improvised explosive device was and what it could do to a family. Caroline held him as they cried until they fell asleep on the couch.

On the bus, she looks over her shoulder and sees him slumped in his seat. She saunters back to his row and sits directly across from him. He looks her over. She holds a soft leather satchel that contains a MacBook, a Moleskine and a thick textbook.

"Fancy bag," Gordon observes.

"A gift."

"Teaching now?"

"Kind of. Doing a Masters in Social Psychology."

"Palo Alto didn't pan out?"

"No, it did. But I wanna do that work here."

The bus slows.

"This is me," Gordon mumbles.

He grabs the seat in front of her and stands. She takes off her glove and touches his hand and the lightning flashes across his skin again. Her wince tells him she felt it too.

"Gordon," she says softly, "I'm sorry. I shouldn't have left the way I did. I didn't know Emily--"

He holds up his hand to silence her and looks away. When the bus stops and he turns back, she sees his tears. He hops down to the sidewalk. The doors close and he does not look back.

In his apartment, Gordon lights the potbelly stove and scoops some leftover chicken and rice into an iron skillet. Standing over his simmering meal, he feels that familiar emptiness again. Caroline was his best friend, the girl across the street from as early as he could remember. His first kiss, his first... everything. When she left for California, it was like an amputation. He sees his reflection in the tall window; his wild hair, his blue mechanic's work shirt, his hard hands darkened by labors of love... so ill-suited to pampered prosperity. And now so ill-suited to her.

"The hell with it," he says to the window.

Not one more second of brain time on this.

Along one side of the loft are a series of cabinets that rise to the ceiling, accessed by a heavy metal library ladder. Gordon rolls the ladder to the third set of doors, climbs and opens one to reveal a neat bookshelf of bound volumes and periodicals. He runs his finger along the bindings and stops at a translated version of a Russian physics journal. He flips it open to confirm that the article he wants is there, then climbs down, retrieves the skillet and sits at the island, eating with the spatula as he reads. After a moment, he digs his laptop and drawings out of the backpack and starts making notations and adjustments to his designs as the rest of his dinner grows cold. A few flakes of snow flutter silently past the window. His head lolls, then drops onto his forearm. At some point he wakes up long enough to eat a few more bites, stumble out of his jeans and fall into bed. Within minutes, the journal drops onto his face as he falls asleep again.

The bright March sky was splashed with clouds and while Athens was not yet green and leafy, it was redolent with promise. On spring break from his freshman year at the University of Georgia, Gordon stood on the sidewalk beside red metal benches where people ate heaps of food from tinfoil wrappers. He was peaceful, even happy, a Hiroshiman blind to the force about to vaporize him. At T-minus-zero, he turned his head and saw Caroline crossing the street toward him, walking with his friend Warren and wearing black shorts small enough to show off her tanned thighs. Sun glossed her hair and flashed in her eyes. He had not seen her since June, and she looked like a different person. She held her shoulders back, rippling at him like a tigress, drawing him in and terrifying him at the same time, so familiar and yet utterly foreign. The air around her shimmered and blurred everything but her face, her body, her... Her.

Gordon had not known the presence of a woman could challenge him like this, or that his childhood friend might be that woman. That the sight of her, the immediate and permanent need for her, could shatter him into a million fragments that would only gather from this point forward into a form that she might find worthy; that would either be worthy of her or stay shattered forever. He saw her that day as if for the first time, as if she had risen like a redwood from a pot of geraniums slowly blooming by his back door for a decade.

Her easy smile evinced no changes on her side, no fragmentation of her own. To her he was still simple old Gordon. He contemplated the unremarkable thing that was Warren, oblivious to or perhaps equally decimated by the apotheosis of the feminine with whom he dared to 'grab a burger.' Prior to that moment Gordon had very few concrete ambitions, but in the wake of her scent he wanted desperately to sack Rome, to cure cancer, to kick moon dust. He had become a massive, gibbering compass and she his magnetic north. He spent most of the next week in a state of shock, the hollow she had made of him not yet missing its mass. Like a ghost unaware it had died, he drifted to the Lab, tinkered on projects and concepts and prototypes and played his guitar at Martín's, wasted on the emotions to which Caroline's sudden and unexpected magnificence had condemned him.

The following Saturday she and two friends walked into Martín's, where Gordon sat at the bar with Martín and Julia. Martín Espada was in his forties, a former priest who had left the Catholic church for love and eventually found his way back to Christianity for the same reason. He and Julia had migrated from Mexico City fifteen years earlier, shortly after they married, and with a few dollars he had saved they bought the bar. By day, Martín served drinks and tacos and heard confessions across the polished mahogany. At night, he was the drummer in a cover band. When he needed a guitarist, he recruited the wild son of his first and best friend in Athens, George Longmeier, who had recently died in Iraq. Gordon had fronted the band ever since.

That night, Martín and Julia were having a spirited debate about the combination of spices used in a proper mole sauce, while Gordon listened to his ear buds and scribbled on a small piece of paper.

Too loudly, Gordon interrupted. "Ever notice that 'Migra' leads almost directly into 'I Want Candy' by Bow Wow Wow?"

"Jesuchristo!" Martín exclaimed. "Do not mention Santana in the same breath as that pop shit."

Gordon pulled one of his ear buds. "I'm telling you, we should play it."

"You should," Caroline said.

Gordon turned and saw her. Her jeans did even more for her figure than her running shorts had. A charcoal t-shirt hugged her breasts in a way Gordon had to work to ignore.

"We don't have a female singer."

"Sure you do."

She smiled and tipped her head a little.

Gordon gave her an appraising look. He turned to Martín and handed him the ear buds.

"Here, you can pick this up in a few seconds. I already know the guitar. The guys can put their horns down and have a beer."

"And you think little Caroline can sing it?" Martín asked.

Julia looked at Caroline with a warm smile and informed Martín in Spanish that she was not so little anymore.

"Oh yeah, Tío," Gordon said. "I'm pretty sure there's nothing she can't do now."

Later, near the end of Santana's scorching indictment of the border patrol, Gordon waved Caroline onto the stage. She danced, comfortable in the glare and sanguine about the braying of the drunken boys in the audience as Martín hammered his drums and Gordon picked through the final jam to wind down the song. Before it could end Gordon shifted the tune and played with the beginnings of 'Candy.' Martín's hands flew around the timpani with the new, faster beat, so Gordon got out of the way and nodded for him to keep it going. The crowd began to pulse with Martín's energy. When at last Gordon launched into the iconic opening riff, he smiled at Caroline and she stepped to the mic, working the moment, her voice strong and clear, leaning close to Gordon as she sang. At one point, she put her palm to his face. He felt a surge of electricity course over the surface of his skin like a fine sheet of lightning. His guitar screeched. She pulled her hand away as if it had been shocked. No one seemed to notice so they kept going, finishing to a raucous ovation. She touched his arm, kissed him lightly on the cheek and took his hand to hop back down from the stage... and no lightning. By the end of the night she had forgotten it completely. But Gordon had not. When the set was over, he walked directly to the bar *and started drawing furiously on the back of a concert flyer; a network of circuits, then another, all spiraling toward a center point where they formed a sphere.*

The Russian physics journal is stuck to Gordon's face when he wakes up. He reaches up to move it, but his hand is blocked by something hard. Sensing a draft around his body, he opens his eyes and turns his head and the journal flutters down to the bed far below. Rigid with panic, Gordon begins to flail. His hands hit the metal rafters as his feet kick air, and instinctively he grabs the rebar and pulls it close. He looks down at the island, at his laptop and the skillet of chicken and rice, at his jeans by the bed, at the journal open on top of the comforter. Hands trembling on the cold metal, shivering in a t-shirt and briefs, breathing fast and shallow, he is alone, nearly naked and pinned to the ceiling -- by nothing at all.

Chapter 3

Lucidity

Gordon starts to laugh. He knows he is lucid dreaming even though he has never experienced a lucid dream before. Tentatively, he lets go of the rebar with one hand. His torso and legs remain stuck to the rafters. He loosens his grip with the other hand but senses no change in his stability. Grabbing the rebar with both hands again, he pushes away from the ceiling with his feet. His body swings down but then slowly drifts back up until it is stopped once more by the ceiling.

"Cool! This feels so *real*."

He gathers his feet under him and works himself forward until he is effectively sitting upside down on one of the rafters. His hair hangs down like it is not subject to the same rules as the rest of his body. Gathering courage, he puts his arms straight over his head and pushes off. His body drifts as if through water until the minor force of his push is expended, then floats back up. His heels hit the ceiling, then his back, then his head. The physical rules of the dream are becoming more clear to him. Feeling chilled by the draft, he gathers himself again, aims for his jeans and pushes harder off the ceiling but his arms are not braced for the impact. They buckle and his nose smashes against the floor. As he rises, he realizes he forgot to grab his jeans.

While he cups his bleeding nose, his back bumps hard against the metal beams and he decides that he does not like this dream very much anymore. He closes his eyes and imagines a new one.

A sunny day. Summer. Maybe a beach.

When he opens his eyes, the first thing he sees is a bright red stain on the white pages of the physics journal, one drip wending its way down the length of the crease. Gordon lifts his shirt and wipes a thick handful of blood, his back tense as his bare skin grazes the rafters. Absently, he wonders how much heat his apartment must be losing without proper insulation, but gradually he is pulled back to the moment by the terrifying awareness that this is not a dream.

"Shit. *Okay.* Okay. *Shit.*"

His mind races. He needs to get away from the cold roof, get some clothes on, get... what? A doctor? A priest? Jesus, get *down*, for a start. He bunches for another push, this time aiming at the bed. When he hits the comforter he grabs it with both hands but it begins to slip away from the bed. He hangs onto the blanket as he floats up again and this time he notices that he does not rise to the ceiling as quickly as he did before.

The added weight matters. Okay, think.

He grabs a corner of the comforter with one hand and slides the other down the length of its edge until he is holding the other corner, which he stuffs between his feet. Extending himself out long with a corner at each end of his body, he pushes off the ceiling with an elbow to start a flat roll. The comforter winds around him. Coming to rest again, he notices the library ladder and the four-foot gap between the ceiling and the top rung. He frees one arm from the comforter and begins to pull himself along the rafter toward the cabinet wall.

At the ladder, he once again pulls his feet up, presses them against the ceiling and with some regret lets the comforter fall to the floor. Slowly, he straightens his legs, reaches down for the top rung and works his way hand over hand to the ground. He hooks one arm through the ladder and gathers the comforter with the other. It seems like a very long way to his jeans where his cell phone hides in a front pocket. For a moment, he sits very still.

What in the absolute fuck is going on?!

Monday. I'm supposed to pick up Wendell... send the wrecker for the car... help Stan fight off the military industrial complex... work with students... file the patent application on Shiva... Stand up without drifting away.

He scans the room for ideas. If he can dive sideways, maybe he can scoop up his jeans, but to get there without floating up will take a hard push and there's a brick wall just a few feet beyond the pants. He turns around and opens the cabinet behind him. A few pairs of jeans hang above a pile of boots and sneakers, a few random tools and a box of shotgun shells. He grabs the pants and works them on with one hand. He pulls out his heavy motorcycle boots, puts them on and relaxes the muscles in his legs. They rise, slowly now. He scoots himself and the ladder across to the next set of doors, digs out a sweatshirt and puts it on. His eyes find the cabinet nearest the stairway. He scuttles over to it and takes out a climbing rope, then hooks a leg around the ladder and plays out half of the rope and ties a loop around his waist. He slides the ladder back to its original spot, eyeballs the distance to the jeans that contain his cell phone and ties that length of rope to the ladder. He lowers down to the bottom rung, squats up his legs and pushes hard at the jeans.

He sails along the floor, hands ready, but just as he is about to grab the pants the rope pulls taut and whips his face and arms to the ground. He is momentarily stunned. The sudden tug pops the top wheels of the ladder off their track and leaves it yawing on one bottom wheel. He claws at the jeans and pulls them close as his feet kick for a floor that is already out of reach. With sickening helplessness, he watches the heavy ladder pirouette and start to fall directly at him. Drifting upward in a slow somersault, he curls into a ball against the impact. Everything goes dark.

The dream involves hammering, or cannons maybe. Gordon feels every pounding blast at the base of his skull. He opens his eyes and realizes that someone is knocking violently on his door.

"Gordon!" Martín hollers. "You are late. Were you drinking again? Stan called me."

"I'm awake," Gordon croaks. "Please help me!"

Martín's key chatters in the lock and he climbs the metal stairs. With a stream of Spanish exclamations, he surveys the wreckage caused by the fallen ladder: skillet dumped on the floor, a corner of the soapstone countertop broken off, the ladder itself on Gordon's bed and most disturbingly, Gordon suspended fifteen feet above it, tethered to a rope, supine and bleeding from the head and nose, barely conscious. Martín stops talking, walks over to the rope and slowly, very cautiously, touches it. He sees Gordon sway a little in midair and crosses himself, praying rapidly in Spanish.

"Tío, please," Gordon rasps. "Help me."

"How, son? What can I do?"

"Pull me down."

Martín grabs the rope and begins to pull very gently. Feeling little resistance, he reels Gordon in and holds him in a bear hug.

"Who did this to you?" Martín's face clouds. "I will tear them apart!"

"No, it's not like that. I don't know what's happening but I'm pretty sure I did this to myself."

"Tell me what you remember."

Gordon recounts as much as he can, from waking up with the journal on his face until the moment the ladder began to fall. Martín's eyes are wide. He pulls a stool closer and begins to set Gordon down but Gordon stops him.

"I'll just float up again." He looks around the room. "Tie me to the island. That post there."

Martín does this. Gordon's feet hover a few inches off the ground as he takes his phone out of his jeans and sees three missed calls from Stan. First, he calls Wendell's house and gets no answer, then he calls Stan and apologizes for his absence, then gives him Wendell's address and asks him to drive Wendell to the Lab.

Martín raises his eyebrows. "And now?"

The hand holding the phone begins to shake. Gordon covers it with his other hand and tries to steady his breathing.

"Now... I need to gain some weight."

Before Gordon gave up entirely on his infrequent workouts, he dabbled in a free weight phase. Luckily, the plates came in handy down in the garage so he saved them. In a few trips, Martín is able to bring up a hundred pounds of assorted sizes. Gordon begins to load his backpack, testing the weight against his hovering body. He is surprised that it only takes fifty-five pounds to keep him on the ground, but the pack leaves him top-heavy. At first, he shuffles across the rug, hesitant to lift his feet, but gradually he begins to understand how to balance himself properly. He reties the climbing rope so that it will tether him to the island but allow him plenty of slack. Martín busies himself replacing the ladder on its track and cleaning up the spilled food. Neither man speaks. Martín makes a trip out to the wood pile, fills the stove and lights the fire. Eventually, there is no more work to distract them so they stand at opposite ends of the island, silent and strange.

"Iron," Gordon says at last.

"What...?"

"That's probably the heaviest workable metal I can get," Gordon explains. "I can coat it with a layer of steel to keep it from rusting." He grabs a pencil and paper. "Here, like this." Gordon starts drawing ovals on the page that begin to connect into the shape of a vest, then leggings. "We could print up a hundred of these little guys in a few minutes. Maybe I can string them together with monofilament or embed them in some kind of rubber sheathing."

Martín walks over to him and puts his hand on Gordon's forearm. Gordon stops drawing and looks at him.

"I have to solve this," Gordon says urgently. "I'm weightless, and I need a better source of gravity. I can't waddle around in this--"

"Son. What is happening?"

Gordon's composure cracks.

"I don't know," he whispers, eyes tearing. "It's like a weird dream, only it's not. I keep trying to understand what could have done this. I thought maybe the electromagnetism in Shiva's sphere? But Stan, the kids, dozens of people have been around that and they're fine. So...?"

"Do you want me to call a doctor?"

"Oh yeah. Let's bring in the local anti-gravity specialist."

He sees the wounded look in Martín's eyes and softens.

"I'm sorry. You didn't deserve that."

"It's okay. This is... frightening."

"Well, I guess I'm lucky it didn't happen when I was outside."

Gordon rubs his forehead and touches the bloody spot at the base of his skull.

"Could have been a lot worse without a ceiling to stop me."

"I think we should pray," Martín says softly.

"Stop it."

"This is a miracle."

"It's not!"

"How else you gonna explain it? Do you think it has something to do with her?"

"With Caroline? Why do you say that?"

"¿Quién sabe? Who knows?"

Gordon stares at him. He remembers the way she removed her glove to touch him, the way the electricity coursed through him again. It was that same lightning sensation he had when they first played on stage together, the feeling that had made him think of the original design for Shiva. He had named the device after the four-armed Hindu god of creation, but Shiva was also known as a destroyer. Could he have harnessed a power that was beyond his control? Once again, he rubs his forehead and looks at Martín as if an answer lay just behind the older man's eyes, as if everything would make sense if he could just bore in there and see it for himself. It is a look that Martín has seen many times, when Gordon brings the full weight of his intellect to bear on a problem and still comes up short. Gordon shakes his head and looks at the ceiling.

"What could Caroline possibly have to do with this?"

Chapter 4

Wizard

Gordon stands in the sun. A thin beard has darkened his jawline, and his hair is even wilder and more unkempt than usual. Around his feet is a halo of cigarette butts. A fourth is locked between his knuckles, one puff from joining the others. At the end of the alley is the sidewalk and the entrance to Martín's. He has been staring at this stretch of wet pavement for almost an hour, ever since Wendell's father came to pick up the car that took Gordon the better part of a week to repair since he would only leave his apartment for a few brief moments each day to work on it.

There is no rational reason to fear the walk, he knows. His backpack is secure, even strapped at the waist. Tucked in his hoodie is a fifteen-foot coil of yellow nylon rope, one end tied to the harness he wears over his jeans and a metal hook on the other end. Worst case, he can snag a telephone wire or maybe a tree branch before he floats away. He knows he has done everything he can to mitigate the risk but this is a different world now. Who's to say the rules will not change again?

He drops the butt and takes one step, and then, another. Then, he runs all the way to Martín's door where he white-knuckles it open and scoots inside. Martín sees him and spreads out his arms.

"G! Welcome back to the living! *Ai* papi, you look like shit."

Gordon gives him a tight smile and nods impatiently. He scrambles onto a barstool, and unzips his hoodie. The rope uncoils to the floor as he grabs the rolled sheaf of paper tucked into his pants. He smooths it flat and leans over it with a pen in hand. Martín comes over. The top page is filled with tiny notations and as it curls he can see that the back of that page and the front of the next one are similarly covered.

"Take a look at this," Gordon implores him. "I need to make sure I'm not missing anything."

"What are all these times?"

"This is my last three months, all meals, events, people, everything I can remember."

"Why?"

Gordon looks at him with wild, bloodshot eyes.

"How else am I gonna solve this thing?!" His hand shakes as he tries to cram another note between two of the items. Martín covers Gordon's hand with his own and looks him in the eye.

"You're not, son. This is not a science problem."

"It *has* to be!"

"No, science is based on things people have observed. Nobody has ever seen this before."

"Some people say they have. But they were... unreliable."

"Stan told me he talked to you." Martín's gaze is searching.

"Yeah, he tried to come by a couple of times."

"I would have, too," Martín says quietly.

"I know." Gordon looks pained. "I'm sorry I told you to stay away. Look, I get the whole God thing, I really do. Y'all can sleep at night. That's beautiful. And maybe it's true, but it doesn't really help me now."

Gordon takes out his cigarette pack, realizes it's empty and squeezes it into a tight ball. He pegs it at the garbage can behind the bar. Martín hands him a glass of orange juice.

"Listen," Gordon continues. "Whether or not this happened because God willed it, I don't care. That doesn't interest me. A tornado is a tornado, whether you're Dorothy or Jesus or whoever. Whatever reason you have for it, it's just wind blowing extremely hard so you have to deal with it. I just have to deal with this."

"Rotating."

Gordon whirls aggressively to face the voice. It is Stan.

"Wind rotating, not blowing," Stan corrects. "Thermal vortex, all that."

Gordon turns to Martín. "I thought we agreed not to tell anyone."

"He didn't," Stan says. "It's not like you to miss a whole week without a call."

Gordon stares. "A week?" he whispers.

Martín walks into the back room. He returns with a plate loaded with food.

"Gordon, eat."

Stan leans close to Gordon. "What is it, drugs? Booze? I can get you some help."

Gordon looks at Stan for an uncomfortable moment and bursts out laughing. He stands up.

"Come on. I gotta show you something."

"First, you eat." Martín's tone is not negotiable.

Gordon sits back down and digs in. As he is eating, a large delivery truck pulls up and blocks the sun from the front windows. It reverses and begins beeping into the alley. Gordon drops his piece of bread, gathers the rope and bolts for the door. When Stan asks where he is going, he hollers over his shoulder.

"Pig iron!"

The apartment is a wreck. Half of the cabinets are open, tools and random mechanical items scattered across the floor. A vice is bolted crudely into the oaken table top, wood shavings still piled around the holes. Its teeth pinch a two-inch oval of black metal with hooks at one end and holes at the other. Similar ovals of varying sizes and thicknesses lay scattered on the table around it. A scuba vest has been cut and cannibalized for its rubber and sewn into foot-long tubes. Gordon unties the yellow rope from his harness and drops it on the floor as he walks to the table. Stan pauses at the top of the stairs and twangs the climbing rope that runs the length of the loft space. He fans the air.

"Jesus, what died in here?"

Gordon walks to the window and throws it open. He grabs a flattened pack of cigarettes from a drawer by the oven, fluffs it up and offers one to Stan, who declines. He lights one on the burner and blows the smoke into the room, spreading it around with his hands.

"Uh, not helping." Stan sets his backpack down on a chair and walks over to the Shiva unit, then to the table where he appraises the debris. "So what are you working up? A weighting system?"

Gordon has been fiddling with the metal oval in the vice grip. He freezes. "Saturday!" Frantically, he takes out the sheets of paper and scans back through the dates. "It was a week ago Saturday that I laid down the bike. How the hell did I forget about that?"

"Okay, Tornado Boy, can you maybe rewind to before the flying monkeys ate your brain and tell me what the hell is going on?"

"You're gonna wanna sit down."

Stan sits on a barstool and Gordon stands by another. He opens his jacket. For the first time, Stan notices the climbing harness. Gordon unclips the large carabiner that is attached to the barstool and clips it onto his harness. He walks over to the rope, clips into it and lowers his pack and hoodie to the floor. As his feet rise from the hardwood, Stan gasps and leans away from him. Gordon floats up until he is horizontal, held there by the anchor point at the center of his body.

"Flying monkeys, huh?"

"What the...?" Stan whispers.

He walks over and looks closely at Gordon's back and his sides and up at the ceiling, then walks from head to toe and back again waving an arm between Gordon and the rafters above. He runs a finger along the waistband of the harness, then looks up yet again. Stepping back, he reaches and shoves Gordon's shoulder, sending him pivoting in a circle. Stan notes that Gordon's arms are floating by his sides, loose and relaxed, rising to the natural limit that his pectoral and shoulder muscles will allow. Gordon's knees bend slightly and his legs also seem relaxed.

"Completely weightless," Stan says softly.

"Just like zero G."

"Except the hair..." Stan lifts a strand and drops it.

"Unaffected. Blood too. I had a little accident and bled onto an old journal from way up there." He jerks a thumb at the ceiling.

"When did this start?"

"Monday night."

"And what might have--?"

"On the table." Gordon points at the papers. "Everything that's happened. Goes back three months. Except for that bike wreck. I completely blanked on that."

"So this started on Saturday then?"

"No, that had to be an anomaly. Everything after that, all night, all next day, was just like usual."

"Can you think of any other anomalies?"

"Well, when I was a kid I used to run really fast and jump and float across the lawn. I'm pretty sure it was a dream, but it's really vivid in my memory."

"Yeah, I've heard other people say that, too. Never seen a kid do it, though."

Gordon holds the rope and flips himself upside down, grabs his backpack and jackknifes his legs down so his feet touch the ground. He lifts the pack straight up and puts it on, then unclips from the harness. Crossing to the table, he lifts one of the ovals and shows it to Stan.

"Yeah, so I think iron in a steel casing would be fine," Gordon says.

"For what?"

"Gen two of this." Gordon thumbs his shoulder straps. "Body weight."

"Hey," Stan says quietly. "And I know you're doing exactly what I would do if... Jesus, this is nuts. But, have you taken a moment and thought about what this means?"

"You sound like Martín now."

"No, not that way. Not like miracles or anything. Just in terms of evolution. Maybe this is a genetic mutation. You said 'gen two.' Maybe you're gen one of People two-point-oh."

"That's as good an explanation as I can think of." Gordon smiles. For the first time in days, he can feel himself relaxing, comforted by Stan's rational responses. Then, his brow tightens. He grabs his forehead and rubs. "But it doesn't keep me from floating up to a frigid death."

"Okay." Stan lays a hand on Gordon's shoulder. "Let's get Shiva going on those ovals. I see your plan there, a vest and some leggings. Good to keep the weight lower on your body, more stable. Also, you should put some on your arms to help maintain proprioception."

"How did you know that was an issue? It really freaks me out when I wake up and I don't know where my arms are."

"I read about astronauts once, how they had issues with that in zero gravity. Even a little bit of arm weight should remind your brain of where your hands live."

"We can scale down the leggings and do them for my arms."

"Easy, yeah." Stan looks at Gordon, suddenly more serious. "Tomorrow I'd like to draw some blood and have Ravi see what's up with your DNA, if you don't mind."

"Guess when you're married to a geneticist you start seeing double helixes everywhere."

"Yeah well, he probably sees defense contractors in his sleep. Lord knows I've been bitching about them long enough."

Gordon turns the oval piece around and studies it. He is looking at the small loops at the end of it.

"Hey, I just realized Shiva can do these in sheets. Let me show you." He draws an enlarged view of an oval with rings on all four sides. Then, he draws ovals with rings that interconnect with all four sets of rings. As he draws, Stan looks over his shoulder. "See, we can just fabricate around the negative spaces between the loops and print them already interlocked. No assembly at all."

"Actually," Stan corrects him, "you can do the whole vest in one shot. Not just sheets."

"Yep, I see it. You can scan my torso with that app you coded for the car build."

Stan takes out his phone as Gordon clips back into the barstool and takes off the backpack and his shirt.

"Whoa, what happened there?" Stan winces at the scar on Gordon's ribs.

"From the bike wreck."

Stan walks around Gordon and captures images of his torso and arms. Gordon rolls up his pants for the leg scans, then flips open his laptop, imports the scans and starts to mock up the design. Stan walks toward the stairs, raising his phone to his ear.

"Hey, don't even tell Ravi right now," Gordon calls to him.

"I know," Stan says, twisting an invisible key to lock his mouth shut.

Gordon's calculations tell him the vest will weigh about forty pounds. He tweaks the designs for the leggings and arm weights to bring the total to sixty. He looks up and sees Stan still on the phone so he continues to run through some other options on his design screen. Stan points at the phone and shakes his head as he walks downstairs. After about twenty minutes, Gordon hears him climb back up.

"You know," Gordon says, "that crash couldn't have been weightlessness."

"Why?"

"Well, the bike wouldn't slide. It would roll over the other way. It would have gone upright and just fallen or drifted off the road."

"You're right."

"If anything, it was too much weight pushing sideways on the tires at too acute of an angle. The shear overcame the friction of the rubber."

Stan looks at the screen over Gordon's shoulder.

"Hang on." Stan points at one section of the rendering. "You know you can just do a multi-layer weave of this loop sequence and skip the oval element altogether. Kind of like a thick wool sweater made of metal. Like chain mail."

"Kind of like this?" Gordon tabs to a different screen.

"Yeah, like that."

"I ran it through the calcs, and the density is not high enough to hold the weight I need. Sucks though. Woulda been a lot more comfortable than this rig."

Gordon flicks the screen away and brings up another one.

"But as I was doing it, I got this idea for a fused weave of interlocking pyramid shapes, which I scaled way down. Like, way waaaay down. I measured that model against the molecular numbers for titanium. Turns out we can still hold rigidity at a scale small enough to allow an equal volume of photons to pass through."

He looks up at Stan, who seems skeptical.

"Nothing to do with weighting my body," Gordon clarifies. "I was just thinking we might be able to print a sheet of transparent titanium."

"Like that Star Trek movie?"

"No, they did aluminum. Titanium would have better rigidity."

"Dude, seriously? You did this in twenty minutes?"

Gordon smiles and takes two pairs of tinted safety glasses from his pack. He puts one on and hands one to Stan, then taps the screen. Downstairs a low thrumming begins and a higher note starts to spin up. Across the room, glowing blue lines form on the metal sphere, widening and becoming more intense as the ball of blue light begins to grow.

"Not bad for a delinquent townie, huh?"

"Your words," Stan grins, "not mine."

Chapter 5

Departures

The socks feel a little weird on Gordon's arms, but the bare metal would have been worse. He smiles at the woman behind the register, scoops up his big bag of dri-fit gear and heads for the door. The vault of blue sky above him is no longer terrifying. His weight feels even and solid, his strides confident if slightly heavy. The vest rides snug against his torso, velcroed together under his work shirt and hoodie. For the first time in a week, he feels almost normal.

Almost.

He decided to take one more day away from the Lab to adjust, to practice moving, mostly just to clear his head and regain some equilibrium. And to shower. He feels as if he has recovered from a flu. The jostle of pedestrians along Broad Street feels foreign to him, their tempo quick and his slow and halting. Mild agoraphobia drives him around the corner and back to Martín's. He is nearly there when he sees a familiar head bobbing toward him in the crowd.

Caroline.

She is looking down at her phone. He ducks into an alcove and presses against the door. As she walks by, he holds his breath, watching her hair bounce along the angle of her cheek, wishing he could see her eyes but relieved that she is not looking at him. When she smiles at her screen, he feels the impulse to run to her, to hug her and make everything just like it was before she left for California. But when he thinks of who she must be smiling at, the feeling dies.

In the apartment, he tosses his shopping bag onto the table and sits down. The optimism he felt about his progress on the mobility problem has vanished. In its place is a darkness he does not understand. For most of his life, Caroline has been there to share everything, good and bad. She has had relationships and he has too. When they were not otherwise committed, they have come together physically. It seemed like a rhythm that would just go on, if not forever then at least a while longer. Yet he never thought of it as love, until now.

He notices a manila folder on the chair next to him; the chair where Stan put down his backpack. He picks up the folder and recognizes it as the one that Stan was reviewing with Dr. Carson, and opens it and begins to read. North Industries is headed by Elliott D. North III, the heir of its deceased founder. North is young and aggressive, a former all-Pac 12 quarterback at Stanford and hero of its most memorable bowl victory in decades, all teeth and hair and twenty-first century edge as he pumps armaments into failing economies around the world. His stated 'mission' is to take warfare out of the trenches and into a more sophisticated future, to "leverage technology into overwhelming military superiority." Which countries might be the ones to achieve that superiority is unclear from the fine print in his brochure. The endowment proposal that North has presented to the university is breathtaking, both in its generosity and its presumptuousness. Gordon feels his neck grow hot.

The funds would not be directed to specific initiatives, but rather would be placed into a general account for use by the university according to priorities determined by its officers, trustees and board members. However, North would be granted a first review and option to invest in any intellectual property developed by university laboratories. Essentially, North would get a free peek up the skirts of any interesting projects happening on campus. A right of refusal would of course be held by the inventor, in accordance with patent law. Unsaid was the fact that the burden of protecting those ideas would also fall to the inventor and as any entrepreneur knows, a patent is only as good as one's ability to defend it in court. The idea that an engineering student could square off with a multinational conglomerate to protect her invention is ludicrous, a disparity that every adult involved in reviewing this proposal would have to recognize.

Gordon tosses the papers aside and picks up his phone. Stan answers on the first ring.

"Did you read it?"

"It's a violation of everything the Lab stands for!" Gordon cries. "We invite these kids in to develop their ideas. We can't risk them being taken advantage of. Shit, Wendell's ideas could change his entire life."

"North doesn't give a rat's ass about Wendell," Stan grumbles. "He wants to use Shiva to make guns, millions and millions of them. That's the whole ballgame, right there."

"I'll call Dan Berrigan. We already have a deal in place, just need to sign the paperwork. Hell, he's already building Shivas. He started as soon as the last test was done."

"Gordon, I'm not sure if Jalen has even filed the patent app yet."

"He has. We're good."

Gordon hangs up and thinks about the first time he met Mr. Berrigan. It was October, junior year. He cringes at his state of mind during that raw period. Throughout his life, people have stepped in to help when he needed it most: Martín, Stan... and Dan Berrigan.

The night of Caroline's duet with Gordon was the first time he could recall seeing such a complex solution so clearly. The electric sensation that spread across his skin had also seemed to reach into his body, at once powerful and very gentle, both broad and extremely precise. He had wanted to run back to Stan's Lab, make a proper drawing of the neural network he had felt and then work up some schematics on the CAD machine, but two shot glasses had appeared on his drawing, placed there by an elegant hand in a silver bracelet. He looked into Caroline's blue eyes and knew he would not be doing any more work that night.

They downed the shots and turned the glasses over on the bar. Gordon reached across and snagged a bottle of bourbon, winking at Martín's raised eyebrows.

"Let's go." He grabbed his drawing as they headed out the door.

"What have you got in mind?"

"Nothing good, I promise you."

She grabbed his arm as they walked along Broad Street, pulling on the bottle. They turned into the campus and reeled a bit as they wandered beneath the trees.

"I want to go up high," she murmured.

"Yes." He leaned down into her hair and nuzzled her cheek. "Indeed."

"Up there." She pointed at a tall building. "Now how do you suppose we get ourselves up there?"

Gordon waved his wand hand. "Wingardium leviosa!"

Caroline smirked at him and took another drink. He touched the brick wall.

"It'll have to be from the inside," he concluded. "Nothing to hold onto here."

"Oh thank God. I was worried you might start climbing."

They suppressed giggles as they walked into the silent vestibule. Ahead was a brightly lit room so they angled along the wall to avoid it. There was a door marked 'Stairs' but it was locked. Gordon looked around and saw a bulletin board and tacked to it, a paper-clipped document. He slipped the clip off the bundle without disturbing it, then took another clip from a similar one. Within a minute he had picked the lock and swung the door open.

"Thieving skills," she whispered. "Very sexy."

They began to climb. At first Gordon had to resist the urge to run up the stairs, but after a few stories he was content to make slow progress. Near the top, Caroline pulled him back by the hair and started to kiss him. He set the bottle down and lost himself in the sensation of her lips, the smell of her hair, the feel of her body through her t-shirt and then under it.

"Let's go all the way," she breathed.

"Yes!"

"I mean, up."

She pointed at the remaining stairs. They smiled as they kissed, teeth and lips touching gently. Neither wanted to end the moment but both wanted to see the stars outside. He looped his arm around her waist and they walked on. At the top, another door blocked their way. Gordon made rapid work of the lock, then took off his shirt and used it to prevent the door from slamming behind them. Caroline pressed her palms to his shoulders as she leaned down and kissed his chest. He lifted her shirt over her upraised arms, then undid her bra, ran his rough palms across her nipples and lightly cupped her breasts. They stood embracing, skin to skin, sensing the dark sky around them. Below, the lights of the campus made them feel even more alive, thrilled by the idea that they might be caught in so strange a place. The roof was flat but very rough, so they stood. Slowly, Gordon undid her jeans and slid them down. She did the same for him. Naked, hands on each other's hips, they barely touched at first, teasing the moment and enjoying sights too long hidden by clothes. When they came together again their bodies pressed and moved in lithe synchrony, finding angles and positions as naturally as if they were built for each other. Leaning on the low wall at the edge and facing the same direction, they panted and gyrated slowly together, glancing out over oblivious students and cars passing by. Sensation blurred it all away as they climaxed together and sank to the hard ground to lay tangled for a long while in the cool night air.

Later as they walked hand in hand along the path, sipping bourbon, Gordon laughed softly.

"What is it?"

"Four arms." Gordon spread his out wide. "While we were up there, we were like one body with four arms."

"We were," she murmured, kissing his neck.

"Like Shiva."

"Who?"

"Never mind." He smiled as he took the bottle and drank again.

Gordon walked Caroline to her parents' house and kissed her goodnight. Walking back across the street, he tried not to imagine what awaited him at home. Eight months earlier, his mother Emily had been diagnosed with Stage Four pancreatic cancer. After winter break, she had stopped teaching. The small bungalow had become her entire world and Gordon a fixture in it. She tolerated his long work hours, his nights playing music at the bar and his drunken benders, but she insisted on breakfast at home. Julia would sometimes bring plates of homemade breakfast burritos and Caroline's mother would stop by with coffee and crumb buns. When Emily's pain became more intense, Martín sent a friend over with a small paper bag. Inside was a Ziploc full of little green gummy bears that confused Emily until the young man explained the dosage in each one. Gordon had never missed one of these breakfasts. Still drunk and watching the light rise over Athens, he knew this morning would be painful but he would be there for her again, as always.

When spring break ended, Caroline went back to California. Soon, there was little room in Gordon's life for frivolity. He studied and went to class, worked at the garage, played sets for Martín and in the remaining hours hunkered in the Lab and drew plan after plan for an electromagnetic system tied to a three-dimensional, computer-assisted manufacturing platform. Gradually, the latter activity subsumed the others. His grades suffered, his work tickets piled up at the garage and his shows happened less frequently. The closer he got to an execution of his vision for Shiva, the further he fell from healthy relationships with everyone, not just Caroline. But the idea of her had penetrated his obsessive mind and remained there. Just one more rev, one more prototype and then he could announce his victory, one that he was certain she would be waiting to celebrate with him. She still kept in touch via text but she was growing apart from him in ways that his creative blindness had not allowed him to see.

When at last he had finished version one, when Shiva thrummed and whined and expanded and gave birth to the first rough metal offspring of its blue fire womb, Gordon's life fell apart.

It was summer and Caroline was home. Earlier that week, Gordon had made a reservation for two, a celebratory dinner that he could barely afford. Before Martín or even Emily, he wanted Caroline to know. He dug one of his father's suits out of storage, shined the dried and cracked dress shoes as well as he could and ironed a shirt. He scrubbed his hands raw and scrubbed some more. Wet hair combed back, he arrived at the restaurant early and made sure the table was perfect, and placed the first object that Shiva had produced in the center of it; a rough steel lightning bolt. He sat watching the door for the next two hours, the hollow in his gut growing deeper and colder until finally he could not hold it any longer. She would not answer his calls. No texts, no replies. When he went to her house, her bedroom window was dark. At the door, her sister feigned ignorance but he would not leave. Finally, exhausted, she looked at him mournfully.

"You really didn't know about the guy from California? They left yesterday."

Three days later, Emily died. Gordon took solace in the knowledge that he was there for her on her last good day. They had spent it in the backyard listening to music and as it grew dark, grilling burgers and singing along with his acoustic guitar. Martín and Julia, Stan and Ravi, Jalen Woods; all of the people closest to him, except Caroline. Many of Emily's oldest friends stopped by the house to drink a beer and enjoy the summer night with her. Gordon hid his desolation from everyone and his triumph from all but Emily, Stan and Martín. It had been Emily's day, and she glowed with gratitude for the love with which she departed this life. In the hours before she passed she lay gray and semi-conscious in bed, grasping loving hands with her thin fingers, recognizing those who had gathered to send her off but unable to speak to them. A tall man with long gray hair had leaned close and kissed her gently on the lips, his dark hand warm against her cheek. Gordon saw her eyes light with recognition and then love as she stared at him. With an effort, she whispered to him and he looked back at Gordon with a curious intensity. He nodded and gently removed the leather thong from around her neck. Attached to it was a polished granite almond with three lines scored into its face. As she watched, he walked to Gordon and then looked back at her. She nodded again so he held the necklace open above Gordon's head, and Gordon allowed the man to put it around his neck. Her smile was both proud and relieved as she raised her hand to Gordon. He rushed to her and held her hand as she lay back and looked at the ceiling, whispering what seemed like a *prayer. He leaned in and strained to hear her thin voice.*

"Never take it off."

The tall man stood behind Gordon and stared at him for a long time as he wept over his mother. Then, the man turned and tapped Martín on the arm and they walked out of the room together. Gordon knelt with his face buried in Emily's pillow, holding her hand as waves of anguish constricted his chest. Suddenly he felt very alone, as if her living presence had ebbed away from the body that lay before him. He stood and looked around the room but the tall man was gone. Later, when he asked Martín who the man was, Martín offered only a vague recollection of a conversation with Gordon's father about a relative who fit the man's description. Perhaps he was Emily's brother? Gordon let it go.

Only after his mother's funeral did Gordon finally crumble. He sat in the living room for an entire day, alternately crying and filling sheets of paper with plans for his short- and long-term future. He ignored Caroline's calls and deleted her texts. He spent long moments with his fist closed around the stone his mother had given him, steeling his resolve. He consulted no one, told no one what he had written and at last when hunger overtook him, he brought the sheets into the backyard and burned them in the grill as he made himself a hamburger. Then, he picked up his phone, searched "Catonsville Tool & Die" and placed a call to Daniel Berrigan, president and chief executive officer.

Chapter 6

Guts

The belt takes all of five minutes to design and print. It weighs roughly twenty-five pounds. Gordon attaches velcro strips to both ends, wraps the belt around his waist and lets his open weight vest fall to the floor. He pulls off his arm- and leg weights along with the nylon sleeves he fashioned from the dri-fit gear and pushes off the ground. Exhausted, he floats across the room, smiling at the precision with which he has calculated his equilibrium weight. He drifts off to sleep.

When the phone buzzes in his pocket, Gordon is confused. His head is resting against the brick wall across from where his body weights lay on the rug. He is used to the odd feeling of waking up weightless but the location is unusual. Remembering the belt, he makes a mental note to put away the climbing rope and harness. He pulls out his phone and sees that he has been napping for twenty minutes. The number belongs to Wendell's father.

"Sorry, Mr. Stainfield, I missed your call."

"Yeah, hey. The Deere ain't turnin' over. Was hopin' you could have a look."

"Sure thing. So how's Wendell liking school?"

"No idea. Boy spends all his time locked in that room makin' drawings. Weird stuff, wheels and such."

"He has a lot of talent."

"Wish he'd get out more, maybe throw a ball around."

"More money in those drawings, I'd say."

"Shoot," Stainfield slurred. "I hope so."

"I'll come by after lunch."

Gordon ends the call and puts his phone away. He is about eight feet off the ground. Reaching back, he pushes sideways against the wall and begins a flat spin that stops when his feet touch. He is about to push off toward the open room when a thought stops him.

What if I woke up out there in the middle?

It would have been worse than when he woke up smashed against the ceiling. He'd have to take off the belt, rise to the rafters and work his way down the ladder. He looks down at his unused bed and makes a mental note to add a couple of pounds to the belt design. Then he adjusts his angle and kicks himself off toward the ladder. He snags it as he floats by and lowers himself to the ground.

"Too damn clever for your own good."

Gordon's resolve to hide his weightlessness from the public is strong, fueled by Martín's concern for his safety and his own awareness of how people react to things they can't explain. However, the novelty of drifting around his apartment is wearing off, as is his fear of losing control and floating up into the stratosphere. His weight systems feel reliable and even his misunderstanding of absolute equilibrium does not scare him. It feels almost like his duty to explore the limits of this condition and yet he knows what will happen to him if people like North find out about it. Gordon gears up with dri-fit sleeves and weights and drops the new belt into the meltdown chute next to Shiva, then takes out his phone and punches Berrigan's number. When Berrigan's assistant says he is in a meeting, Gordon leaves a message.

At Martín's, Gordon eats a quick bite and asks for the keys to the old pickup truck they share. Martín prods Gordon's forearm weights and peers into his collar at the row of shining ovals.

"You are safe, G?"
"I believe so, yes."
"Back to work, then?"
"Business as usual." Gordon snorts. "As if."

At the crossroads where he laid down the bike, Gordon stops the truck and walks the line he took through the turn. Near the apex of the curve, he leans and closes his eyes, trying to remember the sensation of falling, hoping for any insight that might help him solve this. The fall was not like the weightless feeling he has now but it didn't really feel like a normal slide either. Driving on, he bumps the old truck onto the Stainfields' lot and climbs down. He doesn't bother knocking on the front door and instead walks around to the garage where the old tractor is parked.

"Disability ran out."

Stainfield's slippers crunch on the gravel. His potbelly protrudes from an open bathrobe, straining a threadbare Bulldogs t-shirt. The leg holes of his graying jockey shorts hang nearly to the middle of his skinny thighs. "Figure workin' this land's easier than going back to the office and wrecking my arms again."

"Carpal tunnel, you said?"

Stainfield's eyes narrow. "*Doctor* said."

"Well, this thing hasn't run in a long time." Gordon slaps the tractor's narrow hood. "I'm gonna have Henry flatbed it in."

"That guy owes me money."

"What for?"

"Clipped my crepe myrtle with his wrecker when he picked up the car."

Gordon walks over to where a tree stands about ten feet away from the gravel driveway. It has a deep scratch along one side of its trunk.

"Sir, this tree is fine. That won't kill it."

"Oh, so now you're a tree expert?"

Gordon looks at Stainfield for a long moment. "Henry'll be more careful next time."

"I figure that tree is worth at least two hundred dollars."

Stainfield follows Gordon to his truck. Gordon reaches into the cab and comes out with a handful of brochures. The top one features a picture of a hypodermic needle.

"My friend Martín, Reverend Espada, has a group that meets at his church. I thought--"

"What's he, a Mexican spic?"

"He's a former priest. He volunteers, counseling drug addicts."

"'Drug addicts?'" Stainfield hisses. "What's he a dealer on the side? That how he gets his customers, havin' those meetings?"

Gordon feels his blood beginning to rise. He takes a slow, deliberate breath.

"We thought maybe Mrs. Stainfield--"

"Mind your own goddamn business! She ain't no addict. Bad enough you got my kid thinkin' he's better'n us. Leave my damn wife alone!"

Stainfield stalks away and the screen door bangs. Gordon hears the cable news channel begin to blare as the front door slams shut. He lights a cigarette and stares at the house, wondering where in the complex machinations of the human genome the code might exist to draw a mind like Wendell's from loins like Stainfield's. The curtains in the window move slightly, then fall back. Gordon shakes his head, climbs into the pickup and drives away.

Rolling along the county road, he feels his phone buzz. He tosses the butt, rolls up the window and answers it.

"Gordon? Dan Berrigan."

"Mr. Berrigan, thanks for calling back."

"Not at all. What can I do for you?"

"Sir, I hate to ask but we need your help at the Lab."

"Yes?"

"There's a defense contractor, North Industries, making an offer of endowment."

"Okay..."

"It's a very conditional offer, one that gives them the right to review all intellectual property created on university grounds."

"What? That's... unconventional."

"I agree."

"What can I do to help?"

"Well I know I don't have a final patent yet, but I was hoping you could let them know that the work we're doing together is off-limits."

"You know, Gordon, this arrangement we have puts you in a risky position."

"I trust you, sir. No paper can take the place of that."

"Well, I'd be happy to make as much noise about this as you want. Not sure they'll listen to a Mom and Pop tool company over a multinational corporation, but..."

"Sir, you'll be a multinational soon, too."

"You're very confident, son."

After they hang up, Gordon dials Stan.

"On my way there now," Gordon says.

"Is that a good idea?"

"Yeah, I'm fine. Just hung up with Mr. Berrigan. He's gonna rattle his saber a little."

"Good man."

"He is," Gordon agrees.

"I meant you."

Gordon parks the truck in front of the bar. He tosses Martín the keys and snags a biscuit from a platter by the register. Martín pours him a glass of unsweet tea.

"Do you remember when we first met Dan Berrigan?" Gordon asks.

"I do, yes."

"Remember the look on his face when I said no?"

"I remember better his look when you said yes."

The kitchen counter was stacked with empty casserole dishes marked with post-its in Julia's handwriting; the names of the kind people who had prepared dinner for Gordon because there was nothing else they could do. Emily was gone. Gordon was alone and had not yet given himself a chance to process his loss, much less return the dishes. Martín showed Berrigan into the house and guided him to the table where Gordon had neatly arranged three piles of paper, one for each of them. But he was not home.

"He'll be right here." Martín pulled out a chair for their guest. "What can I get you to drink?"

"Thanks Martín, just water for me please."

The back door banged open and Berrigan watched a lean young man with wild hair barrel in. Gordon dropped his backpack, hurried to the table and extended his hand.

"Sir, I'm so sorry."

When he realized how dirty his hand was, Gordon pulled it back and rubbed it on his jeans.

"We had a problem at the garage. They needed my help. I'm very sorry."

"No need, son," Berrigan said. "I just got here myself. Why don't you wash up and we'll have us a chat."

Gordon jogged into the laundry room where a Gojo dispenser was mounted above the slop sink. He scrubbed his hands with a sponge, rinsed, scrubbed again, rinsed again. He ran his wet hands through his hair, frowned at his reflection in the dark window and rushed back into the kitchen.

"Slow down, G," Martín whispered. "Don't be too eager."

Gordon forced himself to walk to the table.

"So, what can an old tool maker like me do for a young hotshot like you?" Berrigan asked.

"Sir, I was hoping you could tell me."

"Well if what you showed us on that video is real, that's one hell of an incredible machine you're working on. We're prepared to purchase what you have, patent or no."

Berrigan opened his briefcase and handed Gordon a check bearing an eight-figure number. Gordon stared at it, inhaled deeply and handed it back.

"Thank you very much, sir, but it's not ready. I can't sell it to you without proving that it works perfectly, and I won't sell it outright. I know what it'll be worth once all of the applications for it are developed."

"It'll take people like you to develop those new applications."

"People younger than me." Gordon smiled at the irony; he was only nineteen. "The material science hasn't even matured yet."

Berrigan folded his hands. "Gordon, would you be open to a development agreement? Kind of a joint venture?"

"Mr. Berrigan, I have researched you. Your grandfather was a machinist, then a tool maker. Your father, then you, worked to build your company from the ground up. You never moved your headquarters out of state, even when you were expanding nationally. You took no venture money, gave away no control. What you earned, you used to grow the business. After your experience in Vietnam, you have quietly donated millions to help your church set up an immigration center for refugees of war. I don't recall reading about a single defaulted loan or disgruntled vendor."

Gordon reached into his pocket and took out a small adjustable wrench.

"And your tools last. I've had this since I was ten years old. So yes sir, I would be open to that agreement. In fact, I've already written it up. You do business the way it ought to be done. I would be proud to partner with you."

Berrigan sat back and appraised the young, long-haired man in the dark blue work shirt, a red script 'Gordon' in a white oval on his chest. Just below his rolled sleeve there was a strange word tattooed on his arm. In his quiet way, Gordon had just spelled out the sum total of forty years of hard work and disciplined integrity.

"I wish my sons understood those things," Berrigan said quietly.

Berrigan reached out his hand to Gordon, who shook it firmly. After an hour of discussion, they had sketched the major contours of a deal. Gordon had two specific additions that were not negotiable: that the company purchase the block of buildings that encompassed Martín's bar, the garage and the apartment spaces above them, and deed them to Martín, and that it commit to funding the Lab at the university. After silently waiting out Martín's objections, Gordon looked at Berrigan. When the older man asked him why he wanted things written that way, he sat back and looked at the pictures on the wall. There was one of his mother standing at her lectern at the university and one of his father with Martín in the alley between their two businesses. He recalled the many hours that Martín had spent with him after his father had died, coaxing him away from the streets and into Stan's Lab

where everything had changed. Unconsciously, he touched the word tattooed on his right forearm as he looked Berrigan in the eye.
  "It's in my blood."

"Berrigan put a lot of faith in me that day."
  Gordon slides off his barstool and puts on his backpack.
  "I think you put more faith in him than he did you, G." Martín says. "Shiva will make him a very wealthy man."
  "Machines can't do that by themselves. It takes a person with integrity and vision. That machine in the hands of a different kind of man is a frightening idea."
  "North?"
  "Yeah," Gordon sighs.
  Martín walks around the bar and gives Gordon a hug. "What you build, it is beautiful. Don't ever stop this work, son."

It is nearly two o'clock, but Gordon wants to check in with Stan and see how Wendell and the other students are doing at the Lab. The sunshine persuades him to walk across campus instead of taking the bus. He is deep in thought as the shadow of a tall building crosses his path.
  "Four arms, huh?"
  Caroline's eyes flash in the sun. The gloss on her hair is silken against her radiant skin.
  "That's the building, isn't it? I didn't realize you were thinking about your invention when we were up there."
  "I wasn't. Not 'til after."
  He notices her left hand, where a large diamond gleams in the sun, then looks at her eyes, which she averts.
  "Gordon, we have a lot to talk about."
  "Five years."
  "I'm sorry. You wouldn't take my calls, or--"
  "You didn't come to her memorial."
  "I didn't think you wanted me there."
  "Oh *bullshit*, Caroline. Even your con artist father showed up."
  "He's not--"

"Listen," Gordon cuts in. "Just... have a nice life. Okay?"

He turns and hurries away. She jogs after him and grabs him by the back of his hair. Instinctively, he yanks his head free and sweeps a vertical forearm across to bat her hand away. When he sees her eyes, he freezes. She is crying.

"Gordon Lightfoot Longmeier, you will stop and fucking talk to me, goddamn it."

Chapter 7

Adaptation

They walk for a while in silence. Something about Caroline has always charged the air with urgency, with presence. Even the smallest moments seem to have something at stake, and this is no exception. Gordon feels as if his day, his trajectory, has been altered, as if her orbit were the only one possible for his tumbling satellite of a heart to enter. For this reason he does not simply walk away, although the truth is that he probably could not break free of her even if he took off all of his body weights and let himself float out into the blue.

"So who's the lucky guy?" he asks at last.

"No one you know. He's from--"

"California."

"Yeah."

"Your sister told me after you left."

Caroline nods.

"So how did you meet?"

Caroline's eyes light up. "When I first got to Stanford, it was incredible. Like this whole other universe of people doing incredible things. And the country out there... Gordon, you have to see Yosemite! It's the most beautiful--"

"What's all that got to do with him?"

With one quick glance, she lets him know he hit a nerve. "I was young, just this girl from Georgia. He was larger than life."

Gordon rolls his eyes at her obvious mythologizing, but she doesn't notice.

"You know," she continues, "he was playing quarterback on national television every week, taking me out to the family ranch, showing me a whole new world. I guess the whole thing, David, all of it... just kind of swept me off my feet."

"Not like tatty old Athens, I guess. Or me."

"Gordon, you and I were never exclusive. And you were in the Lab every waking moment. I know that leaving when I did was not--"

"Human?"

"Okay, I deserved that. But if we're gonna be friends..."

"Really? Friends."

"Well, what else could we be at this point?"

He tries to reply but cannot. The scent of her rushes into him and wells like a sob in his chest. After a moment, his voice returns.

"Caroline, you can't marry him."

"Gordon, don't."

"You can't."

"I can."

Gordon sees the lie in her eyes. She lays a hand on his chest, then turns and walks away. He smiles. To him, a lie is almost as good as a promise.

"Well, I'll just have to adapt then," he calls after her.

Later that night, Gordon leaves the Lab with Stan and Wendell. It is Friday and they are in good spirits, having completed several promising tests of a transparent titanium prototype. Earlier, Stan drew a vial of Gordon's blood for Ravi, which gave Gordon an oddly hopeful feeling. Rational, scientific inquiry and hard answers, no matter how disappointing they might be, had always comforted him. Gordon walks out of the building feeling light and free, the first time he has felt that way since gravity abandoned him.

"Might play a set tonight if Martín can round up the guys on short notice," Gordon says to Stan.

Wendell is confused.

"Sorry bud." Gordon pats Wendell's shoulder. "Still have to be twenty-one to get into the bar at night."

"Tell that to the undergrads," Stan cracks. "Hell, you've been playing there since you were sixteen."

"Fifteen. But don't tell Wendell."

Wendell smiles.

"G'night, guys. G, maybe Ravi and I will make it over there later."

Gordon walks back across campus, typing a text to Martín. The reply is nearly instant and very positive. He has been eager to play again. By the time Gordon gets to Broad Street, he has already gotten everybody but one horn player on board. He is pumped.

He stops by his apartment, eats a quick dinner and walks down to the bar. Martín has already put out the 'Live Music' placard and is beginning to move tables out of the main room. Gordon helps him clear enough space for dancing, then goes backstage and starts hauling out the speakers that he will stack at either side of the stage to augment the small curved row hanging from the ceiling. Martín slides open the big windows at the front of the bar, as he does each time they do a sound check when the weather is warm.

"Good advertising," Martín says to the tall, leather-skinned man with long gray hair who walks in and sits at the bar.

Martín shakes the man's hand with a warm smile. As he tunes his guitar, Gordon tries to remember where he has seen him before. Soon, lost in the sounds of his warmup, he forgets about the man and starts to get excited for the show.

It is the first set Gordon and Martín have played with the band in nearly two weeks. Everybody is excited, no one moreso than Gordon. All of the mad energy of his confinement is buzzing in his head. He takes a seat on the window side of the bar, drinking bourbon and chatting with Martín and Julia as the place begins to fill up. His leg pumps like a piston. The two women playing warmup are working through an energetic set, their crystalline vocals and muzzy guitars sweeping away the residue of everyone's work week. Martín's two young bartenders hustle as more rounds are ordered and people crowd in. The sidewalk is alive with spring. Martín drums on the bar, keeping time with the song. As it ends, a roar sends the ladies off with a smile. Gordon stands, downs the rest of his drink in one gulp, punches Martín on the sternum and bounces on his toes. When he realizes that he is rising nearly three feet off the ground with every hop, he stops and smiles sheepishly. Julia's eyes are wide. Martín rolls his.

They make their way through the crowd and step up onto the stage. Gordon calls out the two women's names again and whips up a strong ovation for them. Martín snaps his drums as the bass and horn players step around to the sides, one of them standing next to a keyboard he plays on certain songs. Gordon plugs in and pretends to fiddle with the tuning of his guitar even though he already knows it's tight. They all glance at each other and Gordon nods at Martín, who kicks them right into a fast Los Lobos song. Gordon leans down and lets his hair screen his face, working the pick through two loud bars before he whips his head up and looks around. People seem happy, out from under winter, smiling and drinking. He steps into the mic, a small but constant part of him aware of Caroline as he sings to the room full of undergrads. Up there as a teenager and later as a college student, he always felt like a townie crashing a university party. He wore that feeling onstage and off like armor, like his tattoo. It drove him to work harder but it also kept him grounded.

They work through some old classics to get the crowd fired up. Gordon sees Stan and Ravi at the bar and points at them, then starts playing back and forth with Martín on 'Couldn't Stand the Weather' before leaning into the hard work of mimicking Stevie Ray's guitar riffs. They use 'Voodoo Child' as a bridge to Hendrix, and from from there it is a short hop to Santana where Martín's heart lies. As they wrap up 'Black Magic Woman,' Gordon takes a long sip of bourbon, shields his eyes from the lights and sees Caroline standing against the wall. He leans over to Martín and says something, then steps to the mic.

"A beautiful woman once gave a boy an awkward name." His words slur a bit. "But she did it for love. This is for her."

Gordon starts to play 'If You Could Read My Mind' by Gordon Lightfoot, but his tuning makes it sound like a lion singing a Christmas carol. He closes his eyes and lets the song flow, driving raw electric notes through the gentle ballad, letting the music sear against the emotion of his memory. He has never played this before, and he doesn't know where it will go. He senses the crowd growing impatient, so he turns and cocks his head at Martín, who nods. Gordon breaks the song off abruptly and punches the first notes of Led Zeppelin's 'Good Times, Bad Times.' Martín works the drum parts expertly between the guitar breaks. Gordon looks directly at Caroline when he sings, "My woman left home with a brown-eyed man, but I still don't seem to care." She purses her lips, finishes her drink and starts for the door. They end the song before she can get through the crowd.

"That woman, there," Gordon calls from the stage. "Caroline. Stop her."

Martín scowls at Gordon from behind the drum kit. The tall, gray-haired man, who has been sitting at the bar since before the show started, rises to leave. He smiles at Martín and waves but in his anger Martín barely nods.

"She promised she would sing with me. One song, just like she did right here years ago. For old time's sake. What do you say?!"

The crowd starts chanting, "Caroline! Caroline!" She drops her head in defeat, then looks up with a forced smile and starts walking back through the crowd. When she gets on stage, she grabs Gordon's arm.

"What the hell are you doing?"

"Adapting," he grins. "Just keep up."

"Well no Candy, get that right."

Gordon spins out of her grip and rips through a quick riff, then starts hitting the first notes of 'Waitress in the Sky' by the

Replacements.

"I fly a lot," Gordon says to the audience.

Caroline looks at him curiously. Stan laughs and slaps his forehead.

Gordon revs up the intro and starts singing. Caroline dances at a distance until he motions her over to the mic and she joins him, to loud cheers. She smiles. The crowd sings along too, rollicking through to the end. The audience loves Caroline, and Gordon steps back to let her bask in it. He bows to hail her, and she bows to the crowd.

"Wanna stay for one more?" he asks her.

She demurs playfully, then nods.

Everyone cheers again as Gordon begins to play a very familiar tune, at the lowest register his guitar can hit. As he builds it, the horn player joins in. Caroline recognizes it before the audience and rolls her eyes, but by the time they get to the chorus she is beaming. Except for one person, the entire bar sings in unison: "Sweet Caroline!"

Playing his drums, Martín does not smile.

Chapter 8

Hangover

Martín meets Gordon at the door and grabs two handfuls of hoodie. He lifts Gordon off his feet and slams his back into the wall. There is fury in Martín's eyes. He holds Gordon there, pinned, legs dangling, as he snorts deep breaths and tries to calm himself. Gordon's eyes are wide. He has never seen his soulful mentor even mildly angry, much less apoplectic with rage.

Martín opens his mouth to speak, then stops himself with a quick shake of the head. Suddenly, he releases Gordon and stalks off across the empty barroom toward the stage. Gordon drops to the ground and stands, waiting. He looks down into the paper bag he has been holding as if its contents might offer some explanation for Martín's anger. Gordon did not see Martín after the show, so he just helped the other bartenders clean up and went home to sleep. This morning, he stopped by a bagel shop so Martín would not have to cook. He is utterly baffled by Martín's mood.

Martín rounds on him and stalks back. He stops a few paces away, visibly willing himself to relax, to breathe. He looks out the windows at the cold morning sun, glances around at the hundreds of stickers, music flyers and graffiti tags with which students have adorned his walls. His eyes level at Gordon.

"Do not ever use that stage to bully a woman again," Martín growls.

Gordon starts to speak, but Martín raises a finger at him.

"Do not, Gordon. Do not try to tell me she wanted to be up there. She was a good sport, but you were wrong. And you know it."

"You're right, Tío. I'm sorry." Humor lights Gordon's eyes. "I didn't know you cared so much about her."

"It is not about her," Martín says forcefully. "*Any* woman. Any *person*. When you are leading a crowd, it is a sacred duty. You turned that crowd on her. You used that crowd to get what *you* wanted. No man of honor does this. That is a thing for cowards. And you are not a *pinche* coward!"

Martín's voice echoes in the room. Gordon realizes the depth of his emotion. He senses that this is not only about last night, that it may be more about what Martín has seen in the past, in Mexico and even here in the States. The rallies, the con men... and the dead bodies. Martín paces the floor until he calms down completely.

"I'm so sorry, Tío," Gordon whispers. "I didn't know..."

Martín walks to Gordon and embraces him.

"I am sorry too, son. I did not mean to frighten you. Last night, I had to... I left. I did not want to be angry. I am sorry."

"Maybe a bagel will help?" Gordon raises the bag.

Martín takes the bag into the back room and returns with the bagels in a large bowl, along with a platter of smoked salmon, and various spreads and cheeses. Gordon walks behind the bar and pours two glasses of water while Martín fetches a pot of coffee. They sit and eat in silence until Gordon looks up.

"Who was that guy at the bar? Looked like an old Indian?"

"You do not remember him?"

"No. Should I?"

"I suppose not." Martín takes a sip of coffee. "His name is Joe. He is a relative of your mother."

Gordon remembers. He opens the velcro at the top of his weight vest and pulls out the necklace.

"He gave me this -- or she did, when she passed. She told me to never take it off."

"Yes," Martín recalls, "he wears one too."

"Did he tell you what it means?"

They are interrupted as the door jingles and Caroline enters. In dark sunglasses and a long leather coat, her look is quite severe.

"Today, we kill moose and squirrel?" Gordon asks in a thick Russian accent.

Caroline laughs, then winces in pain. "You got me very drunk last night, Bullwinkle."

"Boris."

She struggles to a barstool and sits. Martín pours her a cup of coffee and offers milk and sugar. She takes it gratefully.

"Caroline, I'm really sorry for putting you on the spot like that." Gordon glances at Martín, whose expression is impassive.

"Yeah, well, it couldn't have been that bad. I'm here, right?"

Gordon takes out his phone and holds it up. "If it's any consolation, social media loves you."

"Oh dear God, no."

She lowers her head onto her hands. Gordon notes the absence of a certain sparkly item on her left hand.

"You didn't seem that drunk."

"I wasn't, before. But people do tend to buy you shots after an episode like that."

"I didn't see you leave."

"You were still playing. A kind woman called me a car and poured me into it with two of my girlfriends."

Gordon looks at Martín. "Julia?"

He nods and Gordon thanks him.

"Yes, thank you." Caroline starts to take out her wallet. "That's why I'm here."

Martín waves away the money. "Please, no. Do not insult me."

Caroline nods deeply and puts it away.

"Hey, you got a minute?" Gordon asks her.

"Yeah, I doubt I'll be going anywhere fast this morning."

"Come on upstairs, then. There's something I gotta show

you."

"Please tell me it's not your 'etchings.'"

Martín looks at Gordon.

"Way cooler than that," Gordon says.

"G, be careful."

Gordon winks at Martín, who looks solemnly from him to Caroline and back again. Martín picks up the platter and the bowl and walks into the back room. He does not return before Gordon leads Caroline outside.

She hesitates at the garage door, confused.

"Actually, yeah, I live above the garage now."

"Well, my folks moved out to Oconee so I guess a lot has changed around here."

She follows him in. As she passes through to the stairs, Caroline pushes her sunglasses onto the top of her head and looks around. In the loft space, she stares for a long time at the Shiva unit.

"So you really did get that to work?"

"You remember Shiva?"

"You wouldn't shut up about it. It's why I vowed never to date any more geeks."

"Geeks rule the world now."

"The ones in the Valley think they do, anyway."

Gordon takes off his shirt, revealing the highly polished discs of his sleeveless vest and arm weights. He starts to undo his pants.

"Stop. One night of rock and roll doesn't mean I'm gonna--"

"Get over yourself."

He grins and points to the barstool. As she sits, he kicks off his boots and slides off his jeans. Larger metal discs shroud his lower legs like a catcher's shin guards. He walks over and leans on the island.

"Do you remember when I saw you on the bus that night it snowed?"

"Yeah, of course."

"We touched. Just a little brush on the hand."

"I touched you, yes."

"Why did you do that?"

"I don't know."

"Did you feel it? When you--"

She looks away.

"You did! It was the same as five years ago, right? When you were singing with me that first time."

"How did you know about that?"

"It's why this thing even exists." He points back at Shiva. "Lightning. After that moment on stage, I couldn't get the image of lightning out of my mind. Did you ever see what happens when lightning strikes the desert floor? It melts the sand into a solid form. A beautiful shape, like art. People dig them up, these big glass lightning bolts."

"It was just static electricity. Just a little spark."

"It gave me the idea for flash casting, and that became the key to this whole thing."

"That's what you took your pants off to tell me?"

"You felt it again that night on the bus. You know it wasn't static electricity. But that night, something even bigger happened to me."

"Christ, Gordon, you really are a geek. Is that why you're wearing metal underwear?"

He smiles and nods. With a loud ripping of velcro and a metallic cascade of discs, he takes off his vest and one leg weight. Slowly, he rises a few inches off the floor. He takes one of the arm weights off and begins to rise higher. Caroline sits back, her hands gripping the seat. Her eyes are wide, her mouth agape.

"What the hell...?"

Gordon bends forward and reaches down to her.

"Help me down, will ya?"

She pushes away from him and raises her arms defensively. When he tries to lean closer, the barstool crashes to the floor as she steps further back.

"Come on," he pleads. "It's easier if you help."

Caroline shakes her head, several quick shakes that seem

almost involuntary.

"No!" She's not looking at him. "No. Fuck this."

She runs to the stairs and flees down into the garage.

"Caroline, come on!"

The sound of the slamming door hits Gordon like a punch. He lowers his head, hanging in mid-air in his t-shirt and boxer shorts, slowly rising to the ceiling.

A few hours later, Gordon is somber when he walks into Jittery Joe's to meet Martín, who flashes two fingers at the waiter and points at Gordon and himself. The young man returns with a fresh cup for Gordon and refills Martín.

"Gracias, Jorgé." Martín turns to Gordon. "Talk to me, G."

Gordon looks around at the people sitting near them, then tips his head toward the outdoor tables. The sun has warmed the day, so they settle in outside and Gordon lights up.

"You know how some people...?" Gordon stops. "Like, they have a reaction to something, and you just don't know where it's coming from?"

"Yeah..."

"So Caroline freaked when I showed her that I can... you know."

"Ay güey, I warned you. Maybe you oughta tell people first before you just float around. I nearly pissed myself when I saw you up there. Why'd you tell her anyway? You think it's gonna make her like you?"

"I guess I just had to tell someone else."

"G, I get it. It's like a secret you gotta be dying to tell." Martín looks around at the people on Broad Street. "Do you realize that all you gotta do is stand up and take off your weights and you will be the most famous person in the world?"

Gordon looks up and exhales smoke at the sky. "You know, I never really thought about it like that."

"Pretty cool, huh?"

"Terrifying. Seeing me do that would scare the crap out of most of humanity. You know what they'd do to me? No thanks, pal."

"So why trust her then?"

"Shit, Tío, I don't know. Maybe I just wanted her to think about me again." Gordon's eyes begin to well. "I didn't expect her to run away like I was some kind of freak."

"You *are* though, G. Accept it. *Embrace* it. There's power in it."

"Power? What, the God stuff again?"

"Fame. You got a tremendous chance here, Gordon. Some people, they get a little fame, they use it to do bad things, man. But maybe you can use it to do some good."

"I hear you. But..."

"But what?"

Gordon points out at the street, sweeps his hand across the undergraduates and townspeople.

"Them."

"What about them?"

"They already know."

"Know what?" Martín asks.

"Not about me. About... everything. I mean, they already know everything I might get them to think about with my fifteen minutes of fame. What am I gonna say? Help the poor? End racism, or gun violence? They already know. And they don't give a shit."

"They will if you say it."

"Oh, really. Why is that?"

"Because you're a miracle, man."

"I told you, I don't want nothin' to do with that. This didn't happen to me so I could go out and lie to people."

Martín sees Stan and Ravi and stands up to greet each man with a hug. He pats Gordon's shoulder.

"I gotta split, G. Great set last night. Let's get that going again."

"Please do." Ravi smiles. His short hair is wet and freshly combed. He wears aviator sunglasses. "I barely got out of bed today, it was such a good party."

Martín waves goodbye. Stan and Ravi sit.

"Listen," Stan says. "We gotta talk."

"About what?"

"About your genome," Ravi answers.

"What, is it weird?"

"Well, for starters, seventy-five percent of it is some kind of Native American, I think, but I've never seen it before around here. The closest match is actually Mayan."

Gordon stares at him. "What the fuck? My mother said we were German. And like, Russian or something."

"Longmeier, yeah," Stan nods. "Well, we didn't see any German in there."

"You do have a little Scottish," Ravi offers. "And Jamaican. Anyway, the good news is you're not part sparrow, so this flying thing...? Probably not genetic."

Gordon frowns. "Wait, does this mean my father is not..."

"Your father?" Stan finishes. "Not necessarily. But there's an awful lot they didn't tell you about your heredity."

Gordon chuckles. "Jamaican. Who woulda thought."

"Ya mon," Ravi lilts. "Everyt'ing gon' be irie."

"So, what then? Am I adopted?"

"You can't fake a birth certificate," Stan acknowledges. "And your mom's name is on that. But your dad...?"

Gordon becomes serious. "Doesn't tell us much about my condition, does it?"

"No mon," Ravi answers. "Not a t'ing."

Chapter 9

Wolves

Gordon pulls on his backpack as Stan says goodbye to Ravi, and they walk to the bus stop. They are later than usual for the Saturday Lab session, but since the grad assistants always get the students started on their projects early, neither one is stressed. On the bus, Stan lifts his glasses and rubs his eyes.

"Carson is really pushing this North thing."

"Did Mr. Berrigan speak with him?" Gordon asks.

"Yeah, I think so. Doesn't seem to be slowing him down."

"Well, the kids are safe for now, right?"

"Far as I know."

They hop down at their stop. Stan heads for the entrance but Gordon pauses for a smoke.

"I'd like to say a few words to them when I get in there," Gordon says. "Would that be okay?"

"Dude, you don't gotta ask."

Gordon blows smoke into the air and watches it follow the white clouds drifting across the blue. Heredity and race are not things he spends much time thinking about, but now that he knows he has so much Native American blood, so unexpected and exotic to him, he feels different somehow. Sensing his spirits rise with every step, he walks down the hallway and into the

Lab. Stan gathers the students at the middle of the room. Gordon leans against his table and looks at the group. A mix of high school and college students, fifteen in all, stand in a semicircle. Among them is Wendell Stainfield. He keeps his tinted safety glasses on, but most of the others have either pushed theirs up or removed them. Gordon remembers each of their stories; some are from Atlanta, others from towns across North Georgia and some -- the college students -- from across the country. Their faces are as varied as their origins, shades of brown and beige, some pale, some freckled. Young women and young men.

"Yeah, uh, I just have a couple thoughts I wanna share."

Gordon points back at the double doors.

"Out there are a lot of problems. Y'all know that. But in here there's nothing but solutions. This is a safe haven. Your ideas are safe here. They either work or they don't. If not, you test 'em, fix 'em, try again and keep going until they do. Out there, one word from someone with a big enough mouth and people suffer. Lives change. You see it everywhere... even at home, in your neighborhoods. But in here, *you* have the power. Your minds have the power. Your hands are strong. Your tools create new things. Life gets better because you are in it. So stay in it. Make something new. Improve something old."

Gordon puts his right hand in his pocket and closes it around the small Catonsville wrench.

"Listen, no matter what happens..."

He stops, clears his throat, takes a sip of water. The students closest to him see the red in his eyes.

"No matter what some powerful person tells you about your ideas, no matter if someone with lawyers and money and all that bullshit tries to rip you off, know one thing: They are nothing without y'all. *Nothing*. This is a sacred thing you do, creating, building, dreaming. And listen, anybody can do it if they try. Every little kid is born drawing pictures, making stuff. You're not special because of that, or because of how great your test scores are or how quickly you learn physics. Everybody in this room has that, or you wouldn't be here. The reason y'all are special is because you *commit* to it. You push through the barriers that stop other people. You see something in your mind and you don't give up until it exists. Plenty of people can draw or calculate or even fabricate, but they don't make a goddamn thing. They don't add anything to the world. Y'all do. Y'all are here, now, today, doing that. Y'all's hearts..."

Gordon pauses again, coughs and takes another drink of water.

"Your hearts are what give us hope. Humanity. You give humanity hope."

He glances around at their faces, their eyes. They seem to be waiting for something more.

"Anyway, no matter what happens, here or anywhere, never ever give up. Y'all are special because what breaks most people just makes you stronger, more committed. Remember that. Whatever happens, remember that. That's really all I got to say."

The students begin to filter back to their stations. A couple of them pound fists with Gordon or shake his hand and mumble their thanks. Stan pats him on the back.

"I keep forgetting you have that thing on." Stan pokes Gordon's vest.

Wendell walks up and stands by them silently, not making eye contact.

"Dude," Stan says to him. "Spit it out. What's up?"

Wendell motions for them to follow and walks back to his station. A long object that looks like a snowboard lays across nearly the full length of his table. At either end, it humps up into two semi-circular masses. Wendell flips the board over, revealing spherical rubber treads on the bottom side of each hump. They are connected to the board by steel forks. He grabs his phone, punches up an app, pops an earbud into his ear and says, "Engage."

The board begins to hum. Wendell says, "Go." The spheres begin to spin slowly. He takes Gordon's hand and holds it against one of the spheres. Under the knobby rubber surface, Gordon can feel splayed metal fingers moving past.

"Each spoke is attached to one of these knobs on the tread,"

Wendell explains. "Lets you keep traction on any terrain, even snow. No air -- the tire is basically a sponge with a durable skin. Now, watch out."

Wendell moves Gordon's hand away and says, "Go, Go, Go."

Each time he says it, the wheels speed up until they are two whirring blurs.

"Stop, Stop." The wheels slow dramatically. "Stop. Stop." They come to a halt. Wendell says, "Off," and the humming stops.

Stan and Gordon look at each other and erupt with praise for Wendell, who ducks bashfully away.

"I think it's ready for a field test," Wendell says.

"Hell yeah, it is!" Gordon cries. "Seriously, man. This is incredible. I love the voice interface, too."

"Can't shred and hold a remote at the same time," Stan agrees. "What about bindings?"

"I did those shoe-based," Wendell says, "not board-based. So you don't have to use them if you don't want. See these little steel ridges? You just step onto those with the bindings on and say 'Lock' and you're on. When you want to get off, just say 'Unlock.'"

"And hope no one says 'unlock' while you're riding past," Stan cracks.

Wendell does not smile.

"They also release when certain torque coefficients are met," Wendell continues. "Yeah, with that 'unlock,' all of the commands can be personalized in the app. For different languages, or just plain weirdness."

Now Wendell smiles.

"This is amazing!" Gordon throws an arm around Wendell and hugs him tight. "Unbelievable work, bud."

When he is released from the hug, Wendell looks at Gordon's torso and touches it with a curious expression.

"Something I'm working on," Gordon breezes. "I'll tell you when it's ready."

Satisfied, Wendell turns back to the board. Gordon pats him on the shoulder.

"Patent time, little brother."

Wendell smiles broadly.

"We can get you prior art as of today," Stan agrees. "Are your docs on the server?"

Wendell nods. "Also, for production…"

Stan turns to the students who have been watching the demo and raises his arms like a conductor.

"Local and low-impact," they say in unison.

Wendell smiles again, blushing.

Gordon pats his arm. "It's your turn, bud. Your product. Your call on how it gets built."

"Local and low-impact," Wendell confirms. "That's what I was gonna say. This can be made here in Georgia with a fairly small carbon footprint."

"Good man," Stan approves.

The group disperses, but Gordon stays with Wendell. "Talk me through this fork and power train. It looks like a shaft drive. Both sides?"

"Yeah." Wendell smiles. "Opposite rotations off the same motor give both sides of the wheel power. Two motors, one for each wheel. They run in sync. The bottom of the board is a battery and the top is a solar panel."

"Pretty cool. Show me the gearing."

A few hours later, Stan has assembled the patent filing materials and finished a call with Jalen Woods, their attorney. He walks over to Gordon's table, frowning.

"Minor problem. Pardon the pun."

Gordon looks up. "Legal guardian?"

Stan glances at Wendell. "You said the father was difficult?"

"To put it mildly."

"Wendell can file for the patent himself, no problem. But how do we set up the company?"

"You've had this problem before, right?"

"Frankly, no. We've had absentee parents. That kid Thompson, with the door lock."

"Yeah, his grandparents co-signed his incorporation papers.

How did you set up ownership for that?"

"A trust in Thompson's name," Stan explains, "with them as custodians until he turned eighteen. At first Jalen babysat it for the kid, but the grandparents were cool."

"Not the case here. Wendell's father wanted to sue Henry for a couple hundred bucks because he nicked a tree with his wrecker. He'll grab every penny he can. Let's not put Jalen in the middle of that."

"We can hold off incorporation until he's eighteen."

Gordon frowns. "A lot can happen in six months with wolves like North at the door. Still, that's probably the best bet unless he wants to become an emancipated minor."

"He's got a strong case for emancipation. Let's ask him."

"You better do that without me. The father already thinks I'm a home wrecker because I tried to help the mom kick drugs."

"He's a real peach, huh?"

"Oh yeah. Lovely human being."

By the end of the day, Stan has sent Wendell's patent application to Jalen, supported by Wendell's CAD renderings, schematics and even a separate addendum for the voice controls that he built into the app. It's all in Wendell's name, filed with the USPTO. Wendell leaves knowing that as of this day his intellectual property is his own, legally protected by the U.S. government.

That is, unless someone with deeper pockets finds out about it, chooses to steal it and dares him to sue. Once the product is in the marketplace and generating revenue the risk of outright theft goes down, but then come the copycats; intellectual parasites in faraway countries and sometimes here in the States who differentiate their own offerings just enough to stay legal. Stan despises them, but he accepts their existence the same way he does the fat palmetto bugs that crawl around on humid nights. Gordon, on the other hand, would take a flamethrower to every last one of them if he could.

After the students have gone, Stan follows Gordon out of the double doors and locks the horizontal bolt. He installed it knowing it was redundant to the electronic lock and he created only three keys -- for himself, Gordon and Mr. Williams. As Gordon passes Mr. Williams, the older man gestures at the pathway outside. Dr. Carson stands talking to a blond-haired man in slacks, a pressed shirt and high-end loafers with no socks.

"Elliott North?" Gordon snarls.

"Chill, man," Stan says. "Be cool."

Stan thanks Mr. Williams for the heads-up and leads Gordon out the door. They pretend to chat about voice-activated commands as they walk past Carson.

"Professor Malkovich," Carson calls. "I'd like you to meet someone."

"Yeah." Stan looks the tall man up and down. "I've seen your photo."

"Professor." North offers his hand. "And who is this?"

"Gordon."

North looks at the oval name plate on Gordon's work shirt. "So I see. And do you teach here too?"

"I help out."

"Dr. Carson," Stan interjects, "I trust that you will respect the privacy of the Lab while showing Mr. North around?"

Carson flashes anger at Stan, but regains control and forces a banal smile. North breaks the awkward silence.

"Please, guys, Mr. North is my father. Call me David."

Gordon freezes.

"Elliott *David* North the Third?" Stan asks.

North flashes a winning smile. "Elliott the Second cast too long a shadow. I go by my middle name."

Chapter 10

Engagement

Gordon drifts on his back across the kitchen area, head angled toward the floor, hair hanging down. He wears only pajama bottoms and a new weighted belt just heavy enough to bring him to the ground very slowly. He puts in ear buds and presses Caroline's number again.

"Gordon..." she answers.

"Why did you leave?"

"Oh, I don't know. Maybe because you were *levitating off the ground*?!"

"I'm sorry I scared you."

"How did you do that, anyway? Was it something in those metal things you were wearing?"

Lacking any explanation that would make sense to her, Gordon decides to ignore the question.

"So, David... Would that be David North, by any chance?"

"Gordon, I was badly hung over, and you surprised me. I wasn't scared. There just wasn't room in my mind for something so... surreal."

"Because I met him."

There is a sharp intake of air on the other end.

"Seems like a nice enough fellow, for a rapacious arms dealer who wants to exploit my students' ideas."

"He what?"

"Does he live here now? He looks awfully well-dressed for our li'l ol' Athens."

"He's gonna stay in California for now. He said he has to make some 'business transitions' or something before he can move here."

"Fancy guy like him might take a while to warm up to North Georgia."

Caroline remains silent.

"Where are you living?" Gordon asks.

"My sister's apartment. She's at our parents' Oconee house."

"You should have heard him say 'my fiancée.' Like some guys say 'my Porsche.'"

"Now you're lying."

"Am I, though?"

Silence again.

"Actually, yes, I am. I didn't say much to him. But I've read his work and I have to say, it's riveting. 'Leveraging technology to move warfare out of the trenches.' Seems almost... sanitary."

"Goodbye, Gordon."

"Wait, hang on. I didn't mean--"

The call disconnects. Gordon floats toward the island as a sob wells up that feels like it might choke him. He closes his eyes and lets out a sound that is half cry and half roar.

George's old Yamaha started with one kick. Gordon revved the 650 cc engine until the black smoke cleared to a bluish gray. He chunked it into gear and let out the clutch, riding slowly out of the garage and into the alley. The bike had stood under a tarp while the weather warmed and he got used to the idea of owning it. His father's will had not contained much, but he made sure his son got the motorcycle and that Gordon and his mother both understood their shared ownership of the auto repair business. Gordon stopped and leaned the idling bike on its side stand. He looked up at the sign above the garage, "G.L. Auto Repair," then grabbed the rope and hauled the big door down. Walking back to the Yamaha, he noticed the high mirrors, trumpeted tailpipes and spray of wires across the handlebars.

Gonna have to change those.

Gordon gunned the motor and surged onto the main street, beginning to panic about his preparations for the night. He threaded his way through the back streets to his house, parked the bike and ran up the stairs. After a quick shower, he unzipped the black rental bag and began to put on his tuxedo. He was making good time, tying the shiny plastic shoes and shaking out his hair, when he saw the dreaded little bat wings of a bow tie. He stood in front of the bathroom mirror and began to knot it around his neck.

"Mom!" he called.

"Yes, dear?"

"Is there a rule about ties for this thing?"

Emily appeared in the hallway outside the bathroom door, drying her hands on a dish towel.

"The rule is, wear one."

"Does it have to be tied? Technically?"

"Technically, you should have enough respect for Caroline to make an effort."

He turned back to the mirror to try again.

"Oh yeah, that flower thing?"

"Corsage," *she clarified.*

"Right, that?"

"In the fridge."

Gordon looked at her quizzically.

"Flowers do spoil, you know." *Emily watched him fumble with the knot.* "My goodness, you're as useless as your father. Here, let me."

Taking each end of the tie, Emily spread them wide, then folded one side and pressed it to Gordon's throat as she wound the other around, through and tight.

"Why didn't you tell me you were an expert?"

"How would you ever learn?"

Gordon laughed. "I won't be wearing one of these again."

"Oh, one day the right person will get you into one."

Emily smiled and touched the stone hanging around her neck. Gordon rolled his eyes.

Crunching little bits of gravel under his plastic soles, Gordon walked the cold carton of flowers across the street and rang Caroline's doorbell. The Highsmiths' dog howled until her father answered holding a can of beer. He shook Gordon's hand, but told him to wait outside.

"Kinda chaotic in there. Beer?"

"Yes sir, thanks."

Gordon traded the corsage for a cold brew and sat down on the steps. He was halfway through the beer when he heard the door open again. He stood up, turned around and nearly dropped the can. Gone was the casual, jeans-and-sweatshirt girl next door. In her place stood a radiant woman in a low-cut gown, smiling demurely at the reaction she had drawn.

"Pick up your jaw, son," Mr. Highsmith heckled. "Somethin'll build a nest in your mouth."

Gordon blushed, then stammered, "You look beautiful."

Caroline smiled more broadly, took Gordon's beer and finished it in one go. She turned and handed the can to her father, then hooked Gordon's arm and led him down the stairs.

"Be careful now," Mr. Highsmith said.

"Wait!" Mrs. Highsmith called out. "Caroline Jain, don't you leave without a picture!"

She followed them down the stairs and hunted around until she found the perfect backdrop.

"Gordon, how handsome you look in your tuxedo!"

"Maybe if he'd cut that fuckin' hair," Mr. Highsmith called from the stoop.

Gordon forced a thin smile at him, then offered a more sincere one to Mrs. Highsmith as she took the picture.

"Have a great prom, y'all two!" she called after them.

Gordon kept looking at Caroline as they walked across to his driveway. When he got to the bike, he stopped and considered her long dress.

"Caroline, I'm sorry, I didn't think about..."

"Screw it. I'll be alright. Just don't ask me to wear a helmet."

"That's why I love you."

She stepped close and rose on tiptoes to kiss him. After a moment, she had to use both hands to push him away and get them moving again. Gordon helped her gather and tuck her dress around her legs, then lifted her onto the seat. He put his own helmet on and left hers strapped to the frame. Stepping carefully over the gas tank, he turned out the starter pedal and kicked it. Emily walked outside and waved for them to wait. She raised her phone and snapped a picture of them on the bike, then smiled and blew them a kiss. Gordon ducked and shook his head, but Caroline blew one back. She held Gordon's waist and pressed her cheek to his back as they roared off. They weaved through town and stopped in front of Clarke Central High School. Gordon was surprised to see it closed.

"Um, why are we here?" Caroline asked.

"It's not in the gym? Isn't that where they have all the dances?"

"It's at the Cotton Press."

"Across town?"

"Yeah! Jeez, I was wondering where you were going."

Caroline laughed as Gordon pulled an old flask out from under the gas tank. It had a long velcro patch on one side. He opened it, took a swig and passed it to Caroline, who did the same.

"My dad didn't think I knew about this."

"Ugh! How old is that?"

"Bourbon don't go bad."

He replaced the flask and popped the bike back into gear. Within a few minutes, they pulled up to the parking lot and found a spot by the front where a row of girls stood with their dates, waiting to go in. Gordon did not recognize them in their pancake makeup and sprayed up-do's. He helped Caroline off the bike, staring at her windblown, dirty-blonde hair. If anything, flushed from the cool breeze, she was even more beautiful than she had been before.

"Whoa! Check it out!" slurred a huge boy with a ginger flattop, leering at the neckline of Caroline's dress. "Look at the cans on her!"

Gordon walked over and locked eyes with the massive boy, his nose even with flattop's chin. Outweighed by at least fifty pounds, Gordon was rigid with anger. Flattop puffed his chest and sniffed arrogantly.

"Apologize to her," Gordon growled.

"Fuck y--"

Gordon slammed his forehead into the bigger boy's nose, then ripped upward with a hard knee between his legs. When the boy bent forward,

Gordon grabbed the back of his head and drove the boy's face down onto his other knee. Then, with one elbow, Gordon caught him on the chin and knocked him out. As the boy fell, three of his football teammates rushed Gordon and tackled him to the sidewalk. They flailed at him with their fists until one of the policemen stationed at the door sprinted over and pulled them off. The boys dragged their large friend up to a sitting position and revived him. Gordon lay on his side, bleeding from his lip, his nose and his right hand. He got up slowly and walked to Caroline.

"I'm so sorry."

She moved close to him and kissed him gently on the lips.

"Don't be."

The policeman herded the angry group away from Gordon and Caroline. He poked a finger into the bloodstain on flattop's chest.

"This one's drunk. He's out."

A few of flattop's teammates tried to protest, but the look on the cop's face let them know they were about to be next. They moved off with their large, woozy friend as his date began to cry. One hung back, a tall guy with dreads and tattoos peeking out from under his tuxedo sleeves. The cop pointed at Gordon.

"You. Out too."

Gordon nodded.

Caroline smiled. "He can't dance anyway."

The cop's scowl broke for an instant, then returned.

"Just leave the premises and we'll forget the assault. And wear a helmet this time."

They thanked the cop, who walked away.

"He had it coming," *the dreadlocked player said.*

"Yeah, he did," *Gordon replied.*

"My name's Jalen."

"Gordon." *They shook hands.*

"Hey, I know you!" *Caroline said.* "People say you're gonna play for Georgia next year."

"Yeah."

"His mom teaches physics there!"

"Well, I'm pre-law so I won't be seeing much of her."

Gordon smiled, then winced and touched his cut lip. He held out his hand to Jalen.

"Thanks for not jumping on," Gordon said.

"Looked like you knew what you were doing." Jalen smiled. "I respect that."

"See ya around."

At the bike, Gordon leaned against the seat and held Caroline by the hips.

"I'm sorry I ruined your prom. I just couldn't let that asshole talk to you like that."

Caroline smiled and touched the cut on Gordon's lip. She put her arms around his neck and hugged him tightly.

"You didn't ruin anything."

"Maybe we can go to Martín's and have a little prom of our own."

Gordon carefully worked her helmet on over her hairdo.

"Or maybe we can go over by the river and have something else."

She touched the front of her helmet to his as his eyes grew wide. He lifted her onto his lap and kissed her for a long time, then they adjusted onto the seat, fired up the bike and jetted out into the gathering darkness.

Gordon's forehead touches the kitchen cabinet. He blinks his eyes open and tries to focus through his tears. The idea of Caroline marrying someone else, making those dreams, looking forward to that future... feels like it might crush him if he allows it into his mind. They were each other's first, back on that prom night a decade ago. He remembers the peaceful hours they spent on that pine-scented slope watching the river glide by and not caring at all that they were naked in the evening air. They didn't sleep, but neither did they talk or even move very much. They just lay there, enveloped in the feeling that life was in harmony as long as their hearts were close enough to beat as one. Then, he thinks of her having moments like that with the preening mannequin he met at the Lab. Her smile, for him...

Gordon pushes off of the floor and spins backward toward the ceiling. His back crashes into the metal beams and he welcomes the pain. Grabbing the rebar, he smashes his forehead into it, bellowing in rage.

"NOOOO!!! You cannot marry him! You can't!"

He lets go and drifts away from the ceiling, very still. Suddenly, he flails at the air, kicking and punching until he has exhausted himself, until he begins to sob through his hyperventilation. After a while, his breathing becomes calm again, his mind more clear. He quiets down and focuses on the problem. His brow relaxes, and his face settles into stony resolve.

"No," he says quietly. "It's not about weddings. It's about love."

Chapter 11

Windows

The flatbed belches smoke as the driver attempts to back into the alley. He pulls forward, adjusts his angle and makes another try. From the doorway, Martín watches with amusement until the corner of the truck starts to angle into one of his front windows. He runs out into the street, waving his arms and hollering. Behind him, there is a sickening bump followed by tinkles of broken glass. Martín jumps up onto the running board and screams at the driver, who finally stops. The man is very old, knobby knuckles white on the wheel, eyes terrified behind steel rimmed glasses. Martín relaxes his expression and tries to convey calm.

"Please," he says as gently as he can, "pull forward onto the street here."

The old man leans against the gear shifter and lets it grind until it finds traction. When the truck bucks forward violently, Martín has to grab the mirror frame to keep from falling off. The old man straightens it out as Martín rides along, then stops abruptly at the curb. On the bed is a massive, ancient piece of farm equipment, a tractor that has attachment mounts for a machine of some kind. Martín has no idea what it does. He walks over to his shattered window and begins to move the glass across the sidewalk with his foot. Gordon jogs up the alleyway toward him.

"What happened?"

Martín shakes his head and jabs a thumb back at the truck.

"Oh man," Gordon realizes. "Mr. Shepardson. I told him I'd fix his harvester, but I forgot."

The old man crosses the street toward them.

"Sir, I am very sorry about your window. I will pay for it, don't you worry."

"Actually, Mr. Shepardson, I was about to replace it with a new product we're developing at the Lab. So forget about it."

Martín raises his eyebrows at Gordon.

"Well, Gordon," Shepardson scolds, "you must be very busy these days."

"Sir, I'm sorry I forgot to come by and work on that. I've been... preoccupied."

"Please," Martín says. "Come inside. Have some tea."

The two men follow Martín into the bar. He fetches a broom and dustpan and hands them to Gordon, who sweeps up the broken glass and dumps it into a garbage can. Shepardson sits on a barstool and mops his forehead as Martín fetches a cold pitcher of sweet tea and pours a glass for the old man, who takes it gratefully. He looks at the color photo behind the bar, George Longmeier standing with Martín by a picnic table, their wives seated and chatting happily behind them. They smile, arms over each other's shoulders. In the background, a small, blurry Gordon runs past the table. Gordon walks in and sees Shepardson staring at the photo.

"Your father used to work on that harvester for me," Shepardson says to Gordon. He looks at Martín. "I guess you knew George?"

"Sí, he was like a brother."

"I remember George from when he was a teenager. He used to race those sprint cars on the dirt oval up in Lavonia. Saw him go sideways out of a turn one night in the mud. Spun around twice before he got control of her, but he had the red ass after that. Barreled his way up to second and woulda won if the race'd been longer."

Gordon smiles at Martín.

"Always tinkering around with his rides, looking for an edge. Taught you a lot, did he son?"

"Yes, sir. Everything I know."

"Never thought about the service yourself?"

Martín stiffens. Shepardson does not notice.

"No sir. Don't much like the haircuts."

Shepardson laughs. "Well, it might get you outta fixin' old motors for people like me."

"I'm fine, sir. I love this work."

Shepardson sets down his glass and looks through the broken window. "What're we gonna do with that old thing now?"

"We can drop it on the street and haul it back to the garage with the pickup," Gordon answers.

"No need to haul her. She runs a little."

"What do you mean, 'a little.'"

"Well, she's just finicky about gettin' in gear."

Martín chuckles, recalling the old man's treatment of the truck transmission. Gordon walks out with Shepardson and lowers the tractor off of the flatbed, and maneuvers it down the alley and into the garage bay.

"Where'd you get that rig anyway?" Gordon nods at the flatbed.

"Borrowed it from my nephew."

"Might oughta be little more gentle with the clutch on the ride home."

Shepardson raises his eyebrows, then agrees. As he rumbles away in the truck, Martín walks out to Gordon.

"What did you mean by 'new product?'"

"Shiva can make transparent titanium. I've been looking for a use case to test it out, and you win."

Martín stares at him, astonished. Gordon winks and walks back to the garage where the old man's tractor looms huge and dirty. He sighs and closes his eyes, letting the vision of Caroline on prom night play in his mind. When the sound of Martín breaking out the rest of the glass snaps his daydream, he pulls out his phone and walks back to the bar. He stands about ten feet away from the window and scans the opening with Stan's app, then moves closer and scans the channel in which the window sits. A series of schematic images annotated with dimensions flashes on his screen. He sends them to the Shiva unit in his apartment. After he and Martín have cleared the glass and hauled it to the dumpster, Gordon fetches a hammer and small chisel and works the rest of the trim loose. They retrieve the large sheet of titanium and set it into the opening, then tack the trim back into place. Gordon takes a few steps back, runs and launches his shoulder into the window. The force of the impact rattles the bar door but the window shows no sign of damage.

"Jesu! Easy, man."

"Good. We'll do the door and the other window tomorrow and your place will be a fortress."

Martín's eyes widen as he begins to understand the implications of the new product he is seeing. He turns to Gordon.

"I remember when you first came to our youth group. Just a punk-ass kid. Nobody could handle you."

Gordon looks at the ground.

"Vato, who woulda thought you'd be inventing stuff like this?"

Martín lays a hand on the window and rubs it in a circle.

"Listen," Martín says quietly. "I been thinking about your condition. I don't know why you got it, and probably you don't even know, but man, we gotta figure it out."

"How are 'we' gonna figure it out?"

"You got people who care about you. Julia and me known you a long time. And Caroline..."

"Yeah."

"I just feel like, you can't be alone with this thing. It's too big, man."

"The way I see it, it's some kind of physical anomaly. Ravi said my blood was normal, but it's gotta have a physical explanation. It's not some God thing."

Martín raises his hands. "I ain't here to preach. I'm here as your friend. I just think you need to talk about it. Like, it's gotta be some heavy shit to walk around with."

Gordon rolls his eyes at the pun.

"Maybe come to our group session," Martín says. "We meet at the church, Wednesday nights."

"Yeah, maybe," Gordon mumbles.

"I seen Caroline there."

"At the church? Really?"

"She came by to help out with the younger folks. They're like you used to be, figuring stuff out when life ain't real good."

"Last Wednesday?"

"Yeah, vato. You know she's studying to be a real counselor."

Gordon stares at the window in silence.

"You love her?" Martín asks.

"Honestly? Love? I don't know. But whatever this is, it's killing me."

Martín looks at Gordon with little sympathy.

"You might be the smartest person I know, G. But you might also be the dumbest."

Gordon's face flushes with anger. "What do you know about it?"

"I know love. And I think you got it. I think the two of you have had it for a long, long time."

"Tell her that. She's getting married."

"She got the ring," Martín allows, "but she ain't got the right guy."

Gordon leans back against the window and looks up at the sky.

"He can help, you know," Martín says gently.

"Oh yeah," Gordon snaps. "I forgot. God is love."

Martín's peaceful eyes reflect his amusement.

"No, vato. You got it backwards. Love is God."

"What do you mean by that?"

"When you figure it out, the rest of this stuff will make sense too."

Martín pats the titanium window one more time, smiles at

Gordon and goes inside.

Love is God.
What the hell is that supposed to mean?
As he walks across Broad Street, Gordon takes a sip of coffee and considers the audacity of preachers who claim to know what an omniscient god might be thinking. Thankfully, Martín is not one of those people. If he were, their friendship would have ended before it began, but when he says things like 'Love is God' Gordon wants to throw something at him. He understands what Martín means, that the feeling of love is God stirring within us, reaching through us to connect with that part of another that also comes from God. He even accepts that the deep, almost instinctive connection he has with Caroline is something very different than anything he has felt with any other woman. But he wonders, is it love?

Perhaps love is something he has never experienced before. As he walks south through campus, Gordon looks at the pretty young women all around him. He notes his own animal response as bodies and faces and scents pass by, each woman a universe of thoughts and passions and memories, every one a force of gravity pulling gently on his soul. He wonders if Martín might argue that these inklings of feeling are also God, or if he would contend that there is a moral difference between desire and connection. Is God only present when minds and spirits are joined, or is raw physical attraction not also divine?

He laughs.
Always looking for a loophole.

Gordon reaches the Lab and looks through the window. Inside, Mr. Williams is flirting with a woman whose body-conscious lycra top and tight jeans were still not enough to win her access to the inner sanctum. She looks up at Gordon as he walks in.

"Can I help you?" Gordon asks.

"I hope so," Caroline murmurs.

They walk outside. The relative heat of the previous day has yielded to a more seasonal chill, which feels refreshing in the bright sun. A dark thought settles across Gordon's mind as he studies her face.

"Why are you here?" he asks. "I mean, you never had much interest in the Lab before."

"I don't recall it ever being this nice before."

"We've done well with funding. Catonsville Tool & Die. So tell your boyfriend we don't need his money."

"Fiancée."

"Porsche."

"Gordon." Caroline flashes exasperation. "I didn't come here to fight."

"So why did you come?"

"Do you want me to go?"

"No," he blurts. "Yes. I don't know. I don't know why I feel this way about you. We're clearly--"

She steps close and kisses him.

"I don't know either. That's what I came here to say."

Gordon sets his coffee mug down, cradles her head with both hands and kisses her more deeply. He looks down into her eyes.

"We don't have to know." He wraps his arms around her and pulls her close.

She tenses and pulls back, touching his weight vest with her fingertips.

"You're still wearing this?"

"Long story."

"I've got all day."

"Good. We'll need it."

He flashes her a mischievous look and loops his arm around her waist. They walk off toward the campus, leaving his coffee mug standing alone on the flagstones.

At the apartment, Gordon offers to make more coffee but Caroline interrupts him with another kiss. She begins to unbutton his work shirt and pauses as he lifts her lycra top over her head. He takes over removing his shirt and the weight vest. His feet feel very light on the carpet. She unbuttons his pants and pulls them down, revealing the leg weights. He holds her as they move toward the bed, then slips off her jeans and watches her lay back onto the sheets.

"Um," he mumbles, "I've got a little problem."

"Doesn't look like it." She cocks an eyebrow at his briefs.

"No, a gravity problem. It's what I was trying to show you."

Caroline sits up, intrigued.

"If I take these weights off, I'll float up to the ceiling. If the ceiling wasn't there, I'd probably just keep drifting away."

"What? How...?"

"Honestly, I have absolutely no idea. It started the morning after I saw you on the bus."

"Was it that weird lightning thing?"

"I thought that had something to do with it, but now I don't know."

"Lemme see."

He glides over and retrieves the climbing rope, then ties a loop around his waist and hands it to her.

"Promise to pull me down again?"

"If you promise to be a good boy after I do."

"Define 'good.'"

"I think I meant 'bad.'"

"Okay, I promise."

Gordon rips open the velcro on his arm weights, then does the same for his legs. He rises away from Caroline, who stares wide-eyed as the rope slips through her hands.

"Grab it, please."

Her hand closes tight and stops him abruptly.

"I have a Gordon balloon," she giggles.

Caroline lets the rope play out and watches him bob horizontally above her. Then she pulls him down and lets him out again. He grins as she lays on the bed and begins to reel him in. When he reaches her, he holds on with his arms and legs. She loops the rope underneath her hips and around his waist again, then ties it off. They slip off their underwear and hold one another close. Rolling to sit on top of him, she presses his torso down and laughs as it floats up again. She fingers the piece of granite around his neck but does not comment on it. After a moment, she adjusts her hips, closes her eyes and ignores the rest of him as one crucial part finds its way home.

Afterward, Caroline lays on top of Gordon breathing when he does, feeling her weight keep him safe and grounded. He holds her as her head rests on his chest. The feel of her skin on his fills him with contentment, and his heart beating with hers makes him want to cry with joy. Neither wants to ask the questions that swirl around them, so instead they close their eyes and lay still, savoring the simple pleasure of breathing together.

I love you, he thinks. *And if you don't love me, if this isn't love… then love does not exist.*

Chapter 12

Flight

"Let's take your malady out for a spin."

Gordon smiles down at Caroline. They are both naked and he hovers five feet above her, still tethered by the loop around his waist.

"What do you mean?" he asks.

"You know, go fly around. Freak some people out."

"Nothing in public." Gordon glances at the clock; it is noon. "I know a place, though. I've been thinking about this. But let's eat first."

They dress quickly and head to Martín's. Gordon does not tell Caroline about the new window and instead focuses on the lunch menu. Smiling with satisfaction at the two of them together, Martín brings him a sandwich and her a salad. After lunch, Gordon borrows the truck keys and leaves with Caroline to retrieve the climbing rope and his smaller weight belt from the apartment. They drive west on the interstate until the land opens up, then head north on a smaller road.

"I guess I should ask about your, um, fiancée," Gordon begins.

"No, you really should not."

Gordon drives in silence for a few minutes.

"You said he's still in California?"

"Mostly, but he travels all the time. He's kind of a global citizen."

Global merchant of death.

Gordon leaves these words unsaid. He spots a small turnoff and takes it. The two-lane road leads into a wooded recreation area, then angles toward a clearing where a small lake shines in the sun. He steers the pickup onto the dirt siding and parks.

"Ready?" she asks.

Gordon hesitates, but her enthusiasm makes him smile.

"Yeah!"

He steps out of the truck, finds his smaller belt behind the seat and puts it on. With the rope over his shoulder, he walks with Caroline to the clearing.

"It'll be easier with this at first." Gordon holds up the rope.

"You'll be my man kite?"

Gordon grins as he ties the end of the rope around his waist and takes off all of the weights except the belt. As he bobs up, Caroline ties the other end around her own waist. She pulls him back to the ground and kisses him. He squats down, then swings his arms back as he pushes off. Doing backflips, he rises nearly a hundred feet in the air before the rope pulls taut. On the ground, Caroline whoops with laughter. Gordon pulls himself around so that he lays flat in the air, facing down. He can see for miles in every direction, which he realizes also means that he can be seen from miles away. A small silver SUV is the closest vehicle but its driver does not seem to notice him. Gordon is torn between the nearly ecstatic feeling of flight and the knowledge that he is taking a huge risk. He looks down at Caroline, who waves with both hands. As he looks around again, a large hawk glides by. Something about its proximity triggers a flash of fear, as if he might fall, but the feeling passes as quickly as it came. The rope has begun to curve with slack, which reminds him that his belt will eventually bring him back to earth. He laughs, realizing that his innate fear of falling really ought to evolve into a fear of floating.

He grabs the rope and begins to pull himself down. Absently, he notes that the silver SUV has stopped along one of the side roads. Its brake lights are still on and no one has gotten out, but Gordon pulls faster to get below the tree line before he is seen. By the time he reaches Caroline he has forgotten about it.

"Holy shit, that's cool!" He grins from ear to ear.

"I saw that bird buzz you."

"Scared the crap out of me. For a second, I thought about falling."

"What's it like, though? What's it feel like?"

Gordon looks up at the sky. "It feels a little like floating in a pool, but being up there is more like being in a parachute after you pull the cord."

"When did you go skydiving?"

"Once during college, just a tandem jump. This is way cooler."

Gordon holds his weight belt with two hands, thinking. He reaches down and puts on his leg weights, then hops about ten feet in the air. The added weight brings him gently but steadily to the ground. He unties the rope, smiles at Caroline and takes off running across the clearing. He dives straight out and flies horizontally for fifty yards or so before his toes begin to scrape the grass. He lets his boots drag to slow his flight, then pulls his knees into a crouch, puts the soles of his feet on the ground and skids to a stop. He turns back to Caroline, jogs slowly toward her and dives upward. His body traces a high arc, rising to fifty feet before drifting back down. Caroline realizes he has overshot her so she runs to where he finally touches down and tackles him.

"That was amazing!" she exclaims.

"So are you."

Gordon kisses her and she kisses back. They roll in the grass until he is on top of her and kiss one more time. He flashes her a grin, pushes straight up and backflips away.

"Come back here!"

Nearly fifty feet up, he stops flipping and begins to descend feet-first, as if through water. He lands with his arms raised overhead, legs perfectly straight.

"Okay, that was pretty cool," she admits.

He does it again.

After many more runs and jumps, Gordon feels like he has begun to get the hang of it. He decides to try something new. The lake seems to be about a hundred yards across, so as he sprints at it he adjusts his dive angle slightly higher. He can see his reflection in the water as he glides over it. Too late, he realizes that the pine trees are fairly close to the opposite edge and he won't get his feet down to stop before he crashes into them. The impact knocks the wind out of him. He lays still and slowly catches his breath, looking up at the ancient-looking trunks and spidery branches. A car door slams. He sees the silver SUV pull away but its tinted windows do not allow a glimpse of the driver. He doesn't catch all of the numbers on the Virginia tag.

"Are you okay?" Caroline calls from the other side of the lake.

He flashes her a thumbs-up. He stands, sore but not injured, and plots out a run that seems just long enough to get him back to her side of the lake. He takes a higher angle to compensate for the shorter run and lands fairly close to her.

"Someone saw me."

"Did you hear them laughing when you crashed?"

"Come on, this is serious. If word gets out my life is over."

"Well, not over. But different, yes."

"I should have been more careful."

Caroline runs her hand through his hair, then kisses him.

"Forget it. Even if they did see you, they'll probably think you're using some sort of hang glider or balloon. They won't know it's really just you doing it."

He gives her a dubious look.

"For heaven's sake, Gordon, I've been watching you for an hour and I barely believe what I'm seeing."

So has he, thought Gordon. *Whoever he is*.

As they drive back, they talk about all of the things he ought to try. Speed-climbing El Capitan without a rope. Winning every gold medal in the Olympic jumping events for the rest of his life.

Playing professional sports. *Redefining* professional sports. Flying to Europe without a plane. Foiling crime. Rescuing cats. Gordon plays along, but he knows he cannot do any of these things without sacrificing everything he loves. Living with the hot breath of fame on his neck has never attracted him, but living with the fear of an entire generation of people, fear that has always found a murderous way to express itself, would be impossible. He is unique among humans, untouched by the gravity that keeps the world in place. Not only would he be misunderstood, he would need to be destroyed so that everyone else could sleep at night.

Gordon offers to drop her off at her sister's apartment, but she insists on going to the psych building instead. Watching her walk in, he remembers how abruptly he left the Lab and decides to go back. When he pulls up to the entrance he sees his coffee mug on the flagstones where he left it. He scoops it up and walks in, accepting Mr. Williams' sly congratulations for the beauty of his female companion. Inside the Lab, only Stan and Wendell are still working. Gordon spends a few minutes chatting with each of them. Wendell says he has been learning how to ride a motorcycle and watches Gordon for a reaction, but Gordon does not seem to have heard. Distracted, he mumbles something about getting back to Shepardson's tractor and leaves. At the bar, he gives Martín the truck keys, then carries the rope and the belt up to his apartment and drops them along with his backpack. He walks downstairs, sits on the ground facing the tractor and begins to cry.

Chapter 13

Subterfuge

Well into the night, having dropped Shepardson's transmission and disassembled the clutch, having scanned the broken parts and printed new ones on Shiva and having reassembled the whole thing and tested it, Gordon still wonders why he broke down and cried. Even though he has spent the last few hours elbow-deep in grease, he knows he has had one of the most incredible days that any man in history has ever experienced. But in his heart he also knows that things have changed. He will be hurt, badly. He glances at his phone, silenced since he got back from Martín's. The hours working alone with his hands have been a meditation, just as they have been since his first whiff of hot motor oil and gasoline. Since he first realized that the skills in his fingers could translate into speed on the road, he has worked on engines bolted to go-kart frames, then dirt bikes, then his father's Yamaha. The memory of his long hours spent restoring that motorcycle calms him, as does the feel of hot water and the smell of hand soap. He looks over at the chrome spokes gleaming in the dim light, the flat handlebars, the matte gray tank nearly invisible in the shadows. His heart fills with a mixture of love and sadness as he thinks of his father. Perching on a stack of tires, he lights a cigarette and exhales. Whoever saw him fly, it'll wait until morning. Whichever way Caroline's affections go, at least he had today. Perhaps everything just overwhelmed him, or maybe the lingering shock of flying with the birds caught up at last. Whatever it was, Gordon resolves not to lose control again. He will shower, sleep and face his new reality tomorrow head-on.

In the morning, he wakes and gets dressed. He makes coffee, eats a few bites, streams some music and then, finally, checks his messages. Nothing. He packs up to go. Rather than wait for Henry's flatbed, he decides to simply drive the old harvester out to Shepardson's place. Gordon texts Martín for a ride back from the farm, then clips his truncated triangle to one of the huge rear fenders, pops in his ear buds and settles down for a long, slow ride in solitude. He thumbs the 'open' icon and watches the big door rise. The huge machine roars to life with a plume of black smoke and rolls coal for the first ten yards, leaving a thick cloud in its wake. He waits for the smoke to thin before he closes the garage door, then rumbles onto the street and winds his way out toward the county road. This is a good morning for metal, he decides, so he cues up 'Back in Black.' Angus Young's deliberate riffs seem to mimic Gordon's chugging pace. Soon he is miles out of town and playing air guitar as he steers with his knees.

At the farm, Gordon is not prepared for the extended Shepardson family to run down the dirt driveway and greet him. Three lanky coonhounds lead the way, baying at the sound of the tractor.

"That's you, ain't it?" Shepardson hollers, shuffling briskly at the rear. "In the video? You're wearin' the same damn work shirt you always do. And the hair..."

Shepardson's daughter lumbers up, trailing three children who hide behind her and take peeks at Gordon. Her husband stands a few paces away, hands on hips, cap tipped back on his head. He spits and adjusts his dip with his tongue.

"That wasn't too far from here, right?" the husband says.

Gordon is unsure how to answer them, so he taps his ear buds and shakes his head.

"Metallica!" he yells far too loudly.

In reality, no music is playing. Buying time, he takes out his phone and texts Martín:

"Need you to get here a little faster. Pls hurry!"

He looks up from the screen, pulls his ear buds out and kills the motor.

"What's going on?"

"I seen you flying!" Shepardson cries. "On the news!"

Gordon's stomach drops. He struggles to maintain a neutral expression, to breathe, not to run.

"Not sure what you mean, sir."

Feeling safe up high, Gordon stays seated on the harvester.

"What were you using, a cable or something?" the husband asks. "Looked like it was shot on a cell phone. Is that Shiva person a friend of yours?"

"Who, now?"

"The one who posted it online. 'ShivaDiva.'"

A chill runs down Gordon's spine. "Help me out. Someone named 'ShivaDiva' posted a video of me flying?"

"He's wearin' those metal things right now!" Shepardson's daughter points out. "See, on his legs."

"That WAS you!" Shepardson's grin is victorious. "I knew it!"

"Do those help you balance?" The husband walks closer. "Is that why you put them on when you took the rope off?"

He reaches out to touch Gordon's leg. Gordon pulls it away.

"Please," Gordon says. "This wasn't supposed to come out like this."

The man steps back, lifts his cap to scratch his head and spits again.

"Sorry."

"No man, it's okay." Gordon adds. "Just... I had no idea someone was taking a video."

The sound of an engine draws everyone's attention. Martín fishtails into the driveway, guns the pickup's motor and stops in a cloud of dust. When he hops down from the cab, the children run to the house. The husband bows up defensively.

"Gordon!" Martín yells. "Are you okay?"

"Yes, I'm fine. The Shepardsons were just telling me about a video they saw of me flying."

Martín walks forward, a panicked look on his face.

"No, no, Tío, it's alright. No big deal."

"Okay. We will go then."

Gordon climbs down and follows Martín to the truck. As he gathers his seatbelt, Shepardson jogs up waving a piece of paper.

"Hey, you forgot your check!"

Gordon opens the door and steps out again.

"I didn't mean for the whole family to attack you like that. Just that we've never seen someone we know on the teevee before."

"Makes two of us."

Shepardson hands Gordon the check. Gordon looks at the old farmhouse and the acres of land waiting to be planted.

"Sir, how are y'all doing?"

"We're fine." Shepardson stiffens slightly.

"Okay then." Gordon folds the check into his pocket and shakes the man's wizened hand. "Thank you, sir."

"That *was* you, wasn't it?"

Gordon winks. "Top secret. Mum's the word."

Once they have turned onto the road, Martín looks at Gordon.

"What did you say to that old man?"

"I told him it was top secret."

"Ay güey, you know that just makes people talk even more."

"Yeah, I guess."

On his phone, Gordon finds the video and scans the profile of the person who posted it. No prior videos, account created just a few hours ago. As he expects, it is shot from the direction of the silver SUV across the lake. The camera was too far away to identify Caroline, but the footage of Gordon flying across the lake clearly shows his face, right up to the moment that he slams into the tree. Curiously, the segments in which he is kissing Caroline and rolling on the ground with her have been omitted.

"Here, make a left."

They drive into the recreation area and park close to where the SUV had been. Gordon gets out and scans the ground, holding up a paused image from the video and checking its perspective from time to time. As he zeroes in on the spot, Martín watches two cars moving toward them. As Gordon takes a picture of the ground, Martín honks the horn.

"G, come now!"

Gordon looks up and sees the cars. He runs to the pickup, hops in and slams the door, sliding down into the wheel well as the cars stop and four people get out. They run toward the truck. Martín floors it and sprays gravel at them as he pulls away. Gordon looks back and sees one of them writing something in a small pad.

"Reporters. They probably got our tag."

"I told you to be careful, Gordon."

"Yeah, I know. That video was a message to me. It was posted by someone called 'ShivaDiva.'"

Martín suddenly looks much more concerned.

"Someone who wears boots with Vibram soles."

Gordon holds up the photo he took: a footprint.

Outside the bar, cars are double-parked and a small gaggle of reporters waits by the door. Martín does not slow down. They see more reporters clustered in the alley by the garage door.

"I'm sorry. I didn't mean for any of this to happen."

"Hey, it might be good for business."

"Can you maybe drop me at the Lab for now?"

When they arrive, they see Mr. Williams holding court with another handful of reporters outside the entrance. Gordon slips around to the side door, hood pulled low over his head, and smiles when he hears Mr. Williams relaying a recipe for sweet potato pie in great detail. Only at the last moment do the reporters see Gordon enter the building, but the magnetic lock closes before they can follow. Inside, Stan sits chatting with a woman, an old friend of his who works for the local paper. She has loosely-gathered gray hair and horn-rimmed glasses. She stands when she sees Gordon.

"G, meet Sue Eisenstern. She's cool."

Gordon shakes her hand.

"Love what you're doing here. Stan told me about the latest

patent, the transparent titanium."

"Off the record, I'm sure. Stan's more paranoid than any of us."

"Yes, of course."

"We didn't talk about your burgeoning film career," Stan adds.

Gordon rolls his eyes. He catches Sue staring at him a beat longer than is polite.

"I'm not gonna fly around the Lab, don't worry."

"Somebody's gotta tell the story, you know." Stan opens his palms. "Might as well be a friend."

"When there's a story to tell, Sue will be the first person I call."

"For what it's worth," Sue offers, "you should try to control the narrative before it controls you."

Mr. Williams comes into the Lab, chuckling and shaking his head at Gordon.

"Them newspaper folks are sure fired up to talk to you." He stops short when he sees Sue.

"She's okay, Mr. Williams," Stan explains. "We go way back."

"Y'all know anything about the birdman over there? 'Cause I sure don't. They showed me a video. Have to say, it did look a lot like you, G, and that fine lookin' Caroline Highsmith too. But goddamn if you weren't flyin' around! How'd you do that?"

Sue's eyes widen at the mention of the Highsmith name.

"Mr. Williams," Gordon cuts in. "Please tell Sue about that delicious sweet potato pie that Mrs. Williams likes to make."

"You liked that, huh? People don't listen too closely once an old man gets to tellin' stories. Anyway, just wanted to let you know there's more of 'em camped out by the front entrance now, so maybe slip out the back and find somewhere else to hole up."

"I'll drop you wherever you want," Stan offers.

"Thanks. I appreciate y'all."

Mr. Williams escorts Sue out while Stan does a final round with the students and leaves a grad assistant in charge. He and Gordon walk out the double doors and part, Stan heading to the front entrance and Gordon out the back door. Stan pulls his car around to meet him. On the way home, Gordon calls Martín and tells him to pass the word that Gordon is hiding at the Lab. By the time they get to the bar, the reporters are gone.

"You're a very popular guy," Martín observes.

"With all the fake videos out there, they decide this one is real?"

"It'd be pretty hard to fake flying a hundred feet in the air and then cruising across a lake and slamming into a tree without a single edit," Stan observes.

"So you've watched it?"

"Maybe fifty times. Can't say I blame you. Looked like a hell of a lot of fun."

"It was. Except maybe the tree."

Martín crosses to the window and picks at the corner of the playbill for their concert scheduled for the next night.

"Tío! What are you doing?"

"We can't do this now. It will be a zoo."

"You'll lose a ton of revenue."

"I don't give a shit about the money. We need to keep you safe."

"Like Stan's reporter friend said, it's time for me to control the narrative. This might be a chance to do that."

He walks over and presses the paper back into place.

After a few minutes, Stan walks out the front door and Gordon takes the back exit, which puts him in the alley by the garage entrance. Inside, he sees the Yamaha on its center stand. He wheels it to the overhead door and fires it up before tapping the open icon. When the door rises enough to let him out, he releases the clutch and takes off. As he screams up the alley, he hits the icon again and the door begins to close. He skids onto the street without looking back -- and without seeing a small man with a camera slip around the corner of the garage and under the closing door; a man wearing Vibram-soled boots.

As Gordon blasts through town toward the river, the man walks around the garage snapping pictures. He focuses on the equipment connected to the Shiva pipes and takes shots from many angles. He looks up the stairs to the loft, but as he is about to climb the first step the garage door begins to open. Martín ducks under it holding a shotgun, and walks slowly toward the photographer, then reaches out and takes the camera. He aims the shotgun at the man's face.

"Rather than turn over our security footage to the police, I think maybe you should leave this with me and go away."

The photographer's eyes are wide, his cheeks red. Martín cocks one of the hammers.

"Or we can discuss it, if you would prefer."

The photographer shakes his head vigorously, then nods just as fast, then shakes again.

"I'd like to go," he croaks.

Martín steps aside and nods at the door. He sees that the front of the photographer's pants are wet. The man runs awkwardly out to the street, turns and keeps going. Martín's shoulders sag as he closes up the garage and walks back to the bar. He abhors thugs, and at that moment he feels as if he has just acted like one.

Gordon sees the missed call as he walks down the embankment toward the river. He dials Martín and gets the story, and wonders aloud if the photographer really was paparazzi or if he might be working for North. Martín apologizes for not asking. Gordon agrees to examine the camera when he gets back.

"Hey." The voice comes from behind Gordon.

"What...?" Startled, Gordon looks around. "Hey!"

Caroline sits on the grass just beyond a clump of bushes, in the exact place Gordon was headed; the spot where they first made love. He sits down next to her, his leg touching hers out of habit. Her phone is open to the video, which is paused. They sit in silence and watch the river.

"Weird couple of days, huh?" he says at last.

"That's the problem. No. It just felt really good to be with you again." She looks at the screen. "Nearly a million views. Jesus."

Caroline pulls her knees up to her chest and rests her chin on them.

"You know Mr. Aryan American makes his millions selling

weapons to failing regimes, right?"

She looks at him, frowns, and drops her chin back down onto her knees.

"He's not a bad guy, Gordon. If you got to know him--"

"Fuck that."

"I'm just saying, there's more to him than money or football."

"I don't wanna hear it."

"Everybody thinks of him as the quarterback from the Rose Bowl, but he's very thoughtful."

"Y'all always did want to get out of Georgia," he says quietly. "Your dad to Washington, you to Palo Alto."

"Don't lump me in with him."

"Just, I get it. You started a new life, got yourself engaged, moved away from this place. Why'd you come back?"

"I told you, I'm studying psychology at--"

"Yeah, but really why? There's a million colleges in California can give you a degree. Why here?"

"David has a business plan for Georgia." She looks down at her feet. "And the people I want to help are here."

"People you never gave one shit about when you were here."

"That's not true."

Caroline's eyes meet his, then look away.

"People like I was? Lost souls you and Martín are gonna save?"

"Why are you being an asshole right now?"

"I love you, Caroline. Always have."

"Oh bullshit, Gordon! You never even saw me til I left here. I was always dumb old Caroline, girl next door."

"You're not dumb."

"But I'm not splitting atoms or whatever it is you and Emily were always talking about."

Gordon gives her a wounded look, which softens her for a moment. But her eyes harden again.

"It's not my fault she died, Gordon. I'm sorry I wasn't here. That was wrong. But you never thought about me like you are now. All you thought about was your goddamn science. Your inventions."

"Caroline, I was a kid. I--"

"So was I. But I grew up first. And I moved on."

"So why come back? I was okay til you showed up again."

"Were you? What's 'okay' to you? Walking around in a dream all the time? Ignoring the people right next to you? You're a ghost, Gordon. You always were."

"That's not true," he says weakly.

"What's not true? Your music? Up on stage, is that real? 'Cause I know you're hiding up there, too. I wanted you to be here, with me, and you never were."

"I was. Or I am now, at least."

"You just want what you can't have."

Gordon hears this and it wounds him, although he can't explain why. Rather than plumb the depths of his tortured narcissism, he takes out a cigarette and lights it. Caroline slaps it violently out of his mouth, sending a shower of embers out across the grass.

"What the...?"

"Save that poser shit for your groupies. I'm tired of it."

"Come on, Caroline."

"No." She stands up. "Jesus Christ, Gordon. Get over yourself."

"Why are you leaving?"

"Because you're here, and the guy who first showed me this place is long gone."

Gordon stares after her as she walks up the grassy hillside and out across the parking lot. Not knowing how to process the roil of emotions he feels, he lights another cigarette. He stares at the ember, feeling wasted and drained by the nicotine, his tongue dry and sickly-sweet. His throat is sandpapered raw, yet he still feels sadness welling up in it. Hemmed in by choices he did and did not make, he wants to lash out but doesn't know where or whom to attack. Control, the happy illusion he believed he possessed, now mocks him. How is this his fault? She was the one who left, not him. He has known that forever, or at least believed it.

How did she turn this around on me?

The brown river rolls by, cold and impersonal, sweeping as it did those years ago when he was whole and present and loving and Caroline would sit beside him and not run away. Now he feels utterly, completely, helpless. He feels ashamed, ridiculous, trapped by people who have no idea what his truth really is.

And this gives him an idea.

With a flick, Gordon sends the cigarette cartwheeling into the water. He throws the rest of the pack in after it. By the time he stands up, the little blue box has floated a hundred yards downstream. He shambles up to his motorcycle and kicks it to life, then heads out to the big-box store on the edge of town. When he returns to his apartment, he is wearing a baseball cap low on his head, and carrying a shopping bag full of cloth, cans of spray paint and a set of spandex workout clothes, all of it black.

Chapter 14

Harmony

The church sits on the corner of a ragged block near the outskirts of town. Small bungalows and threadbare, storm-fenced lawns dominate a neighborhood pocked here and there with empty lots. The modest chapel is tidy and well-maintained, certainly not opulent. A rectory extends at a right angle, two stories and brick, solid, utilitarian. Gordon parks the Yamaha under a streetlight and follows the unlit pathway in. Downstairs, he sees a dozen drums arranged in rows on the floor, mostly tall barrels and a few smaller snares. Martín walks around with a plastic bucket, placing a set of mallets on each big drum and regular sticks on the snares. Gordon reaches the foot of the stairs and looks around. Martín does not see him. At the far end, past a semi-circle of chairs, two doors lead to smaller rooms, one of which is lit. At a table, Gordon sees a slim, dark-haired boy sitting across from Caroline. He inhales deeply and walks in.

"Hey!" Martín calls.

Caroline walks out with the boy, her arm around his shoulders. When she sees Gordon she stops short.

"He's ready," she says after a moment. "What do you say, Daniel?"

"Sí, I like to play tonight."

"Alright, amigo!" Martín cheers. "You get the biggest drum, since you're the smallest dude."

Behind Gordon, men and women start to file in. Some are gaunt with addiction, while others bear no visible evidence of their pain. The room is silent as each moves closer to the chairs. Caroline and Martín drag two more seats into the circle, facing the group. Gordon leans against the wall and tries to fade into it.

"Okay, welcome, welcome!" Martín waves everyone in. "Everybody, this young brother is Daniel. Please, welcome him."

Daniel ducks, then looks up and flashes a shy smile. Most of the people smile back and wave hello. A few offer quiet greetings.

"He's gonna play tonight," Martín announces to scattered applause. "And that guy, too." Martín points at Gordon, who turns around and looks behind him at the wall, then shrugs. Caroline smiles for the first time.

"Hey, ain't you the one from the video?" asks a tall man with a graying goatee. A few others look at Gordon and nod.

"No, Bobby, that was someone else," Martín answers.

"Damn, bro, sure looks like him. Mechanic shirt and all. And her...?"

Caroline stands. "Well, let's get started. Everybody remember which drum you played last time?"

They rise and begin to drift back to the drums. Soon everybody wears one. One barrel drum is unclaimed, so Gordon lifts it and puts it on. They shuffle from foot to foot as the energy of the session builds. Caroline sits when Martín puts on his own small drum and takes out his whistle. He faces the rows.

"Okay, new guys?" He looks at Gordon and Daniel. "Just keep up. Listen to the beat and mimic it. Have fun!"

Martín blows three quick blasts on the whistle, then three more. He begins to tap out a fast Brazilian beat on his drum, occasionally tapping the rim and the sides. The barrel drummers find the longer beat within his and begin to pound. Gordon and Daniel watch them, then start to play. Daniel smiles when Gordon messes up and makes a face at him. He follows Gordon, who laughs when Daniel mimics the goofy way he dances to the beat. The snares jump in last, driving sharper notes in between the barrel beats, and the whole room dances slowly from foot to foot as music fills the space. Heads loosen and begin to nod. Smiles appear. Martín dances around in a circle, keeping his manic time. Caroline beams at Daniel, then at Gordon, who leads Daniel around in a circle and beats away at his drum. She sways with the infectious rhythm as the beat goes on and on.

After about ten minutes, Martín wraps up the song and everybody cheers. People who were stooped and withdrawn are now standing taller and smiling at one another. Daniel waves at Caroline, who gives him a thumbs-up.

"Go again?" Martín asks.

The loud consensus is yes.

The group plays another song, then another after that. There are no real melodies, just Martín freestyling over the bass drums and chattering snares. Nobody is worried about precision. They just waddle in a slow dance and pound out the raucous energy that lifts them all. When they finish, they cheer. Martín walks over to a cooler and passes out bottles of water, then asks them to put up their instruments and gather in the chairs. When they are seated, they hold hands and bow their heads.

Martín speaks. "With the strength of us all and with the strength of God, no one will fall. Every heart, every soul, as one. Feel the power of love. You are loved. You are loved..."

A few people join in, quietly repeating, "You are loved."

Gradually, the whole group says it together. Even Gordon, who found himself sitting in the circle without consciously moving there, repeats the words. He glances up and sees Caroline looking at him. With a quick smile, she looks away. Martín ends the session and the group disperses, much more talkative and lively than when they arrived. Caroline follows Daniel upstairs to wait for his mother. Martín and Gordon sit down again.

"What's on your mind, G?"

"Less now. That was fun."

"Come anytime. We're here every Wednesday night."

"Might have to do that. Hey, by the way, I was thinking we

should play some of our own stuff tomorrow night."

"They come to hear Carlos, not Martín."

"How do you know they won't like Martín just as much?"

"Dude..."

Caroline comes downstairs and pulls up a chair.

"He really loved it, Martín. That's the happiest I've seen him since his father died."

"Young brother's dad used to work at that chicken farm north of here," Martín explains to Gordon. "He wasn't quite... documented. They didn't care. They put up their flyers all over Mexico, looking for cheap workers. The family came here from Guanajuato, kept their heads down. One day, he got cut real bad at work. Got sick and died. Never had any insurance, nothing. Daniel don't have no one at home with his mama working all the time. So she sends him to us."

Gordon looks at Caroline and whispers, "Wow."

"This drum group was her idea," Martín explains.

"How long have you guys been doing this?"

"Just a couple of weeks," Caroline answers.

Gordon slowly nods and looks down at his boots. Caroline begins to stand up but Martín stops her.

"Stay, please. You two should talk. You know he didn't come here to look for a new drummer. I will go."

"No," Caroline says firmly. "Stay, please."

She sits back down and folds her arms.

"How come you don't play?" Gordon asks gently. "Drums, I mean."

She shrugs.

"Caroline, I just wanted to see you, that's all. This gravity thing..."

Her eyes clouding with tears, Caroline shrugs again, then stands and slowly walks upstairs. Gordon starts to follow her but Martín puts a hand on his arm.

"Give her a minute," Martín whispers.

The heavy rectory door opens and closes. Gordon sits back down.

"You know she loves you, right?"

Gordon stares at him and then looks away.

"Why you think she's here?" Martín asks.

Now it's Gordon's turn to shrug.

"It's because you're soul mates."

Gordon frowns and looks at his hands. The room grows still as he picks at a callus.

"You know," he mumbles, "I've been thinking about that, our souls."

"You? The atheist?"

"Yeah..."

Martín watches as an idea begins to animate Gordon's expression.

"Okay," Gordon begins. "So you say we're all part of the same energy... That even the matter we're made of is, too. And I can get with that. The problem is human intelligence. Our brains are designed to work with our senses. We believe our souls must be the same as our 'self,' but our self is mostly a by-product of our senses. Our memories. Our bodies. Proprioception."

"Pro... what?"

"That awareness of where your body is, where your arms and legs are. Like, you don't have to consciously think about where your mouth is if you move your hand to it in the dark. That instinctive sense of where it is is proprioception."

Gordon lifts his sleeve and shows Martín the arm weight.

"With this weightless thing, my proprioception was beginning to fail. That's why I wear these. But when I sleep, I take them off. Sometimes I just float and it's like my body goes away. All I feel is my mind. After a while, I can't tell where I stop and the world around me begins. Like there's no body, no self."

"Dude, that has to be freaky."

"It is. But it makes me think about this whole idea of differentiation that we get hung up on. Human intelligence is almost all about differentiation. Telling the difference between ourselves and someone else, friend and foe, what's real and what's imaginary, what will feed us and what will kill us. To us, dying seems like the end of the self, but only because it's *our* brains defining death. You say 'soul' and most people see a ghost shaped like them, floating around with no body, thinking all the same thoughts it did when it was alive. But I don't see it that way anymore."

"Why not? What's different now?"

"I think gravity is what reminds us of who we are. We feel our bodies constantly because of it. But I've kinda gotten free of that."

"I can't imagine forgetting about my body."

"You could. It's easy for our minds to get free once our bodies are out of the way. You start to sense something vast in your consciousness, something connected to everything else around you. It doesn't need a name, really. It doesn't need us to believe in it. It doesn't need anything. It just is. So instead of trying to believe in the God mask you hold up in front of it, just accept that your intelligence is limited by what you are and that this energy around us and in us is not. I can tell you, it's beautiful. It's everything. We use words like 'soul mate' to express that feeling of connectedness outside of our senses, because that's as close as our minds and bodies can get to how beautiful it is. But I think it's even bigger than that. I can't find a word for it, other than harmony."

There is a rustling by the stairs. Gordon turns and sees Caroline standing in shadow on the bottom step, leaning against the banister. She walks into the light and takes a seat.

"Go on," she says.

"I thought you left." Gordon studies her face. She has been crying but now she is inscrutable.

"I didn't. Go on, finish your thought."

Gordon is flustered.

"You were saying, harmony."

"Yeah... It's like those people who were here before. Like Daniel. They're walking around with all this pain. We all are."

She nods.

"They walk in here feeling alone," he continues. "All caged up in their own skin, just a bundle of senses looking out at everything else. Then you hand them a drum and say play, so they do, and after a while that cage goes away. Their senses change. The beat in them synchronizes with everyone else's. They move as one, in harmony."

Gordon can feel his heart pound as he stares into Caroline's eyes.

"One drum session and The Great Atheist has found God?" Caroline smiles at Martín. "Maybe I oughta have your job."

"What makes you think that now you got it right, G?" Martín asks.

"I don't. But I know we're all made up of the same energy -- everything and everyone in this world, probably in this universe. And harmony is the only way we can even begin to feel that connection."

"How about love?" Caroline asks.

Gordon studies her. "Only if it is harmonious."

"Harmony..." Martín considers. "Versus differentiation."

"I think it's just that simple. Every moral choice we face breaks down into those two options."

"I don't know about that," Martín demurs.

"As a priest, most of your job was to convince people not to serve their animal nature and to serve God instead, right?"

"More or less."

"So what did you tell them God wants them to do?"

"Love one another, do the right thing. Be kind."

"Pretty much what Muslims hear at their mosque, too. Basically, live in harmony."

"Okay..."

"You remember my dad's friend Munib? Came here after the war?"

"Yeah," Martín says. "Good guy."

"One of the kindest people I've ever met. So why didn't the two of you feel like you were on the same team?"

"We did."

"Same team, different rule books?"

"We understood each other outside of all that."

Gordon looks around at the room. "So if one of the parishioners here is walking down the street and sees a woman in a hijab, will he smile and say 'salaam alaykum?' Or will he think to himself, there goes someone who really ought to start learning about Jesus?"

"I think he would try to love or at least understand that person."

"Because your church teaches harmony. Not differentiation. But how many other churches do that?"

Martín looks away, thinking.

"But just getting along is not the same as really loving someone," Caroline challenges. "I would say most churches teach that you should actually love everyone."

"And how's that working out?"

Gordon gets up, walks over to one of the dark windows and taps it.

"Put on a hijab and drive twenty minutes in any direction out there. Get out and walk around. You know the looks you'll get from all those good Christians. Hell, I get those looks because I don't go to the barber."

"I get them too," Martín says softly.

"Okay, so imagine you're in Baghdad and you're *not* wearing a hijab..."

Caroline purses her lips and presses her fingertips to them. Gordon sits down again.

"Same reaction, different team. Just because your head is covered. Or not."

"Human nature," Martín murmurs.

"Exactly. That's why you can't just tell people to love one another while you're also saying your team is the only one holding God's true rule book."

"But people don't connect with all that abstract stuff," Caroline argues. "They don't get it."

"I know. I'm not asking them to."

"So why bother with it at all?"

"Because I want to understand. You know me."

Caroline smiles.

"The way I see it, the essence of a unifying intelligence would have to be harmony, not differentiation. From the perspective of the universe, all of our little conflicts are like waves on the beach. The waves keep coming, keep smashing the water apart, keep reclaiming it, keep cycling it back into the ocean. The water might get stuck in the sand for a while, but it gets back to the ocean one way or another. It starts again. We die, we disperse, we start again as something else. If we worry about the form we are in now, if we hang onto that differentiation, we can't harmonize with the universe. We put our own will ahead of God's."

Gordon sits back and folds his arms.

Caroline frowns. "So you think if people just 'harmonize with the universe' they'll conquer their fear of death?"

"No. But they might enjoy life more."

Martín shakes his head. "We got all these voices telling us our tribe is the most important thing in the world. Politicians, media..."

"Priests..." Gordon smiles.

"Priests," Martín agrees. "So you're gonna tell some guy who ain't got a high school education that he ought to harmonize with the universe instead of putting on a red hat or a blue hat and feeling like he's okay? Like he's in the group? Safe?"

"I'm not gonna tell him anything. I'm just telling the two of you because I love you and you understand. Besides, it's not really about harmonizing with the universe. It's about walking down the street."

Caroline gives him a puzzled look.

"You have a choice every time you walk past someone on the street. You can scan for clues that differentiate you: what his hair or skin looks like, whether he's wearing your color hat or listening to your music or your favorite politician on his ear buds. Whether he's the enemy or not. Or you can just relax and acknowledge that your soul and his soul are part of the same Soul, that you're both gonna die eventually, and that your deaths will be part of the harmony of all things."

Martín laughs out loud. "Vato, you ain't no atheist anymore."

"Don't get too excited, Tío. I'm never gonna be anybody's disciple. Or role model."

Caroline holds his gaze with an intensity he has not seen in a long time.

"Tonight you were, for Daniel."

As he stares at her, Gordon feels his heart beat faster, sending blood to an extremity that historically has been his moral undoing.

"Well then," he smiles, "I'm happy to help."

Chapter 15

Lies

Gordon peeks around the tall shades he has installed on the front windows of his apartment and sees the crowd that already spills onto the sidewalk in front of Martín's. Earlier, Martín texted that Gordon should use the back door, and now he knows why. While he is watching, a news van pulls up. He turns away as his text dings; it is Caroline, outside. He has not heard from her since the drum session three days earlier, so he walks down and opens the garage door for her. They duck in and close it before anyone gets close and walk upstairs.

"Hey, listen..." she begins. "I just... I wanted to say I'm sorry for that video. I dragged you out there."

"No, you didn't. I had been wanting to try that out. Besides, Martín will make some money off of it."

"So... Why were you at the river that day?"

"Had to get away from all of this." He gestures at the window.

"Um, they're here because you announced a show. Not exactly laying low, dude."

"Stan's writer friend told me to control the narrative."

"Narrative?"

"That video has close to two million views now."

Caroline walks into the kitchen area and finds a bottle of

bourbon. She pours two glasses over ice and Gordon takes one.

"To a new narrative," he toasts. They clink and drink.

"What's all this?" Caroline walks over to a pile of black material on the bed. Next to it is an oddly shaped helmet, a pair of gloves and a heavy looking breastplate.

"My costume."

She knocks on the metal breastplate. "What'd you do, rob a Roman centurion?"

"No, I printed that. The mask too."

She picks it up, recognizes it and bursts out laughing, then tosses it onto the bed and walks back to him.

"You never cease to amuse me."

Downing her drink, she sets the glass down and kisses him.

"What are you doing?"

"Maybe I want what I can't have, too."

Gordon inhales deeply the scent of her hair. They walk to the bed, sweep the costume off and fall together, peeling off their clothes. Before Gordon takes off his weights, he grabs the tether attached to his bed.

"That seems so kinky..." Caroline murmurs.

"Necessary. Or you can just stay on top."

Caroline's skin is warm on his, her cheek soft and familiar against his stubble. They move together easily, naturally, her gentle hip movements growing in intensity, his hands on her back and breasts. They embrace and press tight, eyes closed, bodies melding and moving until they reach the climax together. After a few deep breaths, Caroline opens her eyes.

"Holy shit, Gordon!"

He looks at her, then follows her gaze over his shoulder. They are floating about five feet above the bed. He holds her tightly and begins to feel her weight on him as they descend.

"What the hell was that?" she asks.

He wonders how the effect could have transferred to her.

"What were you thinking while that was happening?" he asks.

"I wasn't. I just felt really close to you. It seemed more... honest, or something, than it was before. There was nothing between us. Just... love."

Gordon's eyes widen a little. He nods and agrees.

"Not the kind with expectations," she adds. "Just the real, pure thing. Like, the sex wasn't even part of that."

"Well, I don't know about that... But I get it. I felt that too."

When Caroline stands and starts to dress, Gordon holds the tether and floats up to the end of it, lost in thought.

"You better suit up, superhero."

He works his way down and hugs her close. They stay rooted on the ground.

"Sorry," she says. "The moment has passed."

"Okay."

"He's coming back tonight. David."

Gordon turns away and looks down at his costume, suddenly feeling ridiculous again. His jaw tightens as he begins to put it on. Caroline touches his shoulder.

"Gordon, I'm sorry."

"Hey, it is what it is."

He turns around and meets her sad gaze.

"But it doesn't have to be," he adds.

In the bar, Martín helps his two bartenders as they struggle to keep up with the crowd's orders. They are filled to capacity. The front windows are open, and the throng outside presses for a view. The television truck has extended its satellite antenna and set up temporary lights. At her barstool, Caroline sips another bourbon and watches the scene with amusement. Julia sits beside her, and Stan and Ravi are on her other side.

The door behind the bar opens and a dark silhouette appears. It seems to have horns. In one gloved hand is Gordon's electric guitar. When he walks out into the light, people realize he is wearing a full Batman costume. They erupt in cheers and laughter. Gordon gathers his cape and hops up onto the bar. It is a long distance to the stage. He rips off the Batman mask and tosses it behind the bar.

"Want me to fly there?" he yells, pointing to the stage.

The room roars. He hands his guitar to Martín and crouches

into a diver's pose. Through the open window, he notices the red light of a television camera so he grins and flaps his cape like wings.

"Okay, ready?"

They roar again. He tenses, dives out over the crowd and plummets into the reaching hands. They groan, but start to cheer again as the hands pass him to the stage. He steps onto the boards, turns around and raises his hands.

"See, I *can* fly!"

The crowd's loud response is a mix of cheers and boos. Martín and the band climb onstage.

"Well, I may not be able to fly, but hopefully I can play."

Gordon turns to the band as they plug in, strum and tweak their tuning. Behind his cape, he takes off the extra weight belt he had disguised as a Batman accessory and drops it behind an amp. With his back still turned to the audience, he begins to play a western sounding riff as Martín starts to gallop on the snare. The song builds until Gordon suddenly jumps about seven feet in the air, twisting his body so his cape floats out around him. A hundred cell phones record the move. As he lands, he slashes at his guitar and Martín kicks the bass drum.

"I'm baaaaack!" Gordon bellows, not quite Steven Tyler but mimicking his rasp. "I'm back in the saddle again!"

The carnival atmosphere of a massive crowd and a news van, combined with warmer weather and plenty of alcohol inside and outside the bar, has everybody feeling good. People dance in the street as Gordon and Martín lead the band through a mix of old classics and their own new music. The crowd continues to grow as the curious wander closer and stay to drink. Halfway through the set, Gordon sees David walk in and edge his way toward Caroline, his face a mixture of tension and mild disgust. Gordon wraps the song he is playing and turns to speak with Martín. Martín smiles and relays the message to the band, then initiates a pattering beat that Gordon answers with a stark repeating riff before he turns to the mic.

"Here come old flattop, he come groovin' up slowly..."

Never once during 'Come Together' does Gordon look

directly at David, but he can tell from David's body language that he may as well have been holding up his middle finger at the tall Californian. David barely sips the drink that Caroline hands him. Halfway through the song, he grabs Caroline's arm and pulls her toward the door.

"What the fuck?" Caroline yanks her arm away.

"That asshole is mocking me," David snarls. "We're leaving."

"We?"

"Fine then, you stay. I'm going to the hotel."

David turns and pushes his way out of the bar. Caroline's tough demeanor begins to melt into tears as she sits back down beside Julia, who gathers Caroline's hair away from her wet cheeks and puts an arm around her.

"He's staying at a hotel?" Julia asks gently.

Caroline nods. "He doesn't like my sister's apartment. Says he feels cramped in there."

"But a hotel room must be even smaller, no?"

"Not the ones he gets."

Julia removes her arm and reaches back for Caroline's drink, which she hands to her.

"May I ask, what do you see in him?"

Caroline looks up at her, then over at Gordon. "Well he's not crazy, for one thing."

Julia tips her head back and laughs heartily, which draws a smile from Caroline.

"He's actually very sweet," Caroline says. "We got engaged at the top of Yosemite Falls, one of my favorite places in California. He lugged a bottle of champagne in a backpack full of ice up three thousand vertical feet. Got down on one knee on a cliff overlooking the valley." She dabs at her eyes. "When he wants to be, he can be very thoughtful."

"And it is different now?" Julia asks.

"No. Yes... I don't know." Caroline watches Gordon lean into a fast little riff and then pivot away from the crowd as Martín begins a solo. "In California, my life is his life. We go to these amazing parties, all these celebrities. Like, some of them even know me now. Not as me, but like, through him. Even my dad..."

Julia watches Caroline's expression cloud over and waits for her to continue. Caroline takes a big swig from her glass, winces and looks at Julia.

"My dad, like, *knew* about David. Like, before I even told him I was dating him. My dad looked at me differently, you know? Like, finally something I did surprised him. Just... it's all that. David's a really cool guy. Everybody loves him."

Caroline's eyes begin to tear up again. Julia pulls her into a hug and whispers in her ear.

"And you wonder maybe why you do not anymore?"

Caroline presses her cheek into Julia's shoulder and shakes her head, then nods. She lifts her face away and stares at Julia through her wet tangle of hair.

"I don't know," she says softly as she brushes her hair away from her face. She looks back at Gordon, who is laughing with Martín between songs. "Honestly, I just don't know."

After a few more songs, Caroline hugs Julia, waves goodbye to Gordon and leaves. The party barrels on until closing time, then continues in the street until a squad car pulls up, its light bar flashing silently in the night. Two officers get out and Martín joins them to encourage the raucous group to disperse. After the people have gone, Gordon wanders over to sit at the bar with his friends. Julia dozes in her chair. Stan recognizes that Ravi is quite drunk, and puts his arm around him.

"We better get this one home," Stan says as his cell phone dings. He removes his arm from Ravi and checks the message, then chuckles and holds up his phone. "Trish came through."

Gordon takes the phone and watches the video that Stan's friend Trish has posted, then passes it around so everyone else can see it. She has given it the same hashtags as the first viral video, and it already has several hundred views. It shows a woman lifting up Gordon's dri-fit shirt and pointing at the breastplate underneath as he swims the crowd toward the stage. Someone asks her what it is, and she says it's metal.

"He's probably got his flying device turned off right now,"

she observes.

The video cuts to the same woman recording Gordon's opening leap into 'Back in the Saddle,' then looking into the camera.

"Guess he turned it back on."

"Why do you want people to believe you have a flying device?" Ravi asks Gordon.

"Because people will ignore almost anything if there's some explanation for it, no matter how ridiculous," Gordon answers. He looks at Martín. "The only thing that really scares them is a miracle."

The wide lawn is crossed with flagstone paths. Gordon and Stan walk purposefully toward the arch and Broad Street.

"Did you know North is down here setting up shop to run for office?"

"Where'd you hear that? It doesn't sound like something he would do."

"Ravi listens to the right-wing radio shows. They were talking about North Industries' planned expansion in Georgia. He wants to build a huge factory. The announcer said, 'someone like that oughta run for office.' You know those yahoos don't say anything on the air that's not written on the back of a check."

"Ravi listens to the right-wing radio shows?" Gordon laughs incredulously.

"He calls it 'opposition research.' I think he just gets turned on by how butch they sound."

Stan waves at his friend Sue, who walks up and gives him a hug and shakes Gordon's hand.

"I saw your new video." She turns to Stan. "That was Trish, wasn't it?"

Stan nods. "We took your advice. Now the comments are all about a secretive young inventor trying to be Iron Man in real life."

"Safer than what they *were* saying," Gordon adds.

Sue still clearly anticipates learning what the real story might be.

"Does this urgent little chat have something to do with that?"

"Yes," Gordon answers. "We're about to meet with our patent attorney to file prior art on a wearable personal flying device."

Sue's eyes widen. "On the record?"

"Not yet, but once something's filed, of course it's in the public domain. So if a reporter were to do a USPTO search, she might break an amazing story."

"Probably national, I'd say," Stan adds. "With a local Athens connection."

"Even if the actual technology is complete horseshit?"

"Who's to say it is?" Gordon knocks on his chest. "Feels pretty solid to me."

"Besides, her subsequent exposé of the 'rejected' filing might get even more attention," Stan speculates.

"Who says a patent filing is even newsworthy?" Sue protests.

"The one after this will be, trust me," Stan counters.

"Oh yeah, the transparent titanium?"

"Yep," Gordon confirms. "You can break that one, too."

"Ahh, I get it. I push your bullshit about flying machines and you toss me a story about invisible metal."

"Transparent, not invisible," Gordon clarifies.

"Sue," Stan soothes. "Every media outlet on the planet will want to know about our titanium. It's a career story."

"And I already have it. So why should I lie for you?"

"You're not lying," Stan corrects her. "We are about to file this. Perfectly legitimate."

"Come with us to see Jalen if you don't believe it," Gordon adds.

"Jalen *Woods*?" Sue asks. "My ex-girlfriend Sandra's son?"

Stan's expression softens. "Yes, that Jalen."

"Not fair, Stanley." Sue's look is wistful. "Well... okay."

The three-story brick building is a couple of blocks away from the North Campus. They arrive in minutes and press the button marked 'J. Woods.' A male voice answers the intercom and buzzes them up. On the third floor, they see a tinted glass door marked with simple sans-serif lettering: Jalen Woods, Attorney.

Inside is a single-room office with exposed brick walls and tall windows at the far end. A small desk sits by the door and a larger one faces it. On one wall is a poster-sized photograph of a Georgia defensive back making an incredible leap to intercept a pass. The name on the back of the jersey is 'Woods.' Along the other wall hangs a row of framed United States Patent Office certificates. A picture of a happy young couple sits on a low shelf behind the desk: Jalen and his wife, Angelique. Jalen is Gordon's height but slightly heavier. His crisp blue shirt strains against muscles that appear to be made of stone. He wears suit pants, leather shoes and tortoise-shell glasses and his hair is long, dreadlocked and tied back. He walks over and raises a tattooed hand to Gordon, who grasps it and pulls Jalen into a quick hug.

"G, we gotta talk." Jalen's brow is furrowed with worry. "Berrigan sent over executed copies of that contract, but I think it's too simple. Hell, you wrote it back in college -- without a lawyer."

"I trust him."

"Stan?"

"It's his baby, Jalen. He knows the guy better than any of us."

"That's a helluva lot of money," Jalen cautions.

"He's already got three Shivas up and running," Gordon says, "and fifty more in production. It's a formality."

Jalen is incredulous. "You let him start without a signed deal? That's fucking crazy."

Gordon just smiles.

Sue edges into the office. Jalen recognizes her and greets her with a hug. He circles back around his desk as everyone sits.

"Sue, can I get you anything? Water? Coffee?" Jalen asks. He looks at Gordon and Stan. "Y'all know where stuff is."

Sue accepts a bottle of water. Suddenly, seeing his friend's vigorous competence, Gordon feels a pang of regret; he doesn't want to waste Jalen's time. The familiar, slow melody of 'Naima' is barely audible on the sound system.

"Coltrane," Gordon comments.

"My mother taught me to appreciate jazz, but Trane taught me to love it."

"Sandra always loved the singers," Sue recalls. "Billie Holliday, Sarah Vaughan."

"I'll tell her you remember," Jalen says warmly. He turns to Gordon. "So, Batman, what are we filing today?"

Gordon smiles but doesn't say anything.

"Man, I thought *I* had some ups..." Jalen waits a beat. "Seriously, what's going on?"

Gordon looks around. "Can y'all keep a secret? I mean seriously, like tell absolutely no one?" They nod. "It's just that, well, I really can fly."

Jalen sits back in his chair and laughs. When Gordon does not, he rocks forward.

"On the real? Like, no machines or nothing? Fly?"

"Yep."

Sue's eyes are wide.

"We agreed, off the record," Gordon reminds them.

"Okay..." Jalen leans in. "So what are we going to do with that?"

"Lie. To the government."

Stan snorts. "With this president? Lying is business as usual."

Jalen does not smile. "Black folks don't tend to do well breaking the law, even when the guy in charge is dirty."

"We can file without your name on it," Gordon offers. "It just needs to be a public filing, not a provisional application or anything like that." He looks at Sue. "So the press has something to write about."

"*You* want the press involved?" Jalen asks.

Gordon nods solemnly. "Not what I would choose, but I think it's necessary."

Jalen sits back and steeples his fingers. "So, you've got two stories kicking around now, the 'miracle' and the 'machine.' And I have to say, I get why you would push the machine. Some crazy folks out there."

"A wise woman told me to control the narrative."

"Control it, not turn it into science fiction," Sue corrects.

She gathers her bag and stands to go.

"I hate to leave right now, but I do have an appointment."

"I'll join you," Stan says.

Jalen walks around and gives Sue another hug.

"Love to Sandra, as always. And don't worry," Sue says to Gordon, "I won't tell anyone about this. Yet."

Gordon shakes her hand. "I trust you. And I'll trust you to tell the real story properly when the time is right."

As Sue and Stan head out, Jalen sits down and crosses his arms.

"So how does this work, anyway? You just decide to fly and then... fly?"

"Not quite."

Gordon takes off his weight vest and hops up easily to touch the twelve-foot ceiling. Jalen makes an involuntary move to run, then laughs nervously and sits back down as Gordon puts his vest and shirt back on.

"That is some freaky... So if you don't keep those on, you just float up... where? Into the stratosphere?"

"Yeah, I guess so. I don't want to find out, anyway."

"You know, we could get you one hell of a contract in the NFL. NBA too, probably."

"And I could win the Olympics for the next fifty years. Yeah, I thought of all that but it wouldn't be right. Besides, I don't think that's why this is happening."

"You think there's a reason for this? What'd you finally get religion or something?"

"Not in any churchy kind of way. But this has sort of forced me to check my assumptions."

"I hear that."

"Martín told me once that all I had to do was walk out on the sidewalk and take off my weights and I'd be the most famous person in the world."

"Pretty much."

Gordon sighs. "If there's a hell, that would be mine."

"So you'll write up some bullshit about a flying machine, file for a patent and let Sue do an article on it, and that's supposed to keep people *away* from you? Dude, you really don't understand."

"Lesser of two evils."

"You could just hide out like Howard Hughes with your big pile of money and let people forget about you."

"I could," Gordon admits. "But where's the fun in that?"

Chapter 16

Fealty

Gordon takes a deep breath and knocks on the screen door. The Saturday sound of televised baseball leaks through, growing louder as the interior door cracks open. Wendell peeks out shyly. When he sees Gordon, he relaxes and opens it wide.

"Hey bud, your dad home?"

"Yeah, he's out back."

On the couch, Wendell's mother sprawls limp-limbed, her chest barely moving. The coffee table is littered with cups, cans and ashtrays, many brimming with cigarette butts. A piece of tin foil lays next to a lighter, pinched into a cup and blackened with residue. Wendell follows Gordon's gaze to the mess, then hurries into the kitchen for a garbage bag and rushes to clean it up.

"Okay then," Gordon calls through the screen. "Gonna head around back."

Wendell does not look up. Gordon walks around to the cement pad where three men sit at a picnic table strewn with beer cans and fast food wrappers. Two large coolers sweat next to an unused grill. A television sits just inside the sliding door, turned to face the patio and blaring play-by-play from SunTrust Park. Smoke hangs over them.

"Mr. Stainfield."

Gordon offers a wave when Wendell's father turns around. Stainfield pulls a stub of cigar from his mouth and spits on the concrete.

"Whatta you doin' here?"

The other men flash looks of recognition at Gordon, and begin a quiet conversation. One takes out his phone to show the other. As expected, Gordon hears Caroline's familiar whoop a few seconds into the video.

"Come to see about that John Deere," Gordon answers. "Sorry I didn't get by sooner."

"Yeah, well, from the looks of it you been busy."

The two men laugh nervously. They stare at Gordon, along with Stainfield. The latter's eyes narrow as he smiles.

"Not gonna be needin' the Deere anymore. Got a new source of income."

Gordon feels his stomach tighten. He glances at the sliding door but does not see Wendell.

"No, it ain't him. Them drawin's ain't quite so lucrative as you thought."

"Sorry to hear that."

"Got hired on to do some land scoutin'. Big company lookin' to set up here in Clarke County."

"I didn't know you had experience with real estate."

Stainfield's smile fades. "Lot you don't know, ain't there?"

"I'm sure there is."

One of the men watching the video squints up through his own cigar smoke. His gray goatee and thin eyebrows are the only visible hair on his square, pink head.

"How'd you do this?" he asks. "This some kinda flyin' belt you got on?"

Gordon tips his head sideways and begins to answer, but Stainfield cuts him off.

"Ain't no flyin' machine," Stainfield answers authoritatively. "Wendell said they ain't got nothin' like that in their Lab."

"Well now," Gordon drawls, "Wendell don't know everything we're workin' on."

"S'pose not," Stainfield allows.

"Pastor Ken said this here's a miracle, Roger," the man holding the phone says to his bald neighbor. "He seen it too."

Roger's brow furrows as his jaw clamps down on his cigar.

"Harlan, ain't nothin' a miracle if a human being done it."

"Well, I'm just tellin' you what Pastor Ken said."

"Pastor Ken thinks the last election was a miracle too."

Roger takes his cigar out and works his tongue over the flecks of tobacco on his lips.

"Well, ain't it? Nothin' but Jesus himself coulda made that man president."

"There's a big difference between a con man squeakin' out the electoral vote and this here fella takin' off like a bird," Roger declares. He turns to Gordon. "Son, are you a miracle?"

The table erupts with laughter. Gordon flashes an easy smile, but he focuses with concern on the man who relayed the pastor's speculation.

"Not hardly," Gordon answers.

Stainfield puffs at his cigar, then accepts that it has gone out and tosses it onto the sparse lawn. He takes a long drink of beer instead.

"Okay then." Gordon waves as he turns to go. "Nice to see y'all."

"Well hang on, now," Roger says. "We'd like to know how you did manage to fly all over that video."

"Without any cables, neither," Harlan adds.

"Nothin' but that shit eatin' grin." Stainfield holds up the paused video. Gordon is skimming across the pond, still unaware that he is about to hit the tree. "She must be one hot number, huh?"

Gordon feels a rush of anger at the thought of Stainfield leering at Caroline.

"Oh, looky there," Stainfield crows. "He's gettin' mad. You two get a little airborne together?"

"Flying Dutchman?" Roger cracks.

They laugh even harder. Gordon feels his neck flush as he struggles to maintain control. He turns and walks away.

"Oh come on," Stainfield calls after him. "Take a joke, why don't ya."

"Just havin' a little fun," Roger adds.

Gordon does not look back, but he pauses to listen once he gets around the corner of the house.

"I'm tellin' ya," Harlan argues, "it's a miracle. Ain't no other explanation for it."

"What do you think," Roger asks, "he's bein' raptured up to heaven or somethin'?"

"Yeah!" Harlan agrees. "I bet that's it!"

"Well he was standin' right there, Harlan," says Roger. "How's it possible he's still walkin' around here if Jesus is lookin' to rapture him?"

"Guy like him?" Stainfield cries. "He don't even go to church. Wendell says he don't believe in God."

Roger laughs loudly. "And you do? You'd steal the beard off o' Santa Claus if he wasn't lookin'."

"The hell I would!"

Stainfield's chair scrapes on the concrete. Gordon turns and walks back to where he left the Yamaha, chuckling at the image of the old men throwing wheezy haymakers at each other. He is surprised to see Wendell sitting on the bike. Gordon's helmet and backpack lay on the ground. Wendell flips the kickstarter pedal out and jumps on it. The recoil nearly launches him off the bike.

"Need to put it in neutral before you kick it," Gordon instructs.

"Can I ride it? Please? I been learnin' on Henry's dirt bike."

"I'm sorry, Wendell. Can't let you do that. What if you get hurt?"

"Ain't gonna get hurt."

"Well, maybe we can do a lesson one day, but not right now if that's okay."

Wendell grudgingly dismounts and stands near Gordon as he hops on.

"I know how to ride," Wendell tries again.

"I'm sure you do."

Gordon reaches out to pat Wendell's shoulder, but Wendell pulls away.

"Coulda rode it," Wendell mutters as he turns and runs inside.

Gordon stares after him, vaguely aware that he has misunderstood the brooding boy but unable to name Wendell's issue. He remembers the men out back and pulls his helmet and backpack on, kicks the starter and accelerates away. Wendell will be a problem for another day. Flying along the county road, Gordon looks at the land on either side and wonders how North might make use of it. Maybe he'll do some good for the local people, but Gordon wants nothing to do with it. As he twists the throttle and enjoys the speed, he wonders if he is being selfish, if even armaments might be acceptable if they provide career prospects to a region that badly needs them. Then he pictures all of those weapons rolling off the line and out the door into the world. Everywhere they went, they would bring death and destruction. Peace is a function of harmony, Gordon concludes, and that would be its opposite. There are an infinite number of ideas and an infinite variety of products that could be manufactured in North Georgia.

We'll just have to come up with better ones.

The road winds north into the Appalachian piedmont, through rolling green hills that promise to rise as mountains if one travels far enough. Suddenly free for the rest of his Saturday and in need of space to think, Gordon inhales the scent of pines and rolls the throttle on. The heat of late Spring has not yet come, but the sun shines high and warm. He has no plan; he merely feels an instinct to wander and maybe to hike, to feel normal again for a moment in his strange new gravity-free universe.

An hour passes and Gordon pulls into a gravel lot near a trailhead that leads into the national forest preserve. He takes off his hoodie and stuffs it into his pack, and considers leaving his weight vest with the bike but decides against it. In his grease-stained jeans, motorcycle boots and mechanic's work shirt, Gordon does not look much like a hiker but he slings his pack onto his shoulders and starts off. The trail is wide and well-maintained, and quickly gains elevation as it meanders through the old-growth forest. About a mile into the walk, he comes to a small clearing amid the tall trees. Years ago, he and Caroline visited this place. A deadfall trunk now lays along one side where a storm must have dropped it, but mostly the place feels the same as it did when they lay there on a blanket that afternoon.

Gordon drops his pack in the grass and lies down to rest against it, but as usual his head drifts up once his muscles relax. He closes his eyes and lets his thoughts wander and dissolve into simple awareness. He feels the high blue sky without seeing it, senses its energy, its pull. The air shimmers with the benign presence of trees, live and still, unsighted but vigilant as they take him in and gauge his intent. Squirrels chatter on his left. Above, there is the call of a raven. His hands brush the warm grass, his arms and legs pinioned by weights yet themselves light and buoyant. A fly buzzes with velocity. Moments come and go as time folds on him in waves, sound and scent awash with purpose, sunlight flooding everything beyond the pink of his eyelids. He dares not open them, as if sight could overwhelm the scenes he has built with the siftings of his other senses.

His mind stirs again. He is a tactile thinker, a man of lines. This thing that has happened to him, this change within and around him, this break with causality, with logic -- it does not work. This weightlessness in another man would be welcomed as a gift and after a while considered a birthright, but to him it is an assignment for which he has no rules. His world has always been divided between what is and what could be; the raw material and the dreams to be built with it. Laying there, he feels his body keenly but he has no idea what to make of it now that it has leapt from the known to the unfathomed. He listens for the spaces between each sound, the air between the rustling boughs, the distance into which birdsong dies. He is trying to draw lines in water, he knows, boundaries and delineations that mean nothing and disappear as soon as he creates them. He is powerless to grasp the intention of a Being so eternal that it might cast away the bedrock rule of his life, gravity, merely to see how he responds. That this was done intentionally, directly and personally to him, strikes him as illogical, but he is human so it feels precisely like that. That Gordon might ever divine that intention without inventing it himself is less certain. But he lays there, arrogant and dutiful, and tries. And fails. And falls asleep.

After a while, he blinks open his eyes. Slowly, he begins to sense something about the creatures around him. They are making choices. The bird lands, chirps, flies off. The squirrel climbs, changes his mind, clatters down, changes it again, goes back up. All around, living things are exercising their will. He notices the limb above. It curves and forks, each fork curving again. To him the limb's growth, driven toward the sun and away from the wind, looks less like a series of choices than do the movements of the frantic little squirrel, but perhaps to one who watches from a position of timelessness they are the same. Like the squirrel, it might very obviously be another organism reacting to the thousands of stimuli visible to a sharp enough eye. As might we.

This thought makes Gordon sad at first, but the more he considers it the less it bothers him. The monumental burden of choice, of cause and effect, of how to spend his fleeting time on earth, has always been a torment to him. He packs his days with studied randomness, leaving room for imagination and effort but also accepting the structures that help him focus. Before gravity fled, his movements were efficient; disorganized to an observer, but calibrated to his own needs. Within his ecosystem he has absolute freedom to pursue whatever serves his ambitions. He finds places that suit his purposes -- the Lab, the garage, the bar -- and scrambles between them, as his mind decides and his heart demands. If he were honest, he would also admit that he does that with people.

Gordon sits up. Suddenly impatient, he grabs his pack and starts down the trail to the parking lot.

Christ, so much to do. Why were you laying around like that?

He reaches the bike and quickly puts on his helmet and roars off, fishtailing as he angles for the paved road. He is agitated, no longer basking in the serenity of the land. Muscling the bike around each curve, he rides as fast as he can toward town. The hour passes in a blur of thought. He feels vaguely like he was close to an understanding, like he was standing at the verge of an awareness or the opening between two heavy curtains and he turned away. He wills his mind to stop, but it won't.

Does the squirrel really know his true place in the forest? Is he the planter of trees? The breeder of pups? Is he food for hawks and foxes and worms? Is he all of these things? What does he think he is? Does he think he chose to be that?

Gordon leans into another turn, then another.

Am I really free?

The motor vibrates, hotter and hotter. He hears Jalen's voice again:

"That's a helluva lot of money."

But do I have any control at all?

I could steer this bike into that retaining wall if I chose to.

But will I? No.

So why not?

Did I choose not to?

The miles fly by as Gordon's mind chews on these questions to avoid another one:

Do I use people for my own selfish reasons?

Am I using Caroline?

Is she using me?

It is well into the afternoon when Gordon arrives at home. With a pang of idler's guilt, he considers going up to his place and starting a new design but instead he walks up the alley to Martín's. He debates telling Martín that he and Julia are now the owners of the entire building, but he notices the couple two seats away. Their American beer and red Georgia sweatshirts signal their loyalties as they stare at a baseball game on the flat screen above the bar. He smiles at them, hoping they have not watched any internet videos recently. Martín sets a glass of water down in front of him.

"Thanks. Hey, I was wondering something."

Martín leans on his elbows and waits for more.

"How do you think the people in Mexico would react to someone like me? I mean, someone who can... do what I do."

Martín stands tall and crosses his arms, then shakes his head.

"Oh, vato, I'm afraid it would not go well for you there."

"Yeah, I kinda figured."

Gordon scans the bottles behind the bar.

"How about a Woodford rocks?"

"You're a grown man, G. But no motorcycling, okay?"

"Scout's honor."

Martín laughs in his expansive way, which invites the couple and Gordon and everyone else to smile and wonder what happened.

"You as a Boy Scout. Now that is funny!"

"Hey! I just went hiking a little while ago."

Martín laughs even louder as he pours Gordon's drink. He opens a bottle of tonic water for himself.

"Salud!" He holds up his bottle to Gordon, then turns to the couple and repeats the toast.

They smile and raise their beers to him.

Gordon picks up his drink and salutes his neighbors and Martín and takes a healthy sip. Above the bar, the picture of his father with Martín catches his eye.

Martín notes Gordon's gaze. "I miss him."

"Sometimes I feel like I can't even remember him," Gordon confesses. "Like the idea of him gets in the way of the real memory."

"It is the same for me."

Gordon nods slowly, drains his glass and slides it forward for a refill.

"Maybe this whole thing would make more sense if we could hold onto a little wisdom after it's over. Maybe bring it back with us in our next life. Otherwise we're just squirrels, burying nuts by instinct because there's a little less daylight today than there was yesterday."

"Is there nothing in between?" Martín asks. "Can we not learn enough to make one lifetime worthwhile?"

"Maybe."

Gordon looks out at the shadows creeping down the facade across the street, then drinks the second glass and asks for another.

"Have to hope so, right?" he concludes.

They sit in silence for a while, watching the game. Gordon takes out his phone and jots a few notes from time to time. The couple gets up, thanks Martín and leaves. Gordon continues to drink bourbon, his expression distant and troubled. Martín sets a bowl of nuts down near him, but Gordon does not touch them.

"Is something wrong, son?"

"No, Tío, no. Just an odd day, is all. I expected to work and got cancelled out. You know I don't do idle very well."

Martín smiles as he pours another drink. "Yes, I am aware."

"By the way, Berrigan signed the contract. So technically I guess I'm celebrating."

Martín's eyes open wide.

"This whole building is yours, Tío."

Martín looks around, slowly realizing what Gordon has said. He walks around the bar and hugs Gordon, smiling broadly.

"Can I tell Julia?"

"Hell yes, tell whoever you want. And Tío?"

"Yes?"

"Thank you. For... everything."

Both men have tears in their eyes as Gordon finishes his drink. He hugs Martín again and heads for the door. He steps into the darkness and feels the bourbon even more in the cool night air. The memory of a drunken stroll across campus with Caroline plays in his mind. He savors the image of her bare skin against the dark sky, the feel of her warmth on him. He has never mastered the subtlety of whiskey drinking, preferring instead to hammer his mind with it at those moments when thought or inhibition seems burdensome. Sensing the brown claws closing around his awareness, he angles for the soft glow of a restaurant. Outdoor seating, perhaps a burger. There is a hostess, a podium. Families.

"One, please," Gordon mumbles, leaden with booze. "Dinner,

yes."

The perky coed leads him into the main dining room. He is about to stop her and ask for an outdoor table when he notices a couple in a booth, a tall man laughing with a woman whose blonde hair shines in the ambient light. Unsteady, he stops to focus.

Of course.

Gordon watches as Caroline's eyes never leave David's. David smiles at something she says, then leans closer and replies. She laughs, beams at him, touches his hand. Gordon's stomach tightens with nausea. He sets his jaw to leave, but a nasty little impulse causes him to turn back.

"Hey, I know a good band for the wedding if y'all are interested," Gordon calls out as he approaches them.

The smile freezes on Caroline's face, but David seems nonplussed.

"Longmeier, right?" David rises and extends a hand. "Gordon?"

Gordon looks at North's hand, swaying slightly.

"You're drunk," Caroline observes.

Gordon's smile is rueful. "Bourbon. Wonderful at night, under the stars."

David sits down. "I would ask you to join us but we're nearly finished."

"Indeed, you are."

Gordon notices the hostess waiting patiently for him by a two-top, but turns back to them. He can feel the wild anger of a fight building in him and he sees something hard and aggressive pass over North's eyes too. But without looking at Caroline, he senses her fear and knows how badly any kind of violence would disappoint her. After a deep breath, he forces a smile.

"Okay then," he says. "Y'all have a good night."

He turns and shuffles away, waving goodbye to the hostess who hurries after him. She catches up with him at the door.

"Sir, is everything alright?"

"Oh yeah, all good. Just lost my appetite is all."

Pine and juniper float on the air as Gordon walks back toward his apartment. Two young people sit huddled on a sidewalk, one crying black mascara onto her nose ring. Gordon thinks about stopping to comfort her, but a look from her friend warns him away. He moves on, contemplating the clear night sky and the streetlit sidewalks, moon-gray as they stretch past the storefronts and plantings of his quirky hometown. With a numb smile, he realizes that he managed to control his violent side and walk away from the man he has begun to hate more than anyone else on the planet.

"Not bad, squirrel," he says to himself, "not bad at all."

"No, not bad at all."

The deep voice startles him. He turns and sees Joe, the tall man with the long gray hair. There is amusement in Joe's eyes. He walks with a loose gait, arms and hands relaxed, shoulders back. Something in his stride seems very familiar. When Gordon stops walking, Joe does too.

"What're you...?" Gordon slurs. "Joe, right?"

"Yep."

"So you're my uncle?"

"Where'd ya hear that?"

"Martín said."

"He's a good man. Takes good care of you."

"How do you know?"

"I keep tabs."

Gordon sways, burps silently and makes a sour face. Joe walks to the low wall that surrounds a tree planter outside the police station. He sits and pats the spot next to him. Gordon follows and sits, swaying slightly.

"Our people don't handle liquor too well," Joe says quietly.

Gordon stares at his hands, then closes his eyes.

"Not exactly a skill worth perfecting." Joe looks at Gordon. "Listen, if you're gonna puke..."

"No, I'm ok. Just tired."

"That Highsmith girl wearing you out?"

"Yeah, well... I guess maybe I'm just wearing myself out." Gordon looks up. "How'd you know her name?"

"Congressman Highsmith, right?"

"She's his daughter, yeah." Gordon closes his eyes again. "Caroline. She had the lightning."

Joe looks sharply at Gordon and stares at him for a long time, then stands up and pats him on the shoulder.

"Careful with the whiskey."

Gordon nods again and presses his face into his palms. After a moment, a thought wakes him up.

"Hey, what are you, some kind of Indian?"

But when he opens his eyes, Joe is gone.

Chapter 17

Larceny

Martín is barely listening. Prowling the deep wooden shelves, his eyes are glued to the rows of vinyl records sheathed in plastic sleeves, hunched like a docent searching for a critical piece of evidence in a lifelong dissertation on taste. He hums as his fingers walk the spines, urgent, precise.

"Seriously, man, I got your whole collection right here." Gordon lifts his phone. "Plus mine and pretty much everyone else's on the planet."

"Not the same."

Martín peers over his reading glasses at the covers, then lifts one album from the shelf and holds it up so he can study the small type.

"No, it's better. None of that crackling or skipping…"

As if awakened from a long sleepwalk, Martín raises his head and looks around the iconic store. Posters and stickers from a hundred bands line the blue and white pegboard walls above wooden bins and shelves. Happy, serene, he inhales the familiar and slightly musty scent.

"This," he says, sweeping one hand across the room, "is rock and roll. And that," he points at Gordon's phone, "is a toy."

"A toy that puts the whole world in your hand."

"Nevertheless, a toy."

Martín cradles his purchase as they walk out onto the sidewalk and over to Broad Street. They angle for the North Campus and continue past the black wrought iron arches into the main courtyard. The Lab is down campus and Martín has parked the pickup in one of the Hull Street lots nearby. They part, and Gordon continues on to the Lab. As he passes the spot where he left his motorcycle, he stops. His helmet lays on the ground and the bike is gone. He walks around in that helpless circle that victims of theft seem to believe will magically conjure their missing items, but when he realizes the futility of it he stops. Scanning the high corners of the surrounding buildings, he sees one camera that might have been able to capture the act. A quick search on his phone turns up the campus security phone number, which he calls to report the theft. Then he calls the Athens police and does the same.

In the Lab, he types up a note with his name and phone number, blows up the text to eighty-point type and inserts a photo of his missing bike, prints two dozen copies, grabs a staple gun and heads out again. After an hour, he has posted about twenty notices within a half-mile radius of the parking spot. He is stapling one to a telephone pole on Broad Street when a tattooed hand pats his shoulder.

"Five thousand dollar reward? You must really love that bike."

"J, hey. Yeah, it was my father's."

"Sorry, man."

"Hey, you're Jalen Woods!"

They both turn and see a middle-aged white man holding a fast food bag.

"I'm a huge fan!"

As Jalen chats politely with the man and signs the sack holding his chicken sandwich, Gordon once again notices the elaborate web of tattoos that cover Jalen's bare arms. He is wearing a dri-fit tank with the logo of the professional football team in Atlanta that paid him many millions of dollars over the course of two contracts, with which Jalen paid for the law degree he earned at the same time. He appears to have come from a workout or a run. He shakes the fan's hand and turns back to Gordon.

"Dude, if you don't want to get recognized, maybe wear something else."

"Says the guy who owns one shirt and wears it every day of his life."

"I own three of these."

"Listen." Abruptly, Jalen's tone is serious. "I wrote up your flying device with those notes you gave me, but you know the application will get rejected. Not enough proof."

"Not *any* proof. But it should buy me a few months, right?"

Grudgingly, Jalen nods. They start up College Avenue and turn right on Clayton. When they get to Mellow Mushroom, Gordon suggests lunch. They grab a table and order a pizza.

"By the way, what was all that with Sue the other day? My mom said they didn't have the best breakup."

Gordon bows his head. "Sorry if that was awkward."

"Not for me, it wasn't. Had to be for her, though."

"Needed to be done."

"Bruh, seriously, what the fuck? I mean, you got this flying thing, yeah. I don't get it, but I get it. But playin' people... that ain't you."

"I'm not--"

"You are. You always said, keep shit simple. Business is only complicated when you're trying to get over on someone, right? With Berrigan and that whole deal, you never lied to anybody. So why now?"

"I didn't lie."

"Oh no?" Jalen picks up a slice and blows on it, then takes a bite.

"No, man."

"You're lying to me now, G. 'Buy me a few months.' For what?"

Gordon sits back, his pizza untouched. He closes his eyes and rolls his head back and forth, then looks at Jalen.

"How am I gonna keep shit simple when gravity doesn't work on me anymore?"

"If that wasn't such a fucked up, science fiction, true thing you just said, I'd say you were making excuses."

"For what?"

"Treating nearly everyone in your life like shit."

"How am I...?"

"Dude, you got people who love you. Who will help you, even with this weird float-away-to-space thing. But people don't hang for long when they're gettin' played."

Gordon's eyes shine with tears. "I don't know what else to do."

"Just... trust. Just be honest and trust that it's gonna work out okay."

"Those Jesus freaks who stand outside the Georgia Theatre with the 'Repent' sign before concerts... What do you think they'll do to me? They'll say this is the devil's work."

"What *can* they do to you? There ain't but a handful of them. There's a whole lot more of us."

"There's a lot more than a handful, you know that."

Jalen sets down his slice.

"Gordon, I am a black man who has lived his whole life in the Deep South. You think for one second that I don't know what crazy white people are capable of? But you gotta live."

Gordon nods.

"It's not just here, either. What the past four years have shown me is that the South has no monopoly on racism. If anything, living in Atlanta showed me we're ahead of a lot of places. Some beautiful, loving people in that city. Some real kindness going on there."

Jalen studies Gordon's reaction.

"You don't look convinced."

"Whattaya want me to do, fly across the North Campus?"

"Yeah, why not? Let 'em see you. Let everyone see you. They're not gonna arrest you or put you in some zoo."

"You think they'll buy the idea that it's a machine doing it?"

"Who cares? Live ya life, bro."

Jalen takes another big bite of pizza and smiles at Gordon. Gordon's somber expression cracks and he laughs as he picks up his slice.

"Besides, this is Athens," Jalen adds. "All kinda weirdos walkin' around here. You'll fit right in."

After lunch, Gordon walks back to the bar and tells Martín about the stolen motorcycle. Martín seems more relieved than upset, a reaction that Gordon questions.

"You know me, G. I worry. It's what family does."

Gordon lights up with a sudden recollection and asks Martín about the camera he took from the photographer who was snooping around the garage. Martín ducks into the back room and returns with an expensive-looking Canon with a stubby zoom lens. Gordon turns it on and begins to scroll through the images. First, he sees the video of himself flying by the small lake and cavorting with Caroline. It includes footage of them rolling in the grass that had been omitted from the version posted online. There are a few shots of the interior of the garage, with closeups and wider-angle pictures of the pipes leading through the wall and up to the Shiva in his apartment. Further in, he sees many views of the shipping container in which the exterior machinery is housed, including extreme close-ups of the locks on the door.

"This photographer," Gordon asks. "What was he like?"

"Very small, very frightened. He wet himself."

Gordon laughs, but Martín does not smile.

"Why did he wet himself?"

"I scared him."

"How...?" Gordon recalls the morning he brought bagels to Martín and wound up pinned to the wall. "Ahh, yeah, I could see that."

He looks at the camera again.

"Any idea who hired him?"

"I didn't ask. Sorry, G."

Martín watches over Gordon's shoulder as he scrolls further back through the camera's memory. There are images of the

Lab's exterior and a few shots of Mr. Williams through the glass doors. Gordon frowns when he sees close-ups of the locks on the Lab's doors and windows. Then Gordon sees a picture of headlights through a snowy night and the side view of a bus in which a blonde woman walks to a seat. He recalls the first night he saw Caroline back in town. There are a few random shots of Caroline and David outside of the nicest hotel in town, then the series skips to what looks like an SUV in a motorcade. Gordon recognizes the vice president in one of these shots, waving at a crowd in front of the same SUV. He lowers the camera and stares out at the room, deep in thought.

"Doesn't look like paparazzi," Gordon observes. "More like some kind of spy."

"Do you think North sent him?"

"That was my original thought. But why would North want pictures of himself?"

"Instagram?"

Gordon scrolls back through and deletes the video and all of the recent pictures until he gets to the one of Caroline on the bus. He scans the heads in the seats but does not see his own, and remembers that she was already on the bus when he got on. The bus stop in the background is the one just before his, near the Lab, by the agricultural buildings.

Why the hell would she get on there?

Gordon hands the camera back to Martín.

"Might want to lock that up. Whether it's North or someone else, they probably want it back."

Martín nods and takes the camera into the back room again. Gordon stares into the distance, trying to divine some connection between the series of images he has seen. He does not notice that Martín has returned until a chuckle breaks his trance.

"What is it, Tío?"

"I said, 'The Spy Who Pissed Himself.' He would have a hard time living that down with his CIA pals."

"Something tells me he's not CIA."

Chapter 18

G-Day

The phone buzzes by Gordon's feet. He's on a creeper halfway under an old Ford Econoline van that drips oil from two places and is barely worth the parts he will use to fix it. Above him, the cracked oil pan is easy to diagnose, but it will require him to put the van up on the lift. He is trying to see what other damage or decrepitude he can remedy in one session, as efficiently as possible, so that Mr. Fulton can get back on the road. The old plumber was a friend of Gordon's father and a loyal customer, so Gordon always makes time for him. After a brief silence, the phone buzzes again. Gordon shakes the numbness out of his arms and wheels himself free of the van. Five missed calls, none from numbers he recognizes. He plays the messages, hoping for an update on his motorcycle but instead hearing nothing but hectoring queries from reporters who saw his number on the flyers. On impulse, he touches one of the numbers and waits for the call to connect.

"Gordon Longmeier?" a male voice asks.

"Yep."

"Uh, Johnny Benton here. Thanks for calling back."

Gordon hears papers shuffling and the click of a pen.

"So, uh... you can fly?"

"Evidently."

"Uh... how, exactly?"

"Combination of magic and technology, pretty much."

"You're an inventor, right? Did you invent a personal flying device?"

"I filed for a patent on one a couple weeks ago. Didn't you see the story in the Banner-Herald?"

"I didn't really understand it. Can you explain how it works?"

"Sure. We apply a combination of ionic de-negativization and thermal extremity to polarized ferric compounds, from which we produce a series of garments -- vests and bracelets -- that defeat gravity."

"Pardon my French, but that sounds like a lot of bullshit to me."

"You're right, Johnny. The truth is I really can fly."

"Listen, if you don't want to give out your trade secrets, I completely understand. But what's your plan? Will it be available to the public?"

"In time, I suppose."

"Any idea how much it will cost?"

"Not sure about that. Still a lot of factors to work through."

Johnny pauses. "Who was the woman in the video?"

Gordon's amusement drains away. He holds the phone away from his ear and stares at the number for a long time. 404 area code... Atlanta. Johnny's voice is tinny and small at that distance, but Gordon hears the word "Highsmith."

"Okay," Gordon says. "That'll be all for now."

He thumbs the red button to end the call and powers down the phone. Fulton's keys are in the ignition, so Gordon starts the van and moves it into position over the hydraulic lift. As he holds the lever and watches the wheels sag and then leave the ground, Gordon thinks about Jalen's advice.

Live ya life, bro.

He drains the oil and removes the pan, mentally cycling through the faces of people he has seen in town and on campus. Very few seem like cranks or religious freaks, or anything more than ordinary people living their own lives. Why should he fear them? Has his paranoia been completely unwarranted? But his celebrity would not be the same as Jalen's if people really knew; if they didn't think it was a machine lifting him off the ground. He had to give them that one little lie.

And then what?

By early afternoon, Fulton's truck is back in working order. Gordon washes up and calls the old man to let him know, then he fetches his bathroom scale, sits at the table and opens his laptop. He gathers the various weight belts he has printed and begins to try different combinations until he arrives at a weight that allows him to hop up and touch the high ceiling with very little effort and drift gently down to the floor. On the screen, he distributes the weight between arms, legs and chest to maximize his comfort, then clicks the print button to send the design to Shiva. As the machine hums to life, he walks to the bathroom, undresses and takes a shower. By the time he has dressed, the last item is lying on the plate and Shiva's sphere has gone dark and retracted.

The next morning, a Saturday, Gordon is outside in the alley in his new, lighter weights. He takes care not to push off too hard with his first step. By the time he reaches the sidewalk he has mastered a sort of gliding walk, as if he's on skates. He heads to Broad Street and down the block to Jalen's building. Glancing left and right at the people around him, he cinches his backpack straps tighter and easily hops up to knock on the third-story window. By the time Jalen wheels around in his seat, Gordon has dropped below the frame. Within seconds, he appears again, smiling broadly. He grabs the sash and waves hello. Below him, people have gathered with their phones raised. Jalen smiles and shakes his head, then turns back to his gaping client. He flashes a thumbs-up over his shoulder to Gordon, who pulls his feet up onto the sash and turns to face the street. He squats and pushes off toward the rooftops on the other side, to a smattering of spontaneous applause. With one more bound, he clears the trees along the side of the North Campus Quad and drifts down onto the grass next to a young woman, who lets out a little cry and drops her books. He apologizes and helps her pick them up, then gives her a quick salute and leaps to the south. Phones follow him as he disappears over the dean's office building.

By the time Gordon reaches the Lab, all of Athens is buzzing. Dozens of videos have appeared online. Gordon's phone begins to light up again but he ignores all of the calls because Caroline's ID is not among them. The students refuse to focus on their projects until Gordon does several leaps to touch the ceiling, but then everyone settles in for a normal work day. Wendell is conspicuously absent, with no call or message. Stan keeps holding up his phone, smiling at Gordon and shaking his head at the number of views the videos are receiving. Later in the day, Jalen calls to say that the last documents have been filed for the transparent titanium patent application and Gordon does a double backflip in the middle of the room. A few hours later, when it is time for the students to go home, Gordon lets them persuade him to jump over the stands and into Sanford Stadium. As they make the short walk up East Campus Road, even Stan has his phone out to record the moment. There is a crowd inside the stadium, which Gordon finds odd for April. Unsure of what to do, he stands on the sidewalk with his hands jammed in his pockets as the kids chant, "Jump! Jump!" The whole moment feels like one of those awful public suicides until with a grin, Gordon raises his arms in surrender.

"Fuck it."

When the traffic clears, Gordon sprints across the street and jumps as high as he can toward the southeast corner of the stadium. He can hear the students cheering behind him as he clears the upper edge of the facade, but when he hears a louder roar from the stands inside his stomach drops. Thousands of Bulldog football fans are gathered for the annual G-Day spring game. As Gordon descends he realizes he will land on the field, very close to where the teams have lined up to run a play. He touches down in the defensive secondary as the ball is snapped and huge men in red helmets begin running toward him. Instinctively, he leaps again just as he is about to be crushed by the flow of the play. Forty feet above the action, he hangs in the air as the players and the crowd fall silent for an eerie moment. When he slowly drops back to the ground, the players stand around him with wide eyes. Some seem angry, but most are too astonished to react at all.

"Sorry, guys."

Gordon begins to jog off the field.

"Science experiment... Kinda screwed it up, though. Sorry."

Two burly policemen run toward him from the sideline. When he sees them, he tries to sprint away but can't get enough traction to really build speed. He takes one more large stride then bounds half the length of the field to get away. The crowd roars. Gordon is all smiles as he lands and leaps again, this time into the stands. He gently settles down among the fans, some of whom record the moment while others pound him on the back and laugh. The cops pull up when they get to the long hedge that separates the field from the stands, faces red and hands on hips. Gordon makes his way from the seats to the stairs, waves goodbye and does a backflip into the upper deck, then one more to exit the stadium. He can hear the crowd cheering as he drifts down to the lawn outside the bookstore and casually walks up the stairs toward the North Campus, nodding at the pedestrians who stare in amazement.

Gordon's text buzzes, from Jalen:

"Dude, WTF? I'm on the sideline."

"You said I should live my life."

Jalen sends a string of five crying-with-laughter emojis, then says the coach made a comment about recruiting Gordon as a wide receiver.

"No way, bud. Those dudes are massive!"

Jalen 'likes' this reply, and Gordon puts his phone away. He decides to limit his leaping to ten or fifteen feet at a time and makes his way up to Martín's.

The bar is crowded with people watching the G-Day game on television, and they applaud when they realize who Gordon is. Martín's smile is thin, his eyes quizzical. Since there are no seats, Gordon walks behind the bar, grabs a water and grins at Martín, who bursts out laughing.

"You are crazy, vato!"

"It was an accident. Really. The kids dared me to jump the stands, so I had to. I had no idea there was a game on. Don't they usually play in the fall?"

"Ain't a real game," says one of the guys at the bar. "Just an intrasquad scrimmage for those of us who can't wait 'til August."

"There's a lot of y'all." Gordon grins.

Another text buzzes in his pocket, from Caroline:

"Nice."

"Did you see it?"

"Look up."

Across the room, Caroline sits at a hightop holding a beer with a mixed group of friends. Gordon walks around the bar and begins to shoulder his way through to her, then pauses and dives up over the crowd to the wall, where he stops himself with his hands, settles down next to her and gives her a kiss on the cheek. A few people cheer but the novelty is clearly beginning to wear off for most of them, which Gordon notes with relief.

"You alone?" he asks quietly.

She nods. "He left yesterday. By the way, that stadium thing would've been better naked, like they used to do in the seventies."

"Don't give me ideas."

"So I guess you're not worried about 'Jesus freaks' anymore?"

"They may not like new technology, but they don't usually kill over it."

A cheer goes up for the red team, which has scored with a long touchdown pass. Gordon doesn't recognize all of Caroline's friends, but the guys seem to be there for the game and the girls for one another's company.

"You sure your cover story will hold?" Caroline asks quietly.

"Should, as long as I don't let anyone else try to use this."

Gordon pats his chest. Caroline smiles and kisses him.

"Or steal it," he adds, raising an eyebrow as he steals a big swig of her beer.

"Hey, get your own!"

She gives him a little punch on his metal breastplate.

"This place is mobbed. Takes forever to get back to the bar."

Gordon looks at the television and sees that they are replaying his odd, brief visit to the stadium. He can't hear what the announcers are saying, but a few people look back at him with curious expressions. He raises his water bottle to them and they quickly turn away. Something in that reaction gives Gordon a brief chill, but the sound of Caroline's laughter breaks the feeling. He turns back and sees the light in her eyes and forgets about everything else around him. Her arm loops discreetly around his waist, and his around hers. For that one instant all feels right in Gordon's world.

In the far corner of the room, a man with a Georgia hat pulled low over his eyes stands to his full height. The dim light makes it hard to see his long hair, which is the same gray as his hat and tucked into the high collar of his fleece sweater. Unnoticed by Gordon and Martín, he slips out the back door and pulls it closed behind him.

Chapter 19

Evidence

"Y'all really need a better hobby."

Gordon smiles at the angry man with wire rim glasses and a thin mustache who aims a tall blue sign at the line of patrons on the Georgia Theatre sidewalk. It bears a long list of God's supposed grievances against the sinful practice of rock and roll.

"You!" the man growls at Gordon. "I know you. You and that Mexican run Martín's bar."

"Naw, he runs it. I just play the devil's music a few nights a week."

Anxious to join Martín and Julia on line, Caroline pulls on Gordon's arm but he doesn't budge.

"Saw you flyin' around at the Dawgs game, too." The man's eyes narrow. "What's that all about?"

"I got a magic iPhone."

Gordon takes his phone out and aims it at the man.

"See? It might make you fly too."

The man flinches away, then turns red when Gordon and Caroline giggle at his reaction. He takes a step closer to Gordon, his face contorted with rage.

"Think that's funny, do ya?"

"Actually? Yeah." Gordon's look is dead serious.

Caroline rolls her eyes and walks across the street to where their friends stand with a growing throng of music fans. Gordon stands his ground.

"There will come a day when you regret your folly," the man says through gritted teeth.

He moves so close to Gordon's face that Gordon can see the dandruff dusting the surface of his glasses.

"So sayeth prophesy," the pastor growls.

"Reckon?"

"I do."

"Okay, how about a selfie in the meantime?"

Gordon moves quickly to the man's side and holds up the camera. Just as the flash goes off, he leaps into the air with a loud hoot. When the man drops his sign and falls into a crouch, the line explodes with laughter. Gordon floats back down in the middle of the street as the small gaggle of demonstrators close ranks around their embarrassed standard bearer. Gordon recognizes Harlan from Stainfield's patio and realizes that this must be Pastor Ken.

"Sorry, bud," Gordon says to the pastor. "Just having a little fun with you."

Pastor Ken flashes Gordon a murderous look and takes his sign back from the protester who picked it up. He raises his chin arrogantly and looks at the crowd.

"Repent!" he shouts. "Repent!"

His group joins in the chant, forming a line to face their bemused audience.

"Sorry I woke them up," Gordon says to the people on line as he walks to his friends.

"I thought you were hiding from those freaks," Martín chuckles.

"Not anymore. Screw 'em."

They make their way into the show and find a spot by the mixing board. Onstage, two tough-looking men fiddle with the mic stands and amps for the opening act. The gear for the main act sits further back, draped with dark cloth. Martín walks up with four Sweetwater 420 tallboys and passes them around, but as Gordon raises his can to touch the others his phone buzzes. It is a text from an unknown number with a 762 area code. An mp4 file is attached. Gordon clicks on the attachment and sees the back of a thin boy with shaggy ginger hair, shot through a window about twenty feet away from him. He is crouched over the handlebars of Gordon's motorcycle, working at the lock with a slim piece of metal. When he looks up nervously and glances around, Gordon recognizes him. Wendell frees the handlebars and turns the lock once more, then climbs on the bike, shifts it to neutral and kicks the starter. It fires up on the first try. Wendell toes the lever down to first, over-revs the engine and lets out the clutch. He hangs on as the front wheel lifts off the ground and the bike careens out of the frame. For the last few seconds of the video, Gordon's helmet rocks back and forth on the ground where it fell.

"Who is this?" Gordon replies.

"I'm at Martín's."

"Please don't share this video with anyone," Gordon types rapidly.

"Ok. Could use the reward money though."

"Be there in a sec."

Gordon looks up and realizes that Caroline saw the video too. He shakes his head and presses a finger to his lips, and she nods.

"This guy's at Martín's now," he tells her. "Sorry, I gotta go."

"But the Drive-By Truckers..."

"Yeah, sucks I gotta miss it."

Gordon gives Caroline a kiss and hands her his beer, then makes his apologies to Martín and Julia and heads for the door. Outside, the church group is loading its signs into the back of a small van. Gordon makes eye contact with the man in the glasses.

"Guess I decided to repent after all."

Gordon salutes, takes two quick steps and leaps the length of the block. Three more leaps bring him to the door of Martín's. He walks in and sees the usual thin Sunday crowd. At the bar sits a pretty woman with dark hair and glasses, casually dressed, fifty-ish.

"Gordon?" she asks. "I'm Professor Miller. I teach English literature."

Gordon walks over and extends his hand.

"Lauren," she says.

"You sent the video?"

"Your master thief was right outside my office window. Something didn't look right to me, ya know?"

Gordon nods sadly.

"I thought you'd be a little happier about it."

"I know that kid."

"Oh. Um, sorry about that. I didn't send it to the cops."

"Don't do that, please. I'll pay the reward."

"No, no, it's okay..."

"I insist. You did the right thing."

The door jingles and Caroline walks in.

"Hey," Gordon greets her. "What about the show?"

"Seen 'em a hundred times. You okay?"

"Yeah. This is Lauren. She's a professor, saw Wendell out the window."

Caroline waves hello, sits down and orders a beer.

"I'll stop by with a check tomorrow," Gordon says as Lauren rises to go.

"Really, no need if you're not going to get your motorcycle back."

"Oh, I'll get it back. Eventually."

Gordon grabs his phone to flip the video to Stan and watch it again with Caroline.

"Why, though?" he thinks aloud.

As if in response, Stan's reply pops up:

"He's a weird kid, but he idolizes you."

"Did his father put him up to this?" Gordon asks out loud.

Caroline shakes her head. "It's not about the money. Stan's right, this is more personal. You're his hero, but somehow just working with you is not enough. He wants to *be* you."

Gordon laughs. "I'm a fucking mess. Who would want to be me?"

"Compared to his situation, yours looks pretty good,"

Caroline answers.

"Well, I don't want him to get in any trouble. The bike has meaning to me, but it's not worth ruining his future." He turns to Caroline. "Wanna see if they'll let us back in the show?"

"No, I've got an early day tomorrow."

Gordon's disappointment draws little more than a kind pat on the cheek from Caroline as she walks out the door. Feeling restless, Gordon follows her out. She turns around and kisses him once, then shoves him with a smile and continues on her way. He heads back toward the theater, but rather than try to enter he jumps up onto the roof of Clarke's Standard next door. When he leans against the wall of the theater, he can faintly hear the music. He closes his eyes and tries to process the wild break with caution that has been his weekend. Not long ago, even a two-story height like this might have given him a twinge of anxiety. Yet in a short time, he has grown comfortable with leaping nearly a hundred feet in the air -- in front of thousands of people. So quickly, people in town have grown used to the sight of his leaps and barely seem surprised anymore. He wonders if it would be the same if they knew it was actually his body and not a machine defying gravity. Probably not, he concludes. People can get used to just about anything if you give them a decent rationalization, but that still might be too much.

After a while, Gordon thinks about Wendell again.

"Master thief."

Hardly. There was always something a little off about the boy, and Gordon has known enough highly intelligent people to expect a little weirdness from someone that smart, but still...

Before Gordon can finish that thought, a whooshing sound followed by a heavy thud makes him open his eyes. Joe squats in front of him, still wearing the Georgia hat. He is grinning mischievously.

"Son, you and me gotta talk."

"Dude, you gotta stop sneaking up on me. It's starting to creep me out."

Joe laughs and slaps Gordon's shoulder, then sits back and

crosses his ankles. His hands rest loosely on his knees. Gordon notes absently that Joe seems very limber for an older man.

"Ain't got tickets for the show?" Gordon asks.

"I was always more of a Jason Isbell guy."

Gordon smiles. "So what's on your mind?"

"You."

"I was afraid you'd say that."

Joe laughs again, then slowly settles into serious mode.

"There's a lot you don't know... and a lot you really can't know, right now at least. It wouldn't help you."

"Okay..."

Joe looks up at the dark sky and closes his eyes. He brings his hands together at his forehead as if in prayer, then lets them fall away as he opens his eyes.

"So, here's the thing. This ain't easy, so I'll just say it. I'm your father."

"Fuck you."

Gordon stands up and walks across the roof, then wheels and walks back.

"What are you, some kind of backwoods grifter or something? Show up here with your line of bullshit... what, looking for money? First you're my uncle and now you're my father?"

Joe remains seated, elbows on his knees and steepled fingertips pressed to his forehead. His eyes are closed again.

"I know this is a shock to you. I'm sorry."

"It's not a shock, it's a load of horseshit. I knew my dad. My mom never said nothing about anybody else."

"No. She didn't tell me either until the end."

"The end...?"

Gordon recalls the moment on Emily's deathbed when Joe removed her necklace and put it around Gordon's neck. Gordon had worn the stone since that day, and he can feel it now against his skin. Joe turns and looks at Gordon with the same hazel-bronze eyes that he has, then reaches into his own collar and pulls up an identical stone.

"I gave her a stone like this before she left. When she asked me to give it to you, I knew you had to be my son."

"You got all that from her giving me some piece of shit necklace? Are you fucking kidding me?"

In one explosive movement, Joe bursts up from the ground and lands right in front of Gordon. He grabs Gordon's weight vest by its edge and rips him close, nose to nose. There is a fury in Joe's eyes that terrifies Gordon.

"I loved her!" Joe snarls. "When she wanted to leave, I didn't try to stop her. That ain't our way. But I loved her. Always. You *will* respect that."

Gordon's fear dissolves into an anger of his own. He stares into Joe's eyes, as if to challenge his right to say any of this. Joe reads this look instantly, coils his body and slings Gordon, backhand, high against the wall. Gordon slams off the bricks, tumbles over the edge of the roof and drifts slowly to the sidewalk, where he comes to rest on his back. Joe's heavy boots slam down on the concrete next to Gordon's head.

"Get up." Joe grabs Gordon's hair and raises his head. "You ain't hurt. Get the fuck up."

The concert crowd begins to emerge from the theater. No one saw either man come down from the roof, but the sight of Gordon prone on the sidewalk and Joe holding him by the hair alarms a few people. One of the larger guys steps forward.

"Hey, leave him alone!"

"Mind your business," Joe says without looking back.

Gordon takes Joe's wrist, removes the hard brown hand from his hair and stands up.

"It's okay," Gordon assures the group. "I'm fine."

Martín sees Gordon and walks over to ask how things went with the bike and Wendell. Gordon looks at him without comprehension, then remembers.

"Oh, yeah. It's all good."

"Hey vato, I got some big news. I talked to the manager in there. Now that we got our own songs, he's gonna let us open for the Truckers in a couple weeks. That's big time!"

Gordon smiles and nods, clearly distracted. There is a wide scratch on his cheekbone that is beginning to bleed.

"Hey man, you okay?"

"Listen, hit me tomorrow on that. I got some shit to deal with now."

He turns and sees that Joe has walked halfway up the block.

"Great news, though," Gordon adds. "Very cool. Now we just need a name."

"Oh, yeah."

"How about 'The Reverend Espada Band?'"

Martín grins. "I like it."

They say goodnight, and Gordon starts after Joe. He is about fifteen feet behind him when Joe turns the corner. By the time Gordon gets to the end of the block, Joe is nowhere to be seen. Standing alone on the sidewalk, Gordon is unsure of what he feels; relief that the brutal man is gone or sadness that he will not learn more about his family. He turns in a circle, looking for a wave of gray hair, listening for boots on the concrete. Then, high above, he hears a faint whistle. He leans back and sees Joe standing on top of the B-of-A building, ten stories up. Joe waves for Gordon to join him. Gordon takes a few steps onto the street, then pauses to consider the strange prospect of jumping a hundred feet in the air to speak with a stranger who claims to be his father -- and who somehow climbed ten stories faster than Gordon could walk ten feet. He looks up at Joe again, then runs and jumps. His arc takes him barely to the curbing at the edge of the roof, where he balances on his toes and tries to steady himself but begins to fall back. Joe reaches out casually and pulls him onto the slick gray surface.

"Thanks. How'd you get up here so fast?"

"Same way you did."

"Come on, man."

Joe steps around Gordon and perches on the edge with his back to the open air, facing in. He smiles, takes one step back and vanishes. Gordon rushes forward in horror but just as quickly as Joe disappeared he bobs back up in front of Gordon. Hanging in the air, he shrugs with open hands as if to say, 'See?' He reaches out and Gordon pulls him back onto the roof. Gordon starts to speak but nothing comes. Instead, he slowly sits down. Joe does the same.

"You're handling your Rising better than most," Joe offers.

Perplexed, Gordon says nothing.

"Emily never told you about any of this?" He looks up at the sky. "Damn, girl. That was reckless."

"What I'm seeing is that you have the same problem I do," Gordon says quietly. "How does that prove you're my father?"

"You have three thin lines on the inside of your right forearm, like parallel scars."

Joe takes Gordon's wrist and pulls up the sleeve of his work shirt. Just above the metal of his arm weight, the word 'facio' is visible in the faint light. Joe presses a fingertip to the tattoo.

"Under this."

He rolls up his own sleeve and holds his arm out to Gordon. On his forearm, there are three identical lines, but they are more pronounced, thicker and darker.

"Yours'll look like this in time. You've only just begun."

"She told me a cat scratched me. I didn't remember that."

"So you covered it up?"

Gordon shrugs. "Better than looking like I tried to kill myself with a fork."

"Can't say as I blame you. Listen, you haven't gotta call me Dad or any of that. You don't know me and I didn't raise you. Hell, I didn't even know you existed 'til Emily put my stone on you."

"What's with this stone, anyway?"

"If you and I were not connected, you could not have kept it on."

"What's that mean, 'connected?'"

"Blood kin or spirit-bonded."

Gordon does not look convinced but he remains silent.

"Anyway, I want nothing from you. That's not our way, taking from kids. Parents give."

"'Our way.' Who's 'us?'"

Joe falls silent and rests his elbows on his knees, his hands pressed together, index fingers to his lips. He closes his eyes and for a long while seems to meditate, or pray. At last, he opens his eyes and looks at Gordon.

"There's a lot... It's a long story, a few thousand years if you get into all of it. You ain't gotta know all that now. But you oughta know what you are."

"'What?' Not who?"

"'What' is 'who.' You are a Lightfoot. I am your father, Joe Lightfoot. We are the last of the Lightfoots, of the People of the Stone."

To Joe's irritation, Gordon begins to laugh. He lets himself fall back onto the roof and laughs until he begins to cry. He lays there for a moment breathing and sniffling, then sits up and wipes his eyes.

"She told me she named me after the Canadian singer."

"Yeah, I figured. Saw your show one night and you kinda said that."

"Why would she lie?"

"Our ways are not for everyone, but I think she wanted to give you a trail back to me. That's why she gave you the stone. Emily was gifted. Science. Physics. She wanted to teach at a big university, do research. It's not like we never had people do that, but she..." Joe pauses and looks down. "Aw hell, maybe it was me."

"You said she left? Left where?"

"One day I'll tell you about it. But for now, you gotta make your Rising without letting it kill you. Like I said, you're doing better than most."

"So this happened to you? The gravity thing?"

"Funny, I never saw it as a 'gravity thing.' Unless maybe the gravity is from above...?"

"Like reversed polarity in a magnet?"

"I guess so. Mine happened a long time ago. It's different for me now. Trust me, you can get through it but it ain't easy."

"You said thousands of years... What're you, Indians?"

"That word." Joe snorts derisively. "No, our family is even older than most of those nations."

Gordon stares in silence.

"Listen, the Rising is a serious thing. You ain't got a choice. You either work through it or it'll kill you."

"Or walk around wearing weight vests for the rest of my life."

"No. You can't avoid it. Sooner or later, it'll catch you."

"So how does it work?"

"You gotta get there on your own, son. My answers are not your answers, but I can tell you what I know. Like when it started for you, there would have been an event of some kind that connected you with your destined path. Anything come to mind?"

Gordon thinks about the lightning and Caroline's touch.

"Could it be a person?"

"Could," Joe allows. "Who?"

"The night before I woke up weightless, I touched Caroline's hand and felt this weird lightning sensation all over my body. I hadn't felt it in years."

Joe looks at Gordon intently. "Electric. Yeah, that's right. That was part of it. You felt it more than once?"

"The first time I felt it was back in college."

"With the same girl, Caroline? You love her?"

"Yes," Gordon declares.

An expression of profound sadness darkens Joe's face.

"So you're telling me Caroline is part of this Rising stuff?"

"It ain't for me to say. But you ain't alone in this. I'm sorry if you felt like you were."

"You knew about me for years. Why didn't you warn me?"

"Would you have believed me?"

Gordon sits very still, staring through Joe and into his own thoughts. At last, he shakes his head.

"You were a wild kid, in a lot of pain. But if you were in any real danger, I would have reached out. Some of us have to go through a lot of disharmony until we find balance. And that you have to do on your own."

Gordon looks out at the rooftops of Athens.

"Joe?"

"Yeah, son."

"Thanks."

Joe smiles and nods, then turns his hat around backwards, stands up and hops off the edge of the building. He plummets to the ground, but just before impact his fall seems to slow and his body to gather. He lands in a squat and explodes upward with the same velocity he had while falling, as if the force had recoiled through him. Incredulous, Gordon watches him disappear into the black sky. As he sits alone on the tallest building in town, Gordon feels a sense of calm settle over him, along with the feeling that a deep truth has been revealed. For a moment, there is no striving in him, no urgent chatter. It is as if he can simply be, without worrying about *becoming*. It is the first moment of real peace that his busy mind has ever known.

Chapter 20

Impact

Gordon wakes up on his back, staring down at the floor from the twin-sized mattress he has strapped to the rafters. His pillow and comforter are secured at their edges with heavy velcro strips. Joe's comment about 'gravity from above' gave Gordon the idea for the upside-down bed, and his sleep since then has felt nearly normal, at least when it's not interrupted by the questions that have whirled in his head for nearly a week. The thought that his condition might not be unique, that it might be part of a known process that ultimately leaves him walking safely without tethers and body weights -- as Joe does -- comforts Gordon. But while Joe's astonishing exit left Gordon thrilled and terrified, his silence since then has been torture.

He no longer questions the idea that Joe is his father; in many ways, it validates the disconnection that Gordon so often felt from George, the kind and cautious man who raised him. Still, he feels no closer to understanding the enigmatic newcomer than he did before. That they are both 'Lightfoots' gives Gordon a sense of kinship; that he still has no idea who the 'People of the Stone' are both frustrates and intrigues him.

Rising...

Gordon rolls over and buries his face in his pillow. The image of Caroline on the bus flashes through his mind.

Why didn't I just walk home that night?

He wonders if any of this would have happened if she had not touched his hand, if the lightning had not flashed on his skin, if she had stayed the hell back in California; if the past had stayed buried, if Caroline...

What? What could Caroline have done?

No, he thinks, *not what she could have done. What* I *could have done. If only I had realized... What?*

Gordon feels the pillow against his face and sees Caroline's smile, inches away, warm and loving, home. Waking up slowly, quiet and close. Before that, sleeping sweetly, relaxed and innocent.

How did I fuck that up so badly?

Another image flashes, Caroline's warm skin, severe silver earring tangled in streaky blonde hair. The curve of her jeans. The onstage blur of her face and scent and sweet breath across the microphone, foreplay in front of a hundred people, loud and lurid, hangover be damned. Wild-eyed velocity, driving harder toward something they both feel compelled to chase, sensation or challenge or transcendence... And yet, David. She's getting married.

"NO!" Gordon screams into the pillow.

He arches his back out of the covers, pulls his legs up and dives hard at the ground. He grips his weight vest where it lays and pulls it on over his bare skin, then grabs the ladder and pushes himself toward the bathroom.

Work.

He turns on the shower to let it warm up, then lathers and shaves his face at the sink, avoiding eye contact with the angry, distracted mess in the mirror. After his shower, he dresses and eats quickly, grabs his backpack and leaves for the Lab. He does not acknowledge the looks or calls from the people below as he glides above campus, jaw set in a scowl of determination, landing only to propel himself forward again.

Sooner or later, it'll catch you, Joe says in his head.

"Fuck that!" Gordon growls as he flies over two older ladies on a bench, oblivious to their shocked reaction. "It ain't gonna catch me. I ain't givin' up my life for this bullshit."

Under his vest, the stone feels suddenly warm against Gordon's skin. As he drifts down toward the Lab, he sees a flash of white and red to his left and realizes that the campus bus is on a collision course with him. He pulls his knees to his chest as tightly as he can, but as the bus rumbles by one of the roof vents catches his hip and sends him somersaulting sideways. He spreads out into a fast-turning cartwheel, aware of the cars moving in either direction around him. Unable to stop, he descends spinning and helpless into the path of an oncoming pickup truck. At the last second, the driver sees him and slams the brakes. Gordon catches the pavement with his hands just as the front bumper taps him in the face. Upside down, wrapped against the pickup's hood, bleeding from his nose and lips, he can feel the hot pulsing of the stone, like an ember with a heartbeat. Like his own heart, it begins to slow when he realizes he is not seriously hurt.

"What the hell, man?!"

The driver comes running around to where Gordon lays on his truck.

"Where'd you come from?"

Gordon jerks a thumb up at the sky, then presses himself off the front of the truck and rotates to land on his feet.

"You okay?"

"Yeah, I'm fine."

Gordon glances at the marks his weight vest has left on the hood of the truck.

"Sorry about the scratches."

"Hey, you're that Gordon, aren't you? Cool! Hey, don't worry about the scratches -- it'll be a good story for the guys." The man grins, then looks at Gordon's nose. "You're bleedin' pretty good."

Gordon wipes a red streak onto his sleeve. He shrugs, says goodbye and does a back layout across the street to the plaza in front of the Lab. The man honks and drives away. Mr. Williams hands Gordon a tissue as he limps toward the double doors of the Lab. Inside, Stan sits at one of the larger tables with a formidable array of papers strewn around him. Gordon shuffles over and drops his bag with a wince, then sits across from Stan and starts to look through the pile.

"You okay?" Stan asks.

Gordon nods.

"So transparent titanium is even more complicated to file than Shiva was," Stan explains.

Gordon holds up one of the sheets.

"Jalen's even making us diagram the molecular processes?" he asks Stan. "Shit, I have no idea what Shiva does to make this stuff. She just prints it."

"USPTO doesn't accept 'she just prints it' for prior art, Wonder Boy."

Gordon looks up. "You haven't called me that in a long time. Thank God."

"Felt right."

"Where's our other Wonder Boy been? Nobody told him about Professor Miller's video, right?"

"Did you really pay her five grand?"

"Yeah, for the video plus her sig on one of Jalen's NDAs."

"She wouldn't have talked."

"Probably not, but things are already bad enough in Wendell's world."

"You just gonna let him keep the bike?"

"I got better ways to get around now."

"Not safer, though." Stan appraises the bloodstains on Gordon's nose and sleeve.

"Long story," Gordon mumbles. "I was distracted."

Gordon quickly tires of the elaborate chemical equations that Stan has generated. He wanders back through the students' work stations, occasionally lifting a 3D model and examining it. The students will arrive in a few minutes, so he is careful to put the pieces back exactly as they were; Wendell is not the only highly-strung young person working in the Lab. Gordon remembers how the stone heated up and feels the tender spot on his chest. He walks out to the rest room and stands in front of the mirror, nostrils rimmed with dried blood, chin caked with a burgundy smear. Forgetting that, he opens his vest and shirt and lifts the small stone. It looks normal, completely incapable of causing the burn on his chest. He glances around the room and begins to lift the necklace over his head. Then, he stops.

The bathroom door opens, and Dr. Carson walks in. Gordon frowns at him as he makes his way to the urinal. He tucks the stone back into his shirt, washes the dried blood off of his face, and pats himself dry. As he is about to leave, Carson clears his throat.

"Everything okay, Mr. Longmeier?"

"Yes sir, why?"

"I heard you had an altercation with a pickup truck."

"All good. I'm fine."

When Gordon walks into the Lab, the first person he sees is Wendell. The boy is hunched over his work station, safety glasses on top of his head, scribbling furiously in a notepad. Gordon walks over and stands by him, waiting to be noticed. On the paper, he sees row after row of agitated capital letters. The word MOM jumps out at him before Wendell senses him there and flips the book angrily.

"Sorry, bud, didn't mean to snoop. You wanna talk?"

Wendell pulls his mirrored safety glasses down and lets his expression go blank.

"Stan says you're making progress setting up production for your landboard."

"Yes sir."

"Hey."

Gordon pats the back of Wendell's shoulder, and the boy flinches as if he's been burned. Gordon tries again, more softly, and lets his hand rest there. Wendell tolerates it.

"It's okay. Whatever's happening with your Mom, it's not your fault."

Wendell turns to face Gordon. His flushed cheeks are taut with emotion, his brow deeply furrowed. Slowly, two streams of tears run down from behind his safety glasses. Gordon pulls him into a hug but Wendell's arms hang limply by his sides.

"She won't stop," Wendell whispers. "It's killin' her, but she won't stop."

Gordon nods and does not let go.

"Don't she want to be with me? I could take care of her. Pop ain't got the money, but I'll have it."

Gordon releases the hug.

"She's not thinking clearly. When someone gets that deep into addiction, it takes over their mind."

Wendell wipes his nose with his bare wrist. Gordon takes the bloodstained tissue from his pocket and offers it.

"What happened to you?" Wendell asks.

"Got hit by a truck."

"What, today? For real?"

Wendell pulls his glasses back up onto his head and looks Gordon over.

"And you ain't hurt?"

"No buddy, I'm Superman, remember? Able to leap tall stadiums in a single bound."

"You ain't!" Wendell smiles.

"Shhh. Don't tell anyone, okay?"

Wendell smiles and wipes his nose.

"Listen. It's Wednesday. You remember my friend Caroline?"

"The real pretty one? Heck yeah."

"She does this thing over at Martín's -- Mr. Espada's -- church. It's a group of people who get together and play drums. I'm gonna go after work today. You wanna come?"

"I can't play drums."

"Neither can I, or anyone else there. But it's fun. Helps folks get their mind off their troubles for a while."

Gordon pats Wendell's shoulder.

"Might be fun. I'll text you the address."

Wendell nods, but his frown tells Gordon he has doubts. Gordon walks back and sits across from Stan, who slides his fist low across the table for a bump. They dig into the documentation, pausing only for questions from students and a brief lunch break. By the end of the day, the proof seems in order. Stan starts a call with Jalen while Gordon makes the rounds and helps the students wrap up their day's work.

"Gonna stop by?" Gordon asks Wendell.

"Yeah, I don't know. My Pop..."

"...don't have to know."

"Lemme see, okay?"

It is dark when Gordon finally leaves the Lab and heads up campus. He has learned to stay below the phone lines and tree limbs at night, and his ground-skimming strides make him look like a particularly swift rollerblader. At the bar, Julia hands him a note from a local reporter who stopped by to inquire about a 'motor vehicular incident' caused by Gordon's 'irrational behavior,' which makes him laugh. Julia looks concerned as he relays the story, but he assures her he is fine. He eats quickly, wads the note up with his napkin and carries his plate back to the kitchen area, then ducks out into the night and heads for the church. Among the cars parked at the curb is Wendell's old Ford, its peeling roof looking woolly in the dim streetlight. Gordon glides down the basement stairs without touching any and bounds happily into the room. The sight of Mr. Stainfield's florid, bristled face and potbelly stops him in his tracks. The man stands with his fists on his hips while the drum group sits in a circle and talks quietly behind him. Gordon does not see Wendell among them.

"I ask him to leave," Martín says from the far side of the circle. "But he want to wait for you."

"Where's Wendell?" Gordon asks Martín, ignoring Stainfield.

"He ain't here and he ain't comin'," Stainfield answers. He takes a step closer to Gordon, who cocks his head with amusement.

"Well then, maybe you'd like to join us?" Gordon gestures at the seats. "All are welcome."

"Ain't no secrets between a father and son," Stainfield growls.

This raises a few chuckles among the people seated behind him. Gordon thinks of Wendell's audacious landboard venture, being grown entirely out of Stainfield's sight, and is tempted to smile.

"You told him I don't need to know about this? What y'all plannin' to do here anyway?"

"This is a drum therapy session that my girlfriend runs for people with issues similar to the ones Wendell is dealing with."

"Oh and what issues are those?"

"Drug addiction in the home, for starters."

Stainfield's face deepens from red to purple.

"What the hell you know about that?!"

"Sir, we're here to help," Caroline says as she walks up behind Gordon. "That's all."

Stainfield's demeanor softens when he sees her, but his anger does not fade. His jaw sets and he jerks a quick nod. Then, he raises a finger at Gordon.

"You damn well ask my permission before you pull any crap like this again."

"Pull any--?"

Caroline jabs Gordon with an elbow before he can finish the sentence.

"Yes sir."

Stainfield turns to leave.

"Girlfriend, huh?" Caroline flashes Gordon a hard look.

Wounded, Gordon stares at her as she walks back to her chair. Just before she sits down, she looks up at him and smiles, then gestures to the empty seat between her and Daniel. Gordon hops over and sits down as Martín initiates the meeting.

Chapter 21

Lockup

Martín's face is ashen when he hangs up the phone.

"Gordon, that was the police. They have your motorcycle."

Halfway down the bar, Gordon's head pops up from the book he is reading. His expression is one of concern more than relief.

"And they have the 'thief' in custody," Martín adds.

"Shit. Where, College Avenue?"

Martín nods. Gordon leaves his book on the bar and heads for the door. When Martín walks over to clear Gordon's plate, he picks up the book: 'Ancient Peoples of the American Southeast.' He smiles and glances out the front window, but Gordon has already bounded away.

At the station, the front desk officer asks Gordon to take a seat while he calls the arresting officer. The man's glance of recognition reminds him of the two policemen who chased him around the field at Sanford Stadium. While he hasn't exactly been laying low, Gordon has not been eager to see those cops again. The door across the room buzzes and a middle-aged detective leans in and nods at Gordon, who follows him into an austere hallway. They enter a large room with several desks, at which sit a mix of uniformed and plainclothes cops. Gordon glances around and does not see the stadium guards, but one of the younger uniforms recognizes him.

"Guess there ain't a law against flyin' around town," the rookie says.

His tone is friendly, but his eyes say otherwise. With Gordon's unkempt hair and local reputation, he has been getting these looks from cops for years -- but never from one younger than he is. He smiles politely at the buzz-cut neophyte and takes the seat next to the detective's desk. The detective glances at his sheaf of papers and addresses Gordon.

"We got a tip from a source outside of Birmingham who was approached to buy your bike."

"Alabama?" Gordon asks.

"Local crank dealer ended up with your bike. Says he got it from a 'friend,' a skinny chick who looks like a heavy user. Says he didn't know it was stolen... Yeah, bullshit. Anyway, he paints it up candy apple red and runs it over to the crew in Bessemer to unload it, which ain't the way to sell something you got legally. We scooped him up there."

"This lady, she's in custody?"

"Well, that's the thing. Her husband says his kid stole it and the kid copped to it. Even if he is a minor... Damn, who rats on his own son? Kid's here in lockup, waiting for a ride to juvie."

"Can I see him? I know who he is."

The detective raises his eyebrows and waits for Gordon to say more.

"Listen, I want to drop the charges."

Across the narrow aisle, the young cop looks up at Gordon, surprised.

"If you do that," the detective warns, "our dealer will probably walk too."

"The boy is a student of mine over at the U. Talented kid, shitty parents."

"Besides, Skip," the young cop interjects, "'cross state lines is felony ain't it? Can't just drop that."

"Keep ya damn rookie ass outta my business," the detective growls. He turns to Gordon. "I get that you wanna protect the boy, but this thing's a little complicated."

"Wendell would never steal the bike for that dealer. He hates his mother using."

"Maybe he was scared for her. Like if she ran up a tab and that dirtbag come to collect."

"I get that your guy oughta be off the streets."

Gordon glances at the rookie and leans closer to the detective.

"Wendell's on his way out of that life. He's already patented an incredible product. He's working hard and he's a good kid. Soon as he turns eighteen, he's free."

"But it *is* your bike, right? The one you reported stolen?"

Gordon sits back and closes his eyes.

"I don't know. Maybe not."

The detective opens a file folder and hands Gordon a glossy photo. The Yamaha has been fitted with garish red fenders and the tank has been sprayed to match them. Ape hanger handlebars now rise from the fork stem and a tall sissy bar has been bolted on behind his saddle, which thankfully survived the makeover. He is sure his father's flask did not. Gordon scowls and hands the photo back. He rubs his face with both hands, then pulls his hair back from his face and inhales deeply.

"It was a gift," Gordon says at last.

Springs creak under the detective's chair as he leans back and folds his arms.

"I gave the bike to Wendell. The flyers were just a joke. I mean, who would pay five grand for that old piece of crap anyway?"

"So his mother stole it from him and sold it?" the rookie asks.

A withering look from the detective turns the younger man back to his pile of papers.

"Son," the detective says quietly, "I know you ain't tellin' the truth. But I think I know why."

He unfolds his arms and extends a hand to Gordon, who shakes it.

"You wanna see the bike?"

"No sir, I wanna see the kid."

In the interrogation room, Gordon sits with his head bowed waiting for them to finish processing Wendell and bring him in.

The click of the doorknob breaks his meditation and Gordon looks up to see a bright green afro above a tight leather dress gripping shapely, athletic legs. Behind this person, the young police officer holds the handcuff chain and yanks it roughly upward, causing the green hair to duck even further down.

"Hey, cut that out!" Gordon stands up. "You're hurting her!"

"Her?"

The young cop laughs as his prisoner raises an unshaven, African-American face. The cop turns both of them around and they leave. Another person catches the door before it closes. Wendell avoids eye contact as he shuffles in and takes the seat across from Gordon. He slumps forward, arms straight down at his sides. Tiny shrugs of his shoulders tell Gordon he is crying. Gordon walks around, sits on the table and puts a hand on Wendell's shoulder.

"Hey bud, it's okay."

"I ain't wanna give it to him," Wendell mumbles into his chest. "Just ride it a little."

"I know. I shoulda let you."

"She told me that guy was gonna hurt her unless she gave it to him."

"What'd your dad say about that?"

Wendell looks up, suddenly very angry.

"He don't do nothin' for her! I'm takin' care of her now."

"Good man." Gordon pats his shoulder again.

Behind him, the door bursts open and Stainfield rushes in, followed by the older detective.

"Get the hell away from my boy!" Stainfield yells.

He grabs Gordon's shoulder and yanks him backward. In one motion, Gordon continues the turn and catches Stainfield by the throat. He lifts the jowly face, stands up and slams Stainfield against the cinder block wall. There is fury in his eyes as he cocks his fist and stares the older man down.

"Easy, Longmeier," the detective says. "Whatever he has comin', let us give it to him."

Gordon slowly releases his grip. Stainfield coughs dramatically, doubles over and begins to moan.

"My neck! Oh hell, my neck!"

"Cut the shit, drama queen," the detective scoffs. "Too many witnesses here for a lawsuit."

Stainfield rises abruptly and crosses to Wendell.

"Let's go, boy."

Wendell looks at Gordon, then stands to follow his father out.

"We'll see you at the Lab tomorrow," Gordon calls after him. Wendell turns back, looking hopeful for the first time, but his father shoves him angrily toward the door.

"Ain't goin' to no Lab," Stainfield growls.

The door clicks closed behind them. Gordon stares at it, fist still balled at his side.

"Let it go," the detective says quietly. "Ain't no changin' people like that."

They walk out and the detective turns toward a door at the back of the hallway. Gordon follows him into the impound section of the parking garage. The bike stands a few bays over, gleaming like a lipstick smear. Gordon turns away, then remembers something and turns to face it again.

"Mind if I check something?"

"It's your bike."

Gordon walks over and feels under the gas tank. The flask is still there, so he pulls it free and puts it in his back pocket. Sloppy tape borders and stray spray marks tell him that whoever painted the tank didn't even bother to remove it first.

"I can't believe they tried to Harley it up like this."

Gordon raps his knuckles on the huge fender that has been mounted over the back tire. The knock sounds duller than he expected, so he feels underneath. When his hands touch duct tape, he pulls out his phone, turns on the flash and shoots a picture up into the fender. A gallon ziploc bag stuffed with dozens of small white pouches has been taped to the inside. He shows the detective the photo.

"Maybe this will help put your guy away?"

"Even a blind squirrel finds a nut once in a while," the detective says with a smirk. "Guess I'm gonna have to hold the bike here while we work that through forensics."

"No problem. When you're done, I'll come get it. For Wendell, of course."

The detective pats Gordon on the back as they walk inside. He stops, feels Gordon's vest again, and shoots him a quizzical look.

"Long story."

"Does it involve trespassing on university property during a football game? Or nearly getting decapitated by a pickup truck?"

Gordon lowers his head.

"Not much happens in this town I don't know about," the detective says quietly. "But there's only so much we can deal with in a day."

"I'll be more careful."

"I doubt that." The detective holds the door open for Gordon. "Say hello to Martín for me. Good work he's doin' over there. Kept your violent ass out of jail, I know that."

Gordon nods grimly as he shakes the man's hand. At the corner, he doesn't cross until the light has changed. He keeps his feet on the ground all the way across, willing himself not to look back at the station to see if he's being watched.

Chapter 22

Deflection

The silver flask glows blue on Gordon's desk as Shiva opens her arms and spreads her electromagnetic fingers. At the boiling center of the lightning sphere, a round object spins into existence. Facing the machine, Gordon stands next to a young man nearly as tall as he is, heavily muscled and shaved up the sides of his head to a dreadlocked mohawk pulled into a scalp knot. Up the back of his neck is a webwork of tribal tattooing, which also extends down his triceps to his elbows. Next to him is a lithe woman in yoga pants and a Lady Bulldogs Track tank top. Shiva finishes her synthesis and winds down. On the platform sits a football helmet, but unlike any Gordon has seen before. The young man touches it tentatively, then lifts it off the metal rods.

"Jesus, Mariana, that's cool!" Gordon exclaims. "Troy, what do you think?"

Troy takes off his safety glasses and nods as he turns the helmet back and forth. Bright red, the top two-thirds of it is shaped like a normal helmet but instead of ending in a facial opening, the opaque material fades into a transparent titanium eye shield. Shaped like the contours of a skull, the titanium begins to perforate just below the cheek and nasal bones, becoming a woven, fang-like gridwork that ends in a solid, eased edge around the jawline. The transparency extends much further back on the temples than a regular face mask opening would.

"The titanium is woven up into the polycarbonate shell," Mariana explains. "It adds rigidity to the plastic, but not a lot of weight. It also makes the eye shield really solid. Troy's had helmets crack on him right at the screw mounts for the face mask. There are no weak points in this design."

Troy lifts the unpadded helmet onto his head and smiles at Mariana through the shield.

"Should be plenty of air flow and better peripheral sight lines," Mariana says.

Inside the helmet, they can see Troy nodding.

"I have the interior padding at my station," she says to Gordon. "We're gonna use the cushion system from one of his old helmets."

"Good to have a smart girlfriend." Gordon winks at Troy. "Great work, Mariana. I don't know if the SEC will approve it, but I sure do."

"Sellout," Stan chides as Gordon walks over.

Gordon flicks his ear and settles into his desk chair.

"Did you ever get that hideous red paint off the Yamaha?"

"Naw, I just painted a big ol' G on it," Gordon drawls. "Actually, they still have it at the impound."

Stan looks over at Wendell's station, where the boy sits staring at Troy, starstruck.

"Why don't you get Troy to sign something for Wendell so he can get some work done again?"

Gordon looks at the boy and chuckles, but his smile fades as Mr. Williams opens the door for a policeman. The cop's uniform is not from Athens. Stan and Gordon walk over and greet the man.

"Is there a Wendell Stainfield here?" the cop asks.

"Right over there," Stan answers. "Is he in any trouble?"

"No sir, just a family situation."

Gordon's stomach drops as the cop walks over to Wendell and

leans down to speak with him. Wendell's expression changes dramatically.

"Hospital? Where?" Wendell asks loudly. "Where is she?"

Even though Stan and Gordon are within a few steps of them, the cop's discreet reply is inaudible.

"Is she dead?!" Wendell's eyes are wide with panic. "IS SHE?!"

The cop stares at Wendell for a beat, then looks back at Stan and Gordon. He leans forward to speak softly again, but Wendell jumps up.

"She *is* dead! I know it. She is!!"

Wendell sprints out of the room, still wearing his safety glasses. The cop, Stan and Gordon all run after him; but the boy is too quick. By the time they get outside, he's gone. Gordon leaps high into the air, leaving Stan and the stunned cop on the ground below. He hangs about fifty feet up for a moment, looking all around. He seems to spot something in the vicinity of the North Campus, but then keeps looking in every other direction as he drops back down to the flagstone path.

"Sir, what in the heck was that?" the cop asks.

Gordon ignores the question. "Was it his mother? Overdose?"

"I can't confirm that." The cop looks around. "Not officially at least, but it'll hit the papers soon enough. Now sir, how did you fly up there?"

"Oh, it's this thing."

Gordon lifts his shirt to show the vest.

"Could I borrow it? I'd like to take a look for myself."

"No!" Stan cries.

"No sir, we can't," Gordon answers more calmly. "It's unapproved technology, still in testing. If you were to get hurt... well, no more football budget for a long time."

The cop gives Gordon a skeptical look.

"Did you see the boy?"

"I thought I did, but it wasn't him."

"Any idea where he might go?"

"His car's in the lot over there," Stan gestures. "But he didn't take his keys. Maybe you should hold onto them?"

Stan leads the man back into the Lab as Gordon starts to bound up campus. He takes out his phone and texts Stan to meet at Martín's, then calls Caroline. When he gets to the bar and Martín unlocks the door to let him in, he notices the 'Closed' sign. In the shadows toward the back of the room, Wendell sits at a table with his head on his arms and Julia's hand on the nape of his neck. Every so often his back heaves with a sob. Martín walks back with two glasses of water and sets them down as Caroline arrives. Gordon starts toward Wendell but Caroline stops him and walks to the boy. Gordon sits with Martín at the bar as a hard pull on the locked door handle causes the bells to jingle; it is Stan. Gordon walks over and lets him in.

"That cop--" Stan sees Wendell and freezes. "G, this could be trouble. That cop really needs to take Wendell to his father."

"I know. But Wendell needs..." *What? A mother? A father?* "...a little space."

Stan drags a seat around. When there is another knock at the door, Martín looks over with concern. It is Stainfield and behind him are his drinking buddies, Roger and Harlan. Stainfield visors his eyes and peers into the bar, then pounds on the door again. Caroline sees him and whispers to Wendell, who jumps up with a panicked expression.

"No! I ain't goin'!"

"Shhh, please," Caroline soothes. "Come with me, back here. Let them handle your father."

Caroline leads Wendell back to the stage. They climb up and walk behind the large curtain to the right, and Gordon waits until they are out of sight before he opens the door. Roger and Harlan have pistols holstered at their sides, but Stainfield is unarmed. Gordon points at the sign: 'No Firearms.'

"Where's my boy?" Stainfield demands. "Where you got 'im?"

His face is florid, his eyes wild.

"Sir," Gordon says respectfully, "I was very sorry to hear about--"

"Never mind about her, goddamn you. Where's Wendell?"

"He's not here," Gordon says. "I spoke with him, and he said he needs some time to process--"

"Process, my ass! He's my son!"

Stainfield walks back to Roger and grabs the pistol from his holster. When Roger protests, Stainfield aims it at him and he quiets down. Gordon slams the door as Stainfield turns and levels the barrel at his face.

"Last time! Where's my boy?"

Gordon stares stone-faced through the window at Stainfield. The older man's pudgy cheeks grow redder, his nostrils flaring as he breathes even faster. His finger twitches on the trigger and to his surprise the barrel explodes with fire. When the smoke clears, there is a nickel-sized dent in the window but Gordon's expression has not changed, as if he has not even blinked. A ring of red begins to form around a black spot on Stainfield's right shoulder. Roger and Harlan stare at Gordon, mesmerized by his unwavering calm and by the miraculous properties of the glass pane in front of him. Even Stainfield's bawling does not distract them at first. Only when he lets Roger's pistol clatter to the sidewalk does the bald man turn to acknowledge his wounded friend.

"Fuckin' ricochet!" Stainfield screams. "I'm shot, goddamn it!"

"You shot yourself." Roger picks up his weapon. "Damn lucky you did, too."

"Get me to a fucking hospital!" Stainfield bellows.

"Wife ain't dead four hours and you're carryin' on like this?" Roger says with disgust. "You coulda murdered that guy there, you asshole. With my goddamn thirty-eight."

Roger grabs Stainfield's uninjured arm, loops it roughly over his shoulder and helps him shuffle away from the bar, ignoring the older man's shrieks of pain. Harlan has not moved. He stares at Gordon through the window, and Gordon stares back.

"You comin', Harlan?" Roger calls.

Harlan does not break eye contact with Gordon as he begins to follow his friends. Through the window, the last thing he sees is Caroline rushing up to hug Gordon, but Gordon does not look at her. He never looks away from Harlan until the man is across the street and a patrol car is roaring up with its siren howling. Two cops rush to the door and push it open, one of whom Gordon recognizes. The rookie looks around the bar and turns to Gordon.

"We heard shots fired. What happened?"

"That dumb motherfucker Stainfield tried to kill me," Gordon answers quietly. "Shot himself instead. He'll be at the hospital if you want him."

The rookie sees the dent in the window behind Gordon and puts his finger into it, then pulls it away quickly.

"The titanium just absorbed the energy of a gunshot," Gordon explains. "It's gonna be hot."

"Titanium...?"

"Yeah. Your man is gettin' away."

The young cop nods and rushes back to his car. His partner looks at the door, then at Gordon, then shakes his head. He sees Martín inside the bar and says a quick hello, then turns and follows the rookie.

Gordon walks to a stool and sits quietly, head bowed forward, eyes closed.

From the back of the bar, Wendell shuffles into the sunlight and looks around at everyone. Martín offers him one of the barstools across from Gordon and sits next to him. Caroline sits on his other side. Gordon still has not looked up.

"Uh, hey, vato," Martín says quietly. "You okay?"

Gordon bobs his head once but doesn't raise it.

"Whatchu doing there?"

"Praying."

Gordon's mind feels like a dark cave, tunneled and narrow yet connected to a vast, open expanse. The darkness is absolute, but not empty. There is a sense of accompaniment, as if a presence stands with him in silence, its awareness palpable and yet also peaceful. The balance of energy between that space and the place from which Gordon views it are in complete harmony. His conscious feeling, if it can be called that, most closely resembles gratitude or joy. He cannot separate the two ideas, so he does not try. He just sits, projecting himself into a place that is neither void nor substance, nor his alone. He has never felt more peace.

'Praying' is the only word he can think of for what he is doing, but when he says it he immediately wishes he had not. Still, it is the only word that might be both honest and comprehensible -- to Martín and to him. 'Meditating' would have implied something more solitary and self-oriented than what he is experiencing. So he lets 'praying' stand.

When he opens his eyes, he is surprised to see Wendell across from him. The boy looks back at him through red rims, drawn and gaunt, as if the last hour of his life has hollowed him out. Gordon stands and reaches out to him, and Wendell steps into the hug. They hold the embrace for a long time, neither one feeling the usual awkwardness or discomfort. When at last they separate, it is a mutual movement, a completion. They turn and sit again. Caroline puts her arm around Wendell and he rests his head on her shoulder. Martín pats Gordon's knee. Still focused on the sensation of prayer, Gordon feels certain that his mind alone could not generate the consciousness he encountered.

"Dude, where are you?"

Gordon startles and looks at Stan, sensing the eyes of the others on him too.

"Sorry," he mumbles.

"No, it's okay. How are you feeling?"

"Good. Yeah, really good."

Gordon ignores Stan's bewilderment and looks at Wendell.

"Shouldn't we go to the hospital?" Gordon asks.

"I don't wanna see him," Wendell mutters.

"I'm more thinking of her," Gordon replies gently.

Caroline takes her arm from around Wendell and turns to face him. She holds both of his hands and looks at him intently.

"It's a good idea. You need to say goodbye to her."

"We'll drive you," Martín offers. "G, maybe you stay here for now?"

Still distracted, Gordon nods. Holding Wendell's hand, Caroline walks him to the door. Martín and Julia follow, but

Martín stops to look closely at the dent in the window. He runs his finger around the outside of it and then into the declivity. For a long moment, he looks back at Gordon, who sits with his eyes closed once again. Then he crosses himself and jogs to catch up with the others. Stan pats Gordon on the back, which brings him out of his reverie once again.

"I'm gonna head back to the Lab," Stan says. "Troy is pretty intent on trying that helmet out for real, but Jalen still needs some documents from Mariana before she can expose it to the public."

Gordon indicates his agreement.

"And those walrus pups need to be soaked in ice water before they get heat stroke," Stan adds.

Gordon nods again.

"Dude, I know you just got shot at, but come on."

With a pronounced blink of his eyes, Gordon manages to focus.

"What? Sorry. Just thinking about something. Nothing work-related."

"What, we can only talk about work?"

"No, it's just... I don't know what to make of it, really."

"Gordon, a man just looked you in the eye and pulled the trigger, thinking he was killing you."

"No, I'm pretty sure that was an accident. He seemed more surprised than I was."

"Still, he did it. It happened."

"It's more about this thing that Joe told me."

"Joe the Indian?" Stan asks.

"He's not..." Gordon stops and looks at Stan. "He's my father."

"Wow," Stan exhales. "Are you sure?"

"Yeah. Yeah, I am."

"Your Mom never told you?"

"She said I was a 'honeymoon baby.'"

"That's all?"

"I guess she was with Joe right before she met my... George. They met in Asheville, North Carolina. She was working as a waitress, saving up for her doctorate."

Stan sees Gordon's frustration at how little he knows about his own family.

"So, how does it feel to have saved your own life?" he asks.

It takes a beat for Gordon to catch up to Stan's meaning. He walks over and opens the door, then stands with his arms on either side of it, stretched out to the hole. When he puts his fingers into opposite sides of it, he sees how thin the material was that remained after it deflected the bullet.

"The metal compressed really well," Gordon observes. "If it were less plastic or if the bullet were smaller, it probably would have gone through. I'd like to shoot a smaller round at a sheet like this, maybe .223, and see what happens."

"Just don't catch the ricochet," Stan cracks. "Were you sure the window would stop the bullet when you were standing there?"

Gordon walks back and sits down. "Honestly, I wasn't even thinking about that." He notes Stan's disbelief. "I was thinking about harmony."

Stan laughs out loud. "What, like a chorus or something?"

"No, more like how that moment, the energy in that moment, was like a big dead tree in the middle of a river. That guy, Wendell's dad, is always in conflict. He's always disrupting the flow. His wife dies, and he's angry at everyone but himself. I was thinking, what a waste. What an awful waste of energy to be that guy."

"Imagine being married to him," Stan muses. "It's no wonder she--"

"Please," Gordon interrupts. "Don't speak ill of her. Her spirit is listening. Don't offend her."

Stan stares at Gordon in disbelief.

"We should go see him," Gordon declares.

"Wendell?"

"No, Stainfield."

Stan's look is even more incredulous. Gordon walks around the bar and takes the pickup keys off the hook below the counter. Stan reckons that Mariana and Jalen will be fine without him and leaves with Gordon. On the way, Gordon calls around and locates Stainfield.

In the emergency room, he and Stan see Roger and Harlan in the chairs. Their holsters are empty. Roger looks up from his magazine.

"Well if it ain't Superman himself."

Harlan sets his phone down and peers over his reading glasses. His pale gray eyes narrow at Gordon.

"Come to finish him off?" Roger cracks. "That junior copper has a close eye on him, so you may have to ambush him outside."

Gordon smiles patiently. "I'm here to apologize."

Harlan raises his eyebrows and puts his phone in his pocket. Roger is momentarily speechless. So is Stan.

"I could've handled things better," Gordon explains. "I chose to answer his aggression with provocation. This was my fault."

"Don't tell him that," Roger says. "He'll have you payin' his medical bills."

Stan watches Gordon, half expecting him to offer to do so.

"I wanna talk to the cop."

Gordon looks down the row of beds and sees polished black shoes under the third curtain. He strides over and opens it. Stainfield is asleep, his left wrist handcuffed to the bed frame. The young cop sits in a chair, looking at his phone. When he sees Gordon he springs up and puts one hand on the butt of his revolver.

"Relax, I'm not here to hurt anyone."

"Show me your hands."

Gordon raises them both and spreads his fingers in the air. He resists the urge to lower eight and leave two extended.

"Can I speak with Mr. Stainfield?"

"They knocked him out. He was moanin' a lot, and I think they just wanted some quiet."

"Why is he cuffed?"

"Uh, maybe it's 'cause he tried to *kill* you?"

"It was an accident."

"Yeah, that's what he said."

"It was. I could see it in his eyes. Y'all ought to release him."

The rookie pulls his elbows back and begins to bow up.

"Don't tell me how to do my job."

Gordon looks at him for a long moment, and as he does the man's face begins to relax.

"Okay," Gordon says, "I understand. If there's anything I can do, drop the charges, whatever, just let me know."

"What's your deal with this family? Why you always tryin' to help them?"

"This man's wife died of an overdose this morning. His son's a student of mine, a good kid. They could use a break."

"Yeah." The rookie's tone softens. "Okay, I'll let him know."

Gordon extends a hand. "Thanks."

The rookie hesitates, then shakes.

"Name's Dean."

"Gordon."

As he walks back to Stan, Gordon feels a tingling sensation on his chest behind the stone. When they pass back through the chairs, Gordon looks at Roger.

"Next time, leave the pistola at home."

Roger's brow furrows for an instant, but then he smiles.

"Sure thing, amigo. Adios."

Chapter 23

Heresy

In the pickup on the way out to the church, Gordon thinks again about the consciousness that he sensed when he was praying. In truth, he realizes, he wasn't really praying -- at least not at first. Not at all, actually. He was just trying to process the idea that his life had nearly ended, that Wendell's mother's life *had* ended and that all of this insane hatred and anger was aimed at him somehow. Very few people get to keep looking into the eyes of the person who has just aimed a pistol at their face and pulled the trigger, point blank. What Gordon saw in those eyes, in that instant, was regret. Stainfield did not want to end Gordon's life, he wanted to end his own pain. Perhaps he had constructed a world in which Gordon was the source of his suffering. Or maybe he didn't even think that much about causality; maybe he was just carrying so much pain that wherever he looked he saw reasons for it.

How do you harmonize with a person like that?

Gordon tries to remember the vastness and the peace he had felt in the dark. It had seemed like it could absorb anything, even Stainfield's pain, and return it as harmony. If only Stainfield could see that too.

The truck rocks over the curb and crunches into the gravel lot.

The church is small, white siding dusted pink with clay at its base, faded tarpaper roof, a single spire. It is Sunday, and there are many cars and trucks in the lot. Gordon hunts for a spot and finally sees one. As he is walking back along the row of cars he notices a large German sedan with California tags. Two people sit in the front seats, speaking animatedly to one another as a third voice, amplified by the speakerphone, joins in. Gordon realizes that it is Caroline and David and that they are having a major argument. He sidles closer to the vehicle but cannot hear what they are saying.

Damn German engineering.

Suddenly the passenger door opens and Caroline barrels out. Over the speakerphone, Caroline's father barks her name but she does not stop. Gordon hears the congressman again.

"Never mind what she says. We'll just book the goddamn show and you'll get that country fucking moron to say his lines."

David reaches across and slams the door, then replies inaudibly. As Caroline stomps around the car, she pulls up with a gasp when she sees Gordon.

"What are you doing here?" she says.

"Pretty much wondering the exact same thing about y'all." He nods at North. "Didn't think they let the devil in the front door of places like this."

She snorts angrily, marches around him and heads for the entrance of the church.

"Really are beautiful when you're mad," he calls after her.

Once again, Gordon hears Congressman Highsmith on David's speakerphone but cannot decipher specific words. Rather than wait and endure an awkward chat, Gordon follows Caroline into the church. She sits at the aisle end of a crowded pew several rows from the back. The rest of the rows appear to be filled as well. A choir sings at full voice, white faces above white robes in front of a mostly white congregation, which Gordon finds odd for a Baptist church. He edges along the wall and secures a standing spot near the back right corner of the room. A closed casket sits across the altar, surrounded by small flower arrangements. At one side, a simple metal tripod holds a corkboard tacked with photos and cards. On the other, a large photo of a very pretty woman sits on a pedestal. At any other time, Gordon would not have connected that picture with the emaciated wreck he saw sprawled on Stainfield's couch.

A movement to his left distracts Gordon; it is David, stepping into the church as he tucks his cell phone into his pocket. He considers the distance to Caroline and the number of people already jammed into the row and seems to hesitate, but then tightens his jaw and strides to her. There is a ripple of communication down the pew as bodies press ever tighter to make room for one more. Clearly irritated, Caroline hisses several times in his ear before settling her gaze upon Pastor Ken as he walks to the lectern. The choir stops singing as Ken removes his glasses and wipes them on his robe. He puts them back on and gazes out over the crowd.

"Death," Ken intones, "comes for us all. We are gathered today to remember a sister in the faith, in the spirit of Christ Jesus, one who fell tragically before her time. Sally May Stainfield, daughter of Gerald and Winona Cobb, wife of..."

Gordon's mind drifts. He scans the crowd and sees Martín and Julia a few rows back from where Wendell sits with his grandparents. Wendell's hair is still wet and combed down and his shirt collar is slightly yellowed. Gerald sits with stiff dignity, but Winona sobs quietly into her handkerchief. Several people away, Stainfield slumps in his suit like a straw effigy. Next to him, Harlan runs a finger around the inside of his collar and stretches his neck to one side, then the other. Next to Harlan, Roger's head gleams like waxed apple, unmoving as he listens to Pastor Ken's rambling blessing. When Roger turns and looks at Gordon, Gordon realizes that Ken has stopped speaking and is staring at him too. Behind his glasses, the pastor's eyes are ice cold. His face begins to flush and his mouth opens slightly as he gathers himself.

"And then there are those who will NEVER enter the kingdom of Christ Jesus!" Ken booms, staring at Gordon. "Whose vanity and godlessness cause them to trespass with impunity! To sully and stain the most holy of places! To bring suffering to innocent people, and pain to those who--"

"Now hold on." Roger stands, to a flutter of shocked whispers. "That fella there ain't done nothin' but kindness to this family. He's here payin' his respects to the mother of his student. He ain't gotta be run down like that, Pastor Ken."

The congregation looks from Roger to Gordon to Ken, confused and upset at the interruption. Gordon brings his hands together in front of his chin as if in prayer and bows slightly to Roger as he mouths, "Thank you." He raises one fist to salute Wendell, then turns and heads for the door. The sun and earthy breeze feel like an embrace as he walks past the gleaming German sedan, pausing to imagine Caroline sitting in the passenger seat next to David, maybe even holding his hand. Gordon sets his jaw and continues on to the pickup. He fires it up, wrestles it around in the tight driving lane and aims for the road. As he reaches the front of the church, he stops when a woman steps into his path. It is Caroline.

"Let me in," she says as she walks to the passenger door.

Gordon does not turn to look at her. He nudges the pickup forward and she lets go of the door handle, then he continues to the end of the driveway. In his rearview mirror, he sees her staring after him. He guns the motor and speeds away.

The Friday morning sky sags cinder gray, swirling with rain. Gordon stands inside the glass doors of the Lab, debating his next move. The storm is aggressive but not electrical, as far as he can see, and as long as he is not grounded it doesn't matter anyway, but he has never flown in the rain or even in a strong wind. He flips up his hood and cinches his backpack tighter, steeling himself for the blow. As he pushes the door open, Stan calls to him from the hallway.

"...meeting!" is all Gordon can hear. He turns around to see Stan jogging toward him.

"Careful, people will think you're doing cardio."

"Maybe I'll get less crap from the fashionistas for my dad bod," Stan mutters. "Hey, so I just got a call from Mr. Berrigan's assistant. They want us at a meeting in Braselton as soon as possible."

"She say what it was about?"

"She did not, but she did say we 'might want to bring a lawyer.'"

"What?! Why didn't Mr. Berrigan just call us? That's not like him."

Gordon digs his phone out of his pocket and punches Berrigan's personal cell number. There is no answer. He tries again with the same result, then calls Jalen and relays Stan's news. All three agree to meet at Jalen's office in thirty minutes.

"Guess I better put on the suit again," Gordon sighs. "Twice in one week."

"Let's hope this goes better than that did."

Stan closes the Lab and drops Gordon at his apartment. Twenty minutes later, they pile into Jalen's Audi sedan and make the forty-five minute drive to Braselton. In the lobby of the Catonsville building, they flop into chairs and wait. Gordon fishes a rubber band out of his backpack and tries to gather his hair into something more orderly, but after a few tries the rubber band breaks and he gives up.

"I feel like I ought to have my playbook," Jalen comments, to confused looks. "When they cut you in the NFL, they always tell you to bring your playbook."

"They can't fire us," Gordon says. "We probably own half the damn company."

"Nineteen percent," Jalen corrects. "And change."

"And a hundred percent of the Shiva patent," Gordon adds.

The elevator dings, and Berrigan's older son Patrick walks out and angles toward them. There are dark circles under his eyes and two days' growth on his cheeks. His suit is rumpled, but his tie is cinched tight.

"Gentlemen," he greets them wearily. "Please follow me."

They walk across the lobby to a set of polished oak doors. Patrick pulls the doors open to reveal a long table. Each seat is occupied except for the two at the heads and three along the right side. Patrick invites them to sit on the right and takes the head seat closest to them.

"Where's Mr. Berrigan?" Gordon asks.

Patrick inhales deeply. "That's why we're here. Dad has had a stroke. He's alive," he adds quickly, "but incapacitated."

"Where?" Gordon presses. "What hospital?"

"He's at home, resting."

"When did this happen?"

"A few days ago. They discharged him today. He can't speak or move the left side of his body."

Gordon stares at Patrick, then looks around at the others, trying to comprehend the situation. When his eyes meet those of Berrigan's younger son, the man looks down at his notepad.

"Since Dad is no longer able to discharge his duties as President and CEO, the board has asked me to begin to perform those duties."

Gordon leans forward, listening closely.

"There has been a proposal before the board for several weeks," Patrick continues, "which Dad has strenuously opposed. It has nearly unanimous support from the rest of the board--"

"'Unable to discharge his duties...'" Gordon cuts in. "Permanently, or temporarily?"

"Mr. Longmeier," an older board member interjects, "we would ask that you please not interrupt Mr. Berrigan."

"It's okay, Porter." Patrick turns to Gordon. "It's a valid question. I would hope that his condition is temporary, and that he regains his full strength. But he is seventy-six years old and it was quite a severe stroke."

Patrick turns back to the group.

"The issue is that this proposal comes with a time limit. We were given six weeks to reply and it's been five already. Dad, God bless him, was trying to run out the clock."

Gordon raises his hand.

"Yes, Mr., uh, yes Gordon," Patrick stammers.

"I'm not familiar with corporate governance or nothing, but this don't smell quite right."

"Smell?" Porter echoes.

He looks at Gordon's wild hair as if he finds it personally offensive.

"Yeah," Gordon answers, "as in, this stinks. And why do you need us here for it? If you're gonna pick the man's pocket while he's sleeping, why call in more witnesses?"

The table reacts in unison, a torrent of angry denials and protests. Patrick looks agonized, yet calm. He raises his hands for silence but it takes a few minutes for order to be restored.

"Gordon," Patrick continues, "you and Mr. Woods and Mr. Malkovich are very important stakeholders."

"So what's at stake?" Gordon asks.

"Frankly," Patrick sighs, "the future of our company."

For the first time, Gordon notices three piles of folders in the center of the table; one at either end, and one in the middle. He points at the one nearest him.

"Is this the proposal?"

"Yes."

Gordon looks more closely at the cover of the top folder.

"North Industries? Are you fucking kidding me?!"

The table buzzes again. Gordon glares at Patrick.

"Your father spent millions of dollars to build the best immigration center in the Southeast for war refugees. Do you think for one second he'd want *his* company to climb in bed with a weapons manufacturer?"

Patrick looks down at the table, ashen. Across the table, Porter coughs loudly and stares at Gordon.

"Mr. Longmeier," Porter says, "you are only here out of courtesy. We don't need your approval for this."

"You need Mr. Berrigan's, and he'd never give it."

Gordon's face hardens as his eyes lock on Porter's.

"What machines, do you suppose, are going to produce pretty much all of the inventory you ship every goddamn day?"

Porter pats the stack of folders.

"This proposal makes all of you *very* wealthy men."

Gordon looks at him with disgust. "The trouble with greedy people is that they think everyone else loves money as much as they do. But some things are more important."

"Mr. Longmeier, our agreements regarding your technology will survive any acquisition or sale." Porter glances at Jalen with condescension. "We have had a team of lawyers anticipating this very objection."

Gordon looks at Jalen, who nods.

"You never counted on a palace coup," Jalen explains. "The original contract assumed the sons would have the same philosophy -- and integrity -- as Mr. Berrigan."

"Perhaps, you should have anticipated market adjustments, Mr. Woods," Porter patronizes.

"At the time that contract was written I was busy anticipating opposing quarterbacks' adjustments," Jalen says calmly. "I was a student at the University of Georgia, same as Gordon."

Porter turns to Gordon. "It might have been good for you to have an adult at the table with you that day, Mr. Longmeier."

"I did. I had Mr. Berrigan."

Gordon looks at the Berrigan sons, who will not meet his gaze, then stands and walks out of the room. Stan and Jalen rise and follow him.

"J, could you take me to Mr. Berrigan's house?"

The Audi cuts through the fog draping the countryside. In a few minutes, its tires crunch to a stop on the tan pebbles of a circular driveway in front of a three-story brick Georgian. Gordon climbs out and walks to the door, where he is greeted by a large man in a gray suit.

"Who are you?" Gordon asks.

"Mr. Berrigan can't have any visitors right now," the man drawls.

"What is this, a lockdown? I'm his friend."

"Family said nobody comes in."

The man starts to close the door, but Gordon stops it with his boot.

"Mr. Berrigan would want to know--"

Gordon sees the man's hand move to the bulge on his hip, his small gray eyes narrow and cold.

"Okay," Gordon concedes. "Okay."

He walks back to the car and gets in. For a moment he sits in slumped silence.

"Let's go back out to the road," Gordon says to Jalen. "Pull around to where those trees are, there." He takes off his suit jacket. "Cool, just stop right here."

When the car stops, Gordon opens the door.

"Y'all don't have to wait for me."

"G," Jalen cautions, "that guy looked like a cop."

"Yeah, I know. But I gotta try."

"We'll wait."

Gordon nods his thanks, turns and runs toward the house. When he jumps, he disappears into the mist above the trees. At the house, a light burns in one second-story window. Gordon drops onto the roof above it, then slides down the drainpipe and lowers onto the sill. He raises the screen, lifts the window and climbs into the room. Dan Berrigan lays sleeping on a large bed, the left side of his mouth sagging open. Gordon tiptoes to the door and presses the pin to lock it, then crosses to the bed and gently nudges the old man's shoulder. When he wakes, Berrigan's eyes light with recognition. He slowly reaches his right hand toward Gordon's and squeezes it hard.

"Do you know what's happening at Catonsville?" Gordon whispers.

Berrigan's brows crease. He nods.

"How can we stop them? Please, tell me what to do."

Berrigan looks at Gordon for a long time. When he closes his eyes, tears run down his cheeks. Slowly, he shakes his head, then lays back onto the pillow.

"There must be something," Gordon pleads.

Outside the door, heavy footsteps approach. Gordon lifts Berrigan's hand and the old man opens his eyes again. The doorknob jiggles.

"Sir?" the guard calls. "Are you okay? How did this door get locked?"

"Please," Gordon whispers. "Can I bring you to the office?"

Berrigan frowns sadly and shakes his head. The guard pounds on the door.

"Sir!" he calls, "are you safe?"

"I'll find a way," Gordon hisses urgently. "I won't let them do this."

With a hoarse exhale, Berrigan tries to speak. Gordon leans closer to hear him.

"...hhhhank you," Berrigan manages.

The guard pounds harder.

With tears in his eyes, Gordon squeezes Berrigan's hand with both of his. He turns and dives out the window as the guard splinters the door frame and enters. Gordon rolls on the lawn, gathers himself into a crouch and springs up over the trees before the guard gets to the window. Watching from his bed, Dan Berrigan's chest rises and falls as he cries in silence.

Chapter 24

Reclamation

Gordon considers the wet grass stains on his dress shirt and suit pants, then pulls them off and drops them on the floor next to his jacket. He puts on jeans and a work shirt and grabs his helmet. If they hurry, he and Jalen can make it to the impound before it closes. Dean, the rookie cop, left a message about his motorcycle while they were in the board room at Catonsville, but Gordon did not look at his phone until he was in the Audi headed back to Athens. Jalen insisted on coming with him to keep everyone honest. Gordon knows that Jalen's football fame will carry more weight with the police than his legal advice, but either way he is grateful to have him along.

"You couldn't keep the suit on for thirty more minutes?" Jalen chides when he sees Gordon.

"What? Oh yeah, no, I looked like I lost a wrestling match with a lawnmower."

"And this is *much* better."

"You sound like Caroline."

"Speak of the devil."

Jalen points across the street. Gordon sees the jaunty stride that Caroline always adopts when the coffee or the conversation is good.

"Shit," Gordon mutters. "I was kind of rude to her at the funeral."

When Caroline sees Gordon, she stops and stares at him. Slowly, she walks across the street and says hello to Jalen. Gordon avoids looking at her.

"Wendell came by the church Wednesday night," she says to Gordon.

Gordon gives her a thoughtful look. "Is he okay?"

"No, he's pretty goddamn far from okay. But his dad ain't locked up, so... thanks for that."

"You think he'll be back in the Lab soon?"

She shrugs.

"So I guess we oughta talk," Gordon mumbles.

Another shrug.

"Fuck it, never mind." Gordon starts to walk away.

Caroline stares after him, then says goodbye to Jalen and heads in the opposite direction. Jalen catches up to Gordon and they continue on toward the police station. After a while, Jalen speaks.

"You remember when the three of us tried to get into that sorority party in high school?"

Gordon nods. "One of them called us 'those townies from Dark Central.'"

"Man, Caroline lit into that Kappa bitch..." Jalen chuckles. "'When he's playin' for the Dawgs next year, you're gonna be on your knees beggin' for his dark cock!'"

Gordon smiles. Jalen grins and shakes his head.

"I wonder what David North would say if he had seen that," Gordon muses.

"She's straight-up Athens, G. Don't give up on her."

At the parking garage, Dean barely takes his eyes off of Jalen as he unlocks the impound. When he starts a running commentary on how Georgia should set up its pass coverages, Gordon nods at Dean and mouths the words 'Kappa bitch' to Jalen. Laughing, Gordon peels off and walks around to the Yamaha. The first thing he notices is that the rear fender has been removed. He turns back to comment on this and sees Jalen's pained expression.

"Uh, hey, Dean," Gordon calls. "Ain't no complicated paperwork or anything for this, right?"

Peeved at the interruption, Dean glances at Gordon, shakes his head and continues speaking.

"Um, because Jalen is one damn expensive lawyer. I'd like to get him off the clock ay-sap. Plus, he and Angelique need to start their weekend."

Crestfallen, Dean agrees that Jalen can go. They walk to the door and Dean swipes Jalen into the station.

"I got it from here, bud."

Jalen shakes Dean's hand. He aims a pistol finger at Gordon and ducks into the station. Gordon's text dings a few seconds later:

"If that motherf'er said one more thing about Cover-2 I was actually gonna start charging your ass."

Gordon closes the screen before Dean can see it.

"Thanks for taking that dumbass fender off."

"Wasn't me," Dean replies. "Forensics was all over this thing. They were pissed that you took that flask."

"Nobody even knew it was there or it woulda been gone already."

Dean accepts this logic, and they head back inside to finish the paperwork. Gordon walks out to the bike and tries his key in the handlebar lock, but it doesn't work anymore. Rather than go back inside and deal with Dean again, he rummages through the trash and picks out a Coke can. He tears it in half, rips two smaller strips from each side and folds them flat. Within thirty seconds, he has sprung the lock and started the bike. He pulls on his helmet and steers for the exit, where he shows the attendant his paperwork.

Feeling self-conscious about the Yamaha's circus makeover, he rolls through town to his garage and quickly closes the door after he pulls in. He kills the motor and rocks the bike back onto its stand. Only then does he finally let himself recall the sight of Mr. Berrigan's tears. He bows his head and closes his eyes, still astride, still wearing the helmet, hands still on the ludicrous ape hanger handlebars. He feels the darkness begin to open up in his mind again, but he wills it closed.

How can God let a man live seventy-six virtuous years and then rip his heart out in one short week?

The darkness opens anyway, and in it Gordon feels a thought begin to form.

That man is not broken. Berrigan is not broken, so don't you be.

But his eyes, Gordon recalls. *So sad. So hurt.*

He is not broken. He lived as he chose. He is a man steeped in truth, an honorable man. This he knows.

Gordon dismounts and takes his helmet off. In his apartment, the Shiva device reminds him of what is actually at stake. He thinks of Berrigan's son Patrick.

"Stakeholder..."

Patrick is beholden to those who are worried about squeezing every drop of cash into their own personal cup, but not at all concerned about the flood of disharmony their greed will send into the world.

How do we stop them?

A pat of butter dances on the iron skillet. Gordon moves it off the heat as he chops onions, peppers and mushrooms into the pan, then whisks and scrambles three eggs. As the spatula lifts and turns the food, over and over, his mind churns. Fascinated by the texture of the coalescing eggs, he pinches off a blob and massages it between his fingers. He studies the sheen it leaves on his thumb. Suddenly, he drops the spatula and grabs his phone. What he types to Stan would be unintelligible to anyone else, just two lines of computer code.

The reply is nearly immediate:

"Jesus. Yes! I forgot about that!"

At the island, hunched over the skillet with a book about the ancient mound builders of the Southeast, Gordon eats in peace. After dinner, he goes down to the garage and removes the Yamaha's gas tank and front fender, the latter of which he pitches in the trash. He looks at the ape hangers and sissy bar, but decides to attack the ignition lock first. He removes it and breaks it down to expose the locking wafers inside the key assembly, then takes it upstairs and pulls up a screen on Shiva's tablet that displays the Yamaha's old key. He adjusts the peaks and valleys to match the key pattern required by the new cylinder and sends it to print. His phone buzzes as he works the new key in and out of the lock.

"Hey..." Caroline's voice is throaty and warm. "You busy?"

Gordon pops in an ear bud and walks down to the garage.

"Just ministering to an old friend."

Gordon takes the reassembled ignition lock housing and slides it back into place.

"Oh?"

"The Yamaha. They really tarted it up."

Gordon walks the tank over to a bench and clamps it in place, then finds his grinder in a cabinet.

"Wanna come by?"

"Sorry," Gordon says. "I don't do threesomes."

"He went back to California."

The grinder crashes to the tabletop as Gordon jumps to the stairs and takes their entire height in one leap. On the other end of the call, he hears Caroline laughing.

"Lemme just wash up," he blurts.

"No, I want you dirty."

Gordon crosses to the window, yanks it open and jumps across to the neighboring roof. In two diagonal leaps, he covers the four-block walk to the apartment. Landing on the roof, he jumps down to the street and bounces back up to the window. He catches the upper trim with one hand and knocks with the other, startling Caroline in bed. She wraps herself in her sheet and squints at the darkened panes. When she recognizes Gordon she stands up and lets the sheet fall away.

"They oughta call you Amazon Prime," she says as he climbs into her bedroom.

Gordon hears her in his ear bud and realizes he never ended the call. He laughs as he strips off his clothing and weights. She catches his wrist when he floats up, pulls him close and holds him as tightly as he does her, safe in each other's arms; warm, then hotter, then sweating, until at last they shiver together with loving release.

In the morning, Gordon wakes up slowly. The scent of Caroline is everywhere, but she is not close. He opens his eyes and sees her down in the bed, still asleep. He is naked, rolled in her extra comforter and pinned to the ceiling. Below, the wrought iron sleigh bed stands between two simple wooden night tables, across from a large armoire of matching wood and surrounded by the pile of decorative pillows she and her sister insist on pyramiding at the head of every bed they sleep in. The items are not new, but they are tasteful. He unravels himself from the comforter and lets it fall to the floor, then works his legs up past the ceiling fan and gathers them close. Pressing to his full height, he reaches down for the bars of the headboard and pulls closer until his face is next to hers. Inhaling the softness of her cheek, he kisses her neck. She murmurs and wakes to see his naked body upside down above her. He laughs into her hair and lets himself up a little. They smile at one another until she reaches up and pulls him in for a kiss. She swings her legs up and locks them around his waist, and they embrace tightly as they hover above the bed. For a half hour, they do not touch the covers as they press into one another and feel the union of their bodies in the cool morning air.

Afterward, Gordon looks down into Caroline's eyes and kisses her one last time, then lets go with his arms and legs. She bounces on the bed, cursing and laughing with him at the same time. When his naked butt hits the ceiling fan, she laughs even harder. Pretending to rub it in pain, he works his way to the headboard and down to where his clothes and weights lay on the ground. When he is dressed, he kisses her once more and heads to the window.

"You do know my parents don't live here, right? You don't have to sneak out."

"Old times' sake."

Gordon grins and rolls out the window sideways, letting his

legs swing over his head and lead him down to the ground. Caroline sees him spring back up past the window and over the neighboring building. She lays back and inhales his scent, sweetened slightly by a hint of motor oil. She rolls onto one side and grabs her phone to cue up some music, settling on Phoebe Bridgers. As she lays back, she notices a few smudges of grease on her bedsheet and slides closer to them and inhales again. She kisses the smears and closes her eyes. Soon, she is asleep, a faint smile on her lips.

Chapter 25

Trespassing

The fire started by accident. At least that's what Wendell swears to Stan after Stan manages to contain it and protect the Shiva a few feet away. Mariana is the only other student working in the Lab and she insists she did not see anything. Smoke alarms are ringing when Gordon arrives and walks into the cloud hanging five feet above the floor. Mr. Williams pokes his head in the door and insists that everyone must evacuate until it has been deemed safe by the fire department, so Stan checks once more that the wet pile of rags near Wendell's desk is completely extinguished, then dumps them into a trash can and takes them outside. The five huddle together on the plaza, shaken by the disruption but eager to return to work. As they wait, a fire truck stops on the campus road, lights flashing. Two firemen hop down and cowboy-walk toward the building. Mr. Williams leads them into the Lab.

In the bushes by the side door, Gordon notices another man. He wears a camo hat and dark t-shirt, right arm in a sling. His pale face and bare left arm stand out like splashes of whitewash. Gordon walks over and stands by the side door as the man tries to back into the underbrush.

"Mr. Stainfield, I can see you."

Stainfield slowly emerges from the bushes, sweeping away needles and leaves with his good arm. He stands looking at Gordon, neither angry nor apologetic, as if he just wandered over for a chat. Gordon sees the corner of Wendell's security card sticking out of Stainfield's pocket.

"Can I help you?" Gordon asks.

"You do a lot of that, don't ya? Helpin'."

"If this is about the shooting…"

"Ain't about--" Stainfield stops himself. "Reckon I might oughta thank you for that, though. You seen it was an accident, right?"

"Yeah, but what led up to it wasn't. Whole thing could have been avoided."

Stainfield reddens. "Shouldn'a had my boy there."

"He needed hel--, he needed someone. Caroline."

"She is a sweet girl. Done a lot for him."

"That's all anyone wants," Gordon says softly.

"Not you, though. You want a whole lot more, I hear."

"Come again?"

"I hear you 'n that Yankee fag started up a business to make money offa him."

Gordon takes a step toward Stainfield, fist clenched, eyes fired with anger. Stainfield raises his good arm in front of his face and backs away. Gordon stops and gathers himself. In his peripheral vision, he sees Stan and Wendell walking toward him. Further away, Dr. Carson stands next to a police car and talks to an officer through the open window.

"Go on," Stainfield taunts. "Take a swing. Plenty'a witnesses this time."

"That 'Yankee fag' has a name: Stan. And he's a good man. More of a man than you'll ever be, you sorry pile of shit."

"Oh, so that makes it alright to steal my son's inventions?"

"The only one doing any stealing around here is you. I'm doing everything I can to keep your ass out of jail. To help Wendell."

"Yeah, like I said."

Wendell comes running up and stands between them. He

turns his back to Gordon, as if to protect him from his father. Gordon puts his hand on Wendell's shoulder and steers him off to the side.

"You ain't gotta come here!" Wendell yells at his father.

"Oh no? Surprise you, did I boy?"

"You know you didn't. But you ain't gotta bother Gordon. He dropped his charges."

Gordon looks at Stan, who raises his eyebrows.

"Wendell," Stan asks quietly. "Tell me again how that fire got started."

"It was a spark from Shiva. I swear it."

"You know Shiva doesn't work like that," Gordon says. "There are no sparks, only magnetically-contained currents."

Wendell's eyes widen, then fill with tears. Gordon puts his hand on his shoulder.

"It's okay, nobody's gonna get you in trouble."

"He wanted to see the Lab," Wendell mumbles.

"Boy, I ain't got nothin' to do with that place," Stainfield protests.

"You said it!" Wendell cries. "You told me to!"

Stainfield looks at Gordon and Stan, his eyes narrowing.

"I heard y'all are stealin' from my son. It's my right to see what the hell is goin' on in there. To protect my boy."

"By making him commit arson?" Stan accuses.

"Ain't nobody committed arson, faggot," Stainfield sneers.

Stan takes a step toward Stainfield, but Gordon holds out an arm to stop him.

"They got some folks in Phillips Prison who'd be happy to teach you the real meaning of that word," Gordon warns Stainfield. "Keep that shit up, and I might have to remember our recent events a little differently."

"Y'all stealin' from my son. That ain't changed."

"That never happened!" Stan yells. "We're protecting his intellectual property!"

Stainfield barks a mocking laugh. "Oh ho! 'Intellectual property,' huh? Protecting it from who?"

"From you, asshole!" Gordon roars.

Wendell looks back at Gordon with wide eyes, then at his father. He gapes to speak, then closes his mouth and runs away.

"Now look," Stainfield grumbles. "You upset the little retard."

"Fuck you," Gordon growls.

He turns and leaps after Wendell, covering the distance between himself and the fleeing boy in two bounds. Wendell sees Gordon, but continues to run. Gordon easily keeps pace.

"Come on, bud. Stop running."

"I ain't goin' back to him again!" Wendell cries.

"No one's makin' you. Just slow down. Let's walk."

Wendell stops running. They turn into the campus and, without speaking, angle through the North Campus gates and on to Martín's. Gordon texts Caroline.

"He tell you to set that fire?" Gordon asks.

"Yeah."

"Why?"

"Get y'all outta there. I wouldn'a let it hurt the Shiva, though."

"What's he want with us?"

"He been talkin' to that guy who hired him, David somethin'."

"North."

"Yeah, him. David told him y'all are helpin' me with my landboard company."

Gordon considers this. There are any number of ways David could have learned that -- all of the Lab's dealings are visible to Dr. Carson and many other administrators at the university -- but a dark part of his mind locks on Caroline. They arrive at Martín's and Gordon holds the door open for Wendell. Inside, Caroline sits at the bar across from Martín. When she sees Wendell, she walks to him and gives him a hug. The boy rests his head on her bosom, closes his eyes and smiles.

"Alright there, playah," Gordon chides. "She's a little old for you."

"What's the emergency?" Martín asks.

"This guy needs some lunch." Gordon pats Wendell's chest. "And we need to review our set list for next week."

"I got you, vato," Martín smiles, reading between the lines. He turns to Wendell. "Hey, young brother, you ever been to the Georgia Theatre? We gonna play there."

Wendell sits at the bar and Martín brings out a menu for him. Gordon puts his arm around Caroline and walks a few paces away.

"Rough morning. His dad came by the Lab."

Her look is a mix of concern and anger.

"Wendell started a fire. His dad told him to."

"Gordon," she whispers, "what the fuck is with these people?"

He says nothing, but in his mind the phrase 'these people' has begun to include her and North as well as the Stainfields.

"Tell me truthfully," he whispers. "Did you talk to David about Wendell's project?"

Caroline pulls away. "Did you call me here to help him, or to interrogate me?"

Gordon looks into her eyes and finds no answers. "He just needs a little normal right now," he says at last.

She takes the seat on the other side of Wendell and within a few minutes they are laughing together. Gordon walks to the far end of the bar and sits with Martín. After a few minutes of hushed conversation, Martín is all caught up.

"This ain't about the boy," Martín concludes.

Gordon nods gravely. Martín glances at Caroline.

"This North..." Martín whispers. "G, you gotta protect yourself."

Gordon grimaces as his phone buzzes in his pocket. "Stan," he mouths to Martín and walks outside to talk.

"Is he okay?" Stan asks.

"Yeah, all good," Gordon answers.

"That fucking guy..."

"It's North."

Gordon explains his connection to the day's events.

"Maybe you should leave his girlfriend alone," Stan cracks.

"I don't know, man. I don't think she'd do that."

"I'm just kidding."

"The whole Berrigan thing, even this bullshit about North running for office. I don't get it."

"Why not? He's a greedy egomaniac. And Shiva is a game-changer for him."

"If that's all it was, he would have come directly to us. He would have thrown money at us until we gave him what he wants."

"Maybe he knows you a little better than you think. Do you really believe money would change your mind?"

Gordon laughs.

"Okay then," Stan continues. "So why would he?"

"It might change yours."

"Fuck off."

"Or Ravi's. That's how he operates. Pressure at the weakest point."

"We have more than enough money to support Ravi's shoe fetish for the next three lifetimes."

"So what does he want?"

"He said Louboutin is coming out with a pair of Cuban heels that are absolutely to die for."

"North, you dumb queen."

"I know. Lighten up. We're not under attack."

"That's just it. I think we are, but I don't know if..." He looks through the window at Caroline, who is completely focused on Wendell. "Never mind."

They end the call, and Gordon paces into the alley. He pauses and looks up at the gleaming blue, then walks back to the sidewalk, mind churning. After a few more laps, he jumps up onto the roof of his apartment and sits with his legs hanging off the edge. He lays back onto the gritty tarpaper and stares at the sky. The simple routines of his life feel like they have been hijacked by a lethal chess match. Once, he could focus exclusively on turning the dreams in his head into products for the world, but now the world is grabbing back, worming its way into his heart and soul... and mind.

Still on his back, Gordon picks up his phone, opens the music streaming app and starts up a song by John Moreland, then lays the phone next to his head and closes his eyes, singing quietly with Moreland's silken gravel and failing again to mimic the soul in it. The set list for next week's debut of The Reverend Espada Band is mostly set, a mix of covers and some originals they wrote. Gordon knows the crowd will be there to see the main act, local legends and national stars. If they have any curiosity about him at all, it won't be for his musical ability. But the idea of playing a venue as revered as the Georgia Theatre fills him with excitement and, for a moment, lifts the gloom that has hung on him since the meeting with the Catonsville board.

The song ends and Gordon begins to feel antsy, needing to work. He is between major projects, always a dangerous time for him. Since his Rising, as he has come to call it, nothing has felt normal. The amorphous task of deciphering its meaning wears on him; too introspective for his nature, too intangible to test or verify. He has cycled through hundreds of possibilities, combinations of life events and personal proclivities, missions both imaginary and far too real. His love for Caroline has grown, as has his need for her, his desire. If she is at the center of this, which he believes, he does not know how he will survive it. She is close enough to his heart to deliver a fatal cut, and the idea that she might be conspiring with someone like North to do so fills him with a cold dread. His love for her has not blinded him to that possibility.

He thinks again about the sadness in Joe's eyes when Gordon admitted that he loved her. There was more to it than empathy, as if Joe were recalling a wound he had felt himself and that he could not stop Gordon from feeling too. Gordon knows that he must protect himself, and he dreads the moment when the mist might clear and reveal his destiny. Yet the obsession, the gravitational pull, the craving for her... remain.

High above, a hawk circles on a thermal. Gordon stares at it, mesmerized by its primal grace. For millennia, it has ridden this air and hunted this land. He knows the hawk can see him with far more clarity than he sees it. He wonders what it must feel, the disdain it must hold in every fiber of its tense and regal body for the landlocked souls below. He takes off his work shirt, then rips off his arm weights and his vest. He stands, the scale now tipped to gravity only by the tiniest of margins, by the dense but delicate metal strapped to his legs. The hawk rounds again. Gordon slowly crouches and pushes upward, closing the distance, drawing close. He sees the small head turn, the golden eyes focus. With an almost casual indifference, it twitches its wings and flies away, yielding nothing, only sky. It traces a wide arc across the blue, banking around and watching as Gordon rises ever higher. Climbing, the hawk does not allow the strange intruder to gain the advantage of a higher position, but it comes no closer. Gordon follows it with his eyes, oblivious to the buildings and the people below. Just he and the hawk, riding warmth and sunlight ever higher until at last one of them remembers and slowly, very slowly, begins to descend.

Chapter 26

Press

"How do you feel about the lawsuit filed against you by the Stainfield family?" the caller asks.

"What?!" Gordon demands. "What lawsuit?"

"It was filed today."

Gordon looks across the desk at Martín and Tyler, the sleepy junior hosting the program for the university's radio station. He scowls and turns back to the microphone.

"Who the fu--, uh, who is this?"

"So you deny stealing your student's invention?"

"Of course I do!" Gordon fumes. "Get the kid on here and ask him yourself. He'll tell you!"

"His father was on Pastor Ken's podcast last night and he said you stole it," the caller insists.

"Don't you think it's a little weird that so many of you people know about this lawsuit and I'm only just now finding out?"

The caller remains silent.

"Mr. Stainfield has a history of strange behavior," Gordon continues. "I don't know what this latest scheme is but I'm sure his son has nothing to do with it."

"He says you brainwashed the boy."

"Are you fu--, are you kidding me?!" Gordon inhales and

composes himself. "That kid is a brilliant student, which Stainfield would know if he paid any attention to him. The boy works with us at the Maker's Lab here on campus. The Lab has helped a ton of kids like him launch great products. Jalen Woods and Stan -- Professor Malkovich, help them file their own patents in their own names, not ours. Stainfield's kid did that. Plus, we have a fund to provide them seed money, which we did for him, too. Stan did that for me when I was a student here. That's what his Lab is all about."

"Stan... that's the gay guy? Should he really be teaching young boys?"

Tyler hits a red button and the line goes dead. "Thanks for the call, but dude, like, this is a music show."

He rolls his eyes at Gordon, who is busy texting Stan and Jalen.

"Alright, y'all, we're here with Martín Espada and Gordon Longmeier from the Reverend Espada Band. Give us a holler, but let's keep it on the music. They're opening this weekend for the Drive-By Truckers at the Georgia Theatre, and they'll be playing some of their new stuff."

He turns to Martín.

"Y'all wanna play something here tonight?"

"Sure, amigo."

Martín taps the conga on his lap. Gordon's guitar leans against the desk.

"Cool, alright! But maybe one more call first?"

"If we gotta," Gordon mumbles, looking up from his phone.

Martín laughs.

The voice on the line is familiar to Gordon. He can see the florid scalp, the thin combover, the greasy wire-rimmed glasses.

"So now you're Biker Jesus, Mr. Longmeier?"

Gordon winces and shrugs at Tyler, who sits forward.

"Caller," Tyler intervenes, "can you please identify yourself?"

"This is Pastor Ken Weaver. I seen that picture on the internet this mornin'. Your boy there seems to wanna do some ascendin' to heaven, but I gotta tell ya, he ain't goin' nowhere but down for what he's doin' to that Stainfield boy. The sins of the greedy are--"

Tyler hits the red button again. Gordon picks up his phone and scrolls through social media posts as Martín and Tyler banter about the new music and the great honor of finally booking a venue that he and Gordon have always dreamed of playing. Gordon stops and taps a picture of a figure suspended in the sky over the rooftops of Athens, arms outstretched and legs extended down with feet close together, as if mimicking the crucifixion. A bird is visible in the nearby sky. When he zooms in, Gordon can see the beatific smile, the closed eyes. It was one of the most blissful moments of his life, descending from his communion with the hawk. But in his sleeveless undershirt, oil-stained jeans and motorcycle boots, he looks more like the name Pastor Ken gave him than a man having a private moment of transcendence. The hashtag confirms that whoever posted the picture agrees. Gordon holds the phone up to the others, and Tyler gasps.

"Long story," Gordon mouths, gesturing that he'd prefer not to tell it on the air.

"Dude," the host mouths back, "please?"

"It's already gone viral, G," Martín says aloud. "Look at the hashtag. You gotta explain it, vato."

Gordon rolls his eyes.

"#BikerJesus is trending," Tyler says. "What's going on there, Gordon?"

"Well, I was laying on my roof looking up at the sky, and I saw this hawk. I had my flying gear with me, so I decided to cruise on up and say hello."

"'Flying gear?'" Tyler asks.

"Yeah, you know, like in that G-day video. It lets me float around like there's no gravity."

"Dude, for real?! I thought that was a fake to promote the football team or something."

"Bruh," Gordon breezes, "haven't you been to Martín's? I wear it sometimes when we play. I'll have it on on Saturday. Come check it out."

"So why the Jesus pose?"

"I wasn't expecting someone to take a picture. I mean, I'm up there, it's a beautiful day, this amazing bird is sharing its sky with me... I'm not thinking about who might be watching."

"You know, we kinda got a song about that," Martín interjects. "'Asuncion.'"

"Not helping," Gordon mutters.

"Where can I get some?" Tyler asks. "Flying gear?"

"Oh, it's not ready yet," Gordon evades. "We haven't even notified the FAA. Still testing it."

As Gordon is talking, a student in the control room catches Tyler's eye and points to his computer, where the student has air-dropped a link to an article in the local paper that got mentions on several national outlets. Tyler scans it quickly.

"But y'all've already begun to patent it?"

He turns the laptop to reveal Sue's piece.

"Yeah, we filed already. Long process, though."

"That's the second life-changing product he has created," Martín adds. "He invented the Shiva machine too. Right here in little ol' Athens. And you should see his bulletproof window!"

Gordon's eyes get wide. He makes a throat-slashing gesture to silence Martín, which Tyler notes.

"Sounds like that one's still top-secret," Tyler chuckles.

"Martín has a vivid imagination," Gordon grumbles.

"So, Gordon..." Tyler leans forward. "What are you? A mechanic? A musician? Or a world-class inventor?"

"I'm just a guy with a lot of hobbies."

"And a lot of money," Tyler adds.

Gordon sits back and crosses his arms.

"I mean, you must have a ton of dough, right?"

Gordon presses his palms on the desk and leans forward.

"So tell me then," Gordon growls, "why would I steal from a teenager?"

Tyler shrinks back.

"Makes no sense, right? That fuckin' Stainfield..." Gordon sees Tyler's shocked reaction to his profanity and realizes his mistake. He pauses and closes his eyes. "Ahh, sorry. Never mind. Let's play some music. That's what we're here for, right?"

The relief in the studio is palpable as Martín and Gordon begin to tune their instruments. After Tyler re-introduces them, Martín starts to palm a soft, slow rhythm on the conga. Gordon's guitar comes in quietly, low notes at first. The drum beat sounds Caribbean, but the distance between the phrases that Gordon plays evokes rural America. It is a gentle melody, stark but not depressed. When he sings the first quiet lines, the students in the control room look up. The imagery is simple, roads and trees and solitary houses. The land in winter. The tempo never really picks up, but Martín notices them nodding along. As the song ends, he watches their silent clapping behind the glass. Gordon doesn't acknowledge them until the last note fades from his guitar.

"Alright. That was beautiful, y'all. What do you call it?"

"Obsidian Heart," Gordon murmurs.

Tyler winds down the show, does another promo for this weekend's concert and thanks Martín and Gordon for stopping by. Gordon gives Tyler a distracted handshake and wanders out of the studio, but Martín stays behind to chat.

Outside, Gordon calls Jalen, then Stan. Martín wanders out during Gordon's second call, sipping a student center coffee and looking contented. Gordon's mounting anger poses a threat to Martín's mellowness, so Martín waves goodbye and starts up campus. Listening to Stan as he reads the legal complaint, Gordon notices students raising their phones and sneaking photos as they walk by. Gordon asks Stan to hang on, then confronts one of the students.

"Hey, what's with everyone?"

"Sorry, man," the young man says. "Just, you're kind of famous. They mentioned you on the national news."

Gordon keeps his leaping to a minimum as he hurries past the stadium and over to the Lab. On the way, he scans the web and sees the news clip, Stainfield vaguely accusing him of taking advantage of his son, the anchorwoman pressing for details, Stainfield evading. Then, a montage of online videos of Gordon flying by the lake, leaping over the football stadium and hovering during one of his concerts. Finally, Pastor Ken denouncing him in no uncertain terms as an agent of the devil himself, corrupting and stealing from young people. The anchor wraps with a comment about a lawsuit brought by 'one of Mr. Longmeier's students' and breathlessly promises 'details to follow on this developing story at the University of Georgia.' Gordon rushes past Mr. Williams and bursts into the Lab, startling a young woman who is trying to assemble a miniature transparent titanium zoo enclosure. Gordon apologizes, then looks more closely.

"Cool," he says. "Just don't do rhinos. They'll charge the people if they think there's not a barrier. Might hurt their noses."

He smiles at her and continues on to Stan's desk. Jalen is already there.

"Countersue?" Stan asks with no preamble.

"Maybe, but who? The network, for defamation?"

"Dude," Jalen laughs, "that channel does nothing *but* lie about people. Seriously though, why don't you just press charges for the shooting and throw his sorry ass in jail?"

"It'll look like we're trying to shut him up," Stan says. "Like revenge. Plus, it'll publicize the titanium window before we're ready."

"Right," Gordon agrees. "This will go away soon enough. We can't risk that."

The Lab door opens and Dr. Carson walks in with another man who Gordon does not recognize. Stan whispers that he is the university president and Jalen turns around.

"Sir," Jalen says warmly, extending his hand, "great to see you again."

The president clasps Jalen's hand and pats him on the arm, then walks off to one side to chat with him while Carson stays with Stan and Gordon.

"Mr. Longmeier," Carson begins, "there's no pretty way to say this. We're going to have to ask you to take a leave of absence while these allegations against you are investigated."

Gordon stares at him, speechless. He looks back at Wendell's work station and sees that it has been cleaned out.

"The Stainfield boy has also been asked to take leave," Carson confirms.

"Did you even talk to him?"

"Oh yes, and he supports you unconditionally. Just as his father said he would, given your influence over him."

Gordon sees a flash of satisfaction in Carson's eyes, as if the administrator has scored a point with some unseen judge. For a moment his anger rises, but he closes his eyes and the deep sense of vastness and peace returns. When he opens them again, Carson is staring at him, mildly agitated.

"Very well," Gordon answers at last. "Our documents will be made available to the court and once they are entered into the public record, to the press. In time, your concerns will be allayed."

"I would hope they would be made available to our committee first."

"Now sir," Gordon patronizes, "I believe our hands are tied, what with the legal proceedings and all."

Jalen and the president laugh loudly at something, then shake hands again as they part. The president waves at Stan and Gordon but continues on toward the door. Carson hurries after him.

"You two are certainly chummy," Stan observes.

"Great guy," Jalen smiles. "Huge football fan."

"Ain't we all?" Stan cracks.

"So what'd I miss?"

"Well, they kicked Gordon off campus."

Jalen gapes at Gordon, who seems unperturbed.

"They need to look into these 'allegations,'" Stan continues.

"Wait, one hatchet job on cable news and you have to leave?"

Gordon shrugs. "It's bigger than that, y'all know it. This is North."

"How?" Jalen wonders.

"I'm not sure. But an idiot like Stainfield doesn't just get on a national news channel without someone's help."

"What about that pastor?" Stan asks.

"Even him," Gordon concludes. "This story's just not big

enough for them. Something's not right."

Gordon walks over to his work station and grabs his Nalgene bottle, George Longmeier's flask and a couple of notebooks and slips them into his backpack along with his laptop. He walks around to the students and says goodbye, then gives Stan a hug and walks out with Jalen, deep in thought. They say very little as they walk up campus and part ways at the arches. Gordon feels an emptiness forming in his chest which he tries to ignore, but as he walks to Martín's it continues to grow. There are malign forces in this world, he knows, and now they have found him.

Chapter 27

Journeys

Grudgingly, Martín surrenders the keys to the pickup and takes Gordon's untouched plate of eggs back to the kitchen. Gordon finishes his cup and slowly rises to leave. His head pounds and despite the strong coffee the inside of his throat still tastes like bourbon. He does not remember making it home the night before or why he woke up on the ceiling with one leg weight still attached, that foot swollen and throbbing inside its untied boot. He vaguely recalls the conversation he had with Martín over dinner at the bar; Martín's concern, Gordon's anger. Powerful people are working to derail Gordon's entire existence, so two-thirds of a bottle of whiskey didn't seem like it could do much more harm. Gordon reels and sits back down, wondering if he might still be drunk. His text dings. Mrs. Jackson has arrived at work, but just barely. The car will be in the parking lot and he should text her for the keys. If not for the emergency call from one of George Longmeier's oldest customers, Gordon probably would have slept the morning away.

He says goodbye to Martín and promises to be on the lookout for anyone who might further damage his life prospects, then puts on his sunglasses and walks out into the overcast. The small office building is less than a mile away but halfway there

Gordon pulls over to retch up his morning coffee. He swigs from the Nalgene and spits, then drinks some more water and continues on. In the lot, he parks in the back corner and closes his eyes. Forty minutes later, his phone dings again. Mrs. Jackson hopes everything is okay and that he might be there before lunch time. He texts her back and struggles out of the truck, scanning for the Volvo SUV which is parked in the third row from the front, a distance Gordon wishes he had considered before choosing the spot that he did. He can see from the angle of Mrs. Jackson's right front wheel that the impact was much harder than she described. Taking a left turn just a little too fast, she had 'kissed' the curb and knocked her front end out of alignment.

"What do you think, Gordon?"

He turns and sees the old woman's concerned brown eyes, crinkled at the edges from a lifetime of laughing through the indignities this world deals out to Black women.

"Ma'am, I think someone could lose a few teeth 'kissing' that hard."

Mrs. Jackson's laugh is deep and sincere, welcoming. Gordon takes the keys and assures her he will have the car back to her in a day, two max. He gives her the keys to the pickup truck and apologizes for its untidy front seat, then accepts a hug of thanks.

"What's this you have on, a bulletproof vest?" She knocks on his chest.

"No ma'am, just a thing I'm working on."

"That your 'flying machine' they were talking about on the teevee?"

"Yes ma'am, it is."

"How wonderful! Let me see you fly, Gordon."

Not at all convinced he can even jump without vomiting again, Gordon sets his water bottle down and leaps about ten feet into the air. Mrs. Jackson howls with glee and gives a few little claps, then asks him to go higher. Already feeling dizzy, Gordon tries to decline but she insists, taking out her phone to record the event for her grandchildren. Realizing he needs to give them a decent show, Gordon crouches low and bursts into a high back flip but over-rotates and comes down spinning too hard. His boots clatter onto the hood of the car next to Mrs. Jackson's, setting off its alarm. He scrapes his hands on the pavement trying to prevent his face from smashing into the ground. Slowly, he gets up as the car flashes and honks. A security guard from the building jogs out to where they stand, his hand on the revolver at his hip.

"Mrs. Jackson, is everything okay?" Tensed and wary, he keeps his eyes on Gordon.

"Oh yes, Anthony," Mrs. Jackson assures him, "it was just a little accident. Want to see the video?"

Anthony's eyes widen as he watches Gordon rise forty feet into the air and crash down on the car. In the meantime, the alarm times out and cuts off. He looks at Gordon.

"You that guy from G-day?"

"Yes, sir."

After a few minutes of pretending to explain his 'technology' to Anthony, the young guard and the old woman return to the building. Gordon gets into the Volvo and sighs as he looks at the lines of blood on his palms, noticing absently that they sting enough to take the pain out of his head. He starts the car and slowly backs out of the spot. There is a low screeling noise when he moves forward, and he has to keep the wheel turned about thirty degrees off center to go straight, but he manages to limp it back to the garage.

The first hour of the job is disassembly, scanning damaged parts and correcting them virtually on Shiva's software, then printing their replacements. As he works, Gordon tries not to think about the lawsuit. He does not share Jalen's confidence that it will quickly be thrown out of court.

What more does North want? He's already got Catonsville. Why come after me personally?

Caroline?

Maybe North actually does love her.

And maybe North knows she doesn't love him.

So maybe she really does love me...?

Gordon carries the new parts back to the Volvo. Willing himself to get lost in the meditation of manual work, he gradually stops obsessing about all of that and even about Caroline. He doesn't even realize he's hungry until the windows are nearly dark and the last piece has been bolted into place.

Suddenly famished, he washes up and walks over to Martín's. Martín and Joe are huddled across the bar in conversation, each a portrait of concern when they look at Gordon. Joe says something to Martín, who nods and pats Joe's shoulder as the older man stands up.

"Come on," Joe says to Gordon.

"Can I eat first?"

"We'll eat on the way."

"Way to where?"

Joe doesn't bother to answer as he walks out the door and climbs into an old Ford Bronco. Martín motions for Gordon to follow.

"Where are we going?"

"Waffle House."

"After that?"

"Back to the beginning."

Joe drives north in silence until they see the familiar yellow sign above an exit ramp. The restaurant's cheerful interior contrasts sharply with the sobriety of Joe's mood. Gordon orders a heaping plate of scattered and smothered and begins to wolf it down. Joe sips a coffee and stares out at the lights on the road.

"Martín'll drop off the Volvo," Joe says absently.

Gordon looks up with surprise, his mouth full.

"He already talked to Mrs. Jackson. All good."

"How'd you know I was done with it?"

Joe offers a slight smile, then looks out the window again.

"So, where is 'the beginning?'"

"Son, I thought I warned you about our people and drinking. You smell like a distillery."

"I guess it's a secret?"

"You ever want to get your life right, you'll give up the booze."

Gordon finishes his meal and pays the bill. They drive on for two more hours, passing through a corner of South Carolina and then up into the North Carolina mountains. Above Asheville, Joe steers onto a smaller road that winds higher into the hills, then onto a dirt road that becomes a narrow mountain trail. After fifteen minutes or so, he abruptly pulls into the brush on the shoulder and parks.

"Where the hell are we?"

"North Carolina. Listen, if you wanna leave that gear in here it's okay. I got a rope, and I'll keep you safe."

Gordon feels a shiver of panic as he contemplates venturing into the unknown without any body weights.

"I'm your father, boy," Joe says quietly. "I won't let no harm come to you."

Slowly, Gordon takes off his weights and lays them in the wheel well as Joe walks around the Bronco. Joe takes a dirt-crusted climbing rope from the back seat and ties one end around his own waist with a figure-eight knot, loops the other end around Gordon's hips and does the same, then gathers the slack onto his shoulder and starts to walk up the road. With little choice, Gordon releases his death grip on the Bronco's door handle and begins to float behind Joe at the end of the rope. They reach a bend and round it to see a straight stretch of road headed northeast.

"Okay, son. Ready?"

"I guess."

Joe pulls Gordon close and instructs him to wind the rope around both hands and hang on tight, then starts to run up the road. After two jumping strides, he lands crouched and explodes upward. The tug nearly pulls Gordon's shoulders out of joint. With terrifying speed, they rise above the mountains and glide up into the black. Joe hollers for Gordon to let go, but he refuses. Joe reaches back and pats Gordon's hands, assuring him it's okay. Gordon unwinds the rope from his hands and with one quick inhale, lets it go. As Joe sails away from him, Gordon tenses with fear but the rope catches and pulls him along and he begins to relax. Riding across the cold night sky, he lets his arms and legs spread out and trail through the thick air, wondering how Joe's momentum continues to carry them so fast. He is almost disappointed when the rope begins to drag him back down to earth.

"How do you keep moving?" Gordon hollers.

Joe looks back and smiles.

"I mean, the momentum from the jump was not enough--"

"You'll see," Joe says. "With someone you're connected to, it kind of just flows. With anyone else, you ain't gettin' too far." He motions at the ground and Gordon looks down. "Get ready."

In a small clearing within a heavy stand of trees, Joe lands squarely on both feet and immediately begins to reel Gordon in. He manages to take up enough slack so that Gordon does not whip around into the trees at the far end of the clearing. Gordon swings in a wide arc as Joe pulls him closer. When Gordon is within five feet or so, Joe ties the rope to his waist. He warns Gordon to watch for low branches and starts to climb up a barely visible trail straight ahead of them. Within a mile or so, he stops again and turns off the trail, pulls Gordon closer and ties him again, then continues into the brush for a few hundred feet until he comes to the base of a cliff. Gordon leans back to see how high it goes, but the vertical wall is covered in thick vegetation that fades into the inky sky. Gordon feels Joe's muscles tighten just before he begins to rise straight up. A hundred feet or so above the ground, he slows and catches the branches in front of him. When he pulls them closer to the rock, Gordon notices a thin seam that runs between an outcropped arete and the main wall. Joe undoes the loop holding Gordon close and lets him drift a few feet up as he works at something in the seam. There is a scraping sound, then Joe wriggles through and pulls Gordon in after him. In the darkness Gordon can't see anything, but the sound of the air around him gives him the feeling that he is in a large open room.

Joe reaches behind Gordon and pulls an old iron door closed across the narrow opening. With a muffled click, lights come on. Gordon's mouth falls open. The walls around him rise clean and curved to a blackened ceiling, as if the soot of many fires had been repeatedly scrubbed from the lower sections. Roughly thirty feet above, three halogen work lights frame an opening that disappears up into the mountain; a chimney, Gordon surmises. The lights angle slightly outward and illuminate the entire chamber, which is a little larger than the Lab and has walls that slope up toward the lights. Intricate carvings decorate most of the visible surfaces except for the floor, which is covered by mats of tightly woven grass. Holding Gordon's tether, Joe walks over to a massive boulder and feeds the rope through a cleat carved into its polished top. As he pulls it through, it tugs Gordon lower until he is seated. Joe hands Gordon the rope and sits down next to him.

"I installed the lights a while back," Joe explains. "Solar cells. Never did like the smell of kerosene."

Distracted by the hundreds of scenes carved into the rock around him, Gordon nods absently. The lower ones are crude, some merely scratches of pigment in the shape of hunters and animals. There are circles, like henges, with stars radiating light into them from above. Higher, the carvings seem newer and more sophisticated. Scenes of life, some of battle. Men in colonial uniforms fighting half-naked braves, and losing. In some places, too high for Gordon to read, text has been engraved into the stone.

"Son, you're struggling," Joe says gently. "I know that."

"No, this is fascinating."

"I mean with your Rising."

Gordon looks at Joe. "I can handle it."

"Thing is, you can't. Not by doing things the way you always do. I know you're learning, but I also know you're afraid. And that's okay. Listen, I just wanted to give you some hope. This place'll always be here for you. Them who you love may not be, but it will. This is your heritage, son."

"What is this place?"

"This is our stronghold. Nobody ever took this place from us. This is our history."

Joe points at one scene, a primitive battle.

"See here? Our people have survived a lot of different nations, a lot of different invaders. Some of those nations built mounds, filled them with their dead, made them higher and grander, even built major cities."

"Yeah, I've been reading about them," Gordon says.

"They thought they would rule this land forever. Then others..."

Joe points higher.

"...Spanish people, came and took those nations down. They brought diseases and weapons that the mound builders had never known before. The builders fought back and got rid of the Spanish, for a while, but they lost most of their people and they never built up those cities again. Still, those builders held on in this land as the people you know now as Creek and Cherokee, until the English came and then the Scots and the Irish and all of them."

He turns around and gestures at another mural.

"The Europeans forced the old nations to move far away, so they could bring in their idea of America. You've heard of the Trail of Tears?"

Gordon nods.

"This land has seen a lot of change. But in all those years, we never left. We're all spread out now, but we're still here. The mound people, the Spanish, the Cherokees and Creeks, the Europeans, the Americans... all flowed in and out like tides. And we kept on. We never built up cities or ruled anyone. But we never let anyone else rule us either. We blended in and kept learning, kept helping where we could. We lived in harmony with the world around us. And we kept our ways."

"The People of the Stone?"

"Yeah." Joe pats the rock they sit on. "This."

Gordon looks down and slowly presses both hands to the surface of the stone. He imagines the hands, like his, that must have pressed on it in a similar way. The cleat through which his rope is tied is easily a foot deep and worn slightly thinner at its center, as if thousands of ropes had rubbed that same spot. The way it is carved makes it look like three raised ridges on the surface of the stone. He touches his forearm and feels the three scars, now harder and more pronounced beneath his tattoo.

"Did our people all have this... Rising?" Gordon wonders.

"No, very few. One in a generation, maybe. Some of them worked it out right here, in this place."

Gordon palms the rock. "Looks like it's gotten a lot of use."

"Like I said, we've been here a very, very long time."

"Tell me about your Rising."

"It'll only waste your time if you try to make my answers work for you."

"But you gotta give me something," Gordon pleads.

"Okay." Joe inhales, then bows his head. "When I met Emily..."

"My mother?"

"Yeah. Everything changed when I met her. She wasn't like any other woman I knew. The closer we got, the more I wanted. Not just from her... from life. Before her, I was pretty simple. Didn't need much, or want much either. But she blew that wide open."

"How old were you?"

"Nineteen. She was eighteen. Nobody ever told me much about the Rising. Mine started when I was around twenty. I was kind of losing my mind over her. I wanted her more than anything in this world, but she wanted... something else."

Unconsciously, Joe slips a finger inside his collar and touches the stone. The sadness in his eyes makes Gordon look away.

"From what I know," Joe says, "this thing has always been about letting go. All the suffering in our lives comes from holding on. Wanting something so bad we think it might kill us not to have it. Holding onto that wanting. All of our weakness comes from that too. Wanting not to suffer, wanting not to die... It keeps us from finding out how strong we really are."

"Sounds very Buddhist," Gordon observes.

"Our stories are older than Buddhism, but yeah."

"So you decided you had to let go of Emily? My mother?"

"I didn't decide anything." Joe's eyes begin to tear. "I'd never have chosen to live without her. But in the end, it wasn't up to me."

"But you said--"

"You'll know the moment for letting go," Joe cuts in. "You ain't gotta look for it. It'll find you."

Gordon points up at an ancient carving of a man high above a group of others, a rope dangling from his waist too high for the others to reach. The man looks terrified.

"Like that guy?"

"Everybody adds a little to our understanding of this," Joe says. "That guy got it wrong and didn't survive. The ones who did, like me, all came through with a different piece of the puzzle."

Joe walks a few steps away, then turns and faces Gordon.

"For us," Joe says, "faith is the only way back."

"From what?"

"Not from, to. To harmony."

Gordon puts his face in his palms and slowly shakes his head.

"So you're telling me this is some kind of God thing?"

"No," Joe says. "It ain't a religion, if that's what you mean. Y'all seem to put faith and religion in the same bucket, but they ain't the same. One's a set of rules that people agree to follow so they can be a community, all believing the same thing. That's religion. Faith, though, that's your own business. That's answering your own questions and believing those answers. All around the world, people are looking at the same sun. They got different words for it, but it don't change no matter what they call it. Mostly we're all looking at the same things, same moon, same oceans, trying to understand them and just naming them different. There's lots of ways to describe the same thing. This is ours."

"I don't follow," Gordon says.

"See," Joe goes on, "whatever you believe about this world, whatever story you been telling yourself about it, none of that matters right now. You might think it's all physics, all action and reaction... and it is, on one level. But that ain't all it is."

Gordon feels the impulse to argue, but he forces himself to remain silent. Joe walks over and sits down on the rock again.

"You ever wonder what God might be?" he asks Gordon.

"'What?' Or 'who?'"

"What," Joe restates. "'Who' is too small an idea for that."

"Yeah," Gordon allows. "I have. The closest I can get to it is that God is the energy that makes up all things. When you get down to the atom, the neutron, the electron... smaller than that, it's just energy. So I think maybe God is in that energy. But I don't really know."

"We see it a little different," Joe says. "We see God as gravity. Or really, we see gravity as God's expression of self in this universe. Before the Big Bang, gravity was in an absolute state. It had total control of everything, total security and comfort. But then it had an impulse to let go and maybe see what else it could say."

Gordon stares at Joe, then starts to look through him as his mind works on this idea.

"After that moment, that impulse," Joe continues, "gravity... God... started to reach out again. Things began to come together. Suns, planets, eventually life. After the chaos of letting go, gravity brought things into harmony."

"So what does it mean that gravity let go of me?" Gordon asks.

"Ahh," Joe smiles. "Now you're starting to see it. We believe that the Rising is God letting us feel a little of what that first moment felt like, when order gave way to chaos, so we can let go too. You can't have true harmony when you grab on to everything too tight and try to hold it close out of fear or wanting or whatever. When you let it all go, it's just the essence of you that stays. If that essence is sincere and true, you and God can be in harmony."

"And that's not a religion?" Gordon asks.

"No, not really. God is a physical presence to us, not an idea. It don't matter what you believe, God is still there. You either harmonize or not, but you're only hurting yourself if you don't. Like in the ocean when there are big waves. You can either ride 'em or drown in 'em, but the ocean don't change either way."

"So all these people..." Gordon sweeps a hand across the ceiling. "They've all been thinking this stuff for thousands of years, but nobody said a word about it to anyone else?"

"How do you think we managed to stay here this long?" Joe smiles. "We found strength where nobody else would even think to look. Listen, all people want. Every person on Earth. It's what they do. Some take what they want and others are just happy with what they're given. But some of us..."

Joe hops up and pats one carving on the ceiling in which a man hovers just above a group of soldiers in Civil War-era uniforms, holding his arms out wide as their bullets fly past him.

"Some find a way to stop wanting and start giving. They find harmony with the world and give themselves to something greater. You can't take anything from people like that because they've already given everything away."

He drifts back down and sits next to Gordon again.

"That man was a Lightfoot," Joe continues. "He chose to sacrifice himself, to lead those soldiers away from this place. He stayed just out of range of their bullets, but close enough to keep them chasing. He taunted them, got them so worked up that they were blind with hate, with the desire to kill him. They chased him right off a cliff." Joe chuckles. "But of course, *they* couldn't fly."

Gordon stares up at the carving and notices that there is no ground below any of the soldiers.

"So now it's your turn, son. I know you're in a fight right now with some nasty people, men who believe in their own power. But they're like hollow trees with no roots. They never reckoned with the beast."

Gordon waits for Joe to explain.

"You wanna beat men like that, first you gotta deal with what's inside of you. It's an animal instinct to claw like a wild thing, to defend the boundaries of who and what you are. And you can win like that, some fights. But some ain't like that. Some are bigger. And they happen inside your own heart."

Joe stands and walks over to the wall, and presses his hand against the stone. After a moment, he turns back and looks Gordon in the eye.

"You wanna rise above that animal instinct, that beast, first you gotta understand it. Harmony, son. Move in harmony with it until you can anticipate what it wants. When you understand it, you can subdue it. And once you do that, you allow something much more powerful to grow inside you. There is no man on Earth as strong as the thing that made him, so get yourself out of the way and let that power work through you. Stop trying to keep the beast alive, and you'll connect with your true strength. And nobody will ever defeat you again."

Chapter 28

Dreams

In the middle of the closing riff on 'Asuncion,' Gordon pops himself off the ground and hovers as he plays. Martín smashes away at the cymbals and the kick drum, and the rhythm section blares to a crescendo. Gordon works his way up the guitar neck as he settles back to the ground, letting the low notes match his decreasing altitude. He lands precisely as the song ends with Martín's resounding thump. They look around the huge room, sweating and exhilarated by the performance, but it is dead silent except for the echoes of the final notes. Finally, Martín laughs and the others join in. Gordon smiles and pumps a fist at him.

"We ready, amigos," Martín says happily.

The band members clap for one another, their happy noise reverberating around Gordon's garage. Gordon takes out his phone and opens the big main door to let in the warm breeze, and the guys begin to pack up. Martín hangs back with Gordon, opens a Coke and pulls up a rolling stool. Gordon hops up onto the stack of tires next to him and lays back against the wall, then slips his flask from his back pocket and takes a deep drink. Martín notes this but says nothing. As the last of the band members leave, in the alley outside a man in a suit approaches tentatively. He sees Martín but not Gordon.

"Uh, hello? I'm looking for Gordon Longmeier?"

Martín slaps Gordon's leg and he sits up. When Gordon recognizes Patrick Berrigan, he drops to the ground and walks out into the alley. Patrick notices Gordon's flask, which he quickly tucks away.

"This is the only address we have for you."

"I live here," Gordon says. "What do you want?"

"Well... it's just that... my father passed away. I didn't want you to hear it on the news or... some other way."

Gordon feels the words more than hears them, as if they were hurled at him by some kind of trebuchet. The impact is cold, immediate. He drops to a squat and sits down, then lays his arms across his knees and rests his face on them. Patrick is still speaking, but Gordon no longers hears him. Behind his closed eyes he sees two soldiers, cropped and brisk outside the screen door of his childhood home. Politely, efficiently, they rip away the foundation of his life and depart with a salute. Awkward and well-intentioned, Patrick fumbles the job a little but achieves more or less the same thing. Martín walks over and puts an arm around Patrick, speaking quietly as he guides the bigger man back to the bar for a drink. Patrick is crying. So is Gordon. The sun shines on both of them.

There is a tiny voice in Gordon's mind.

It's better this way.

Berrigan would not live to see his life's work dealt away to the demons of war that he had always battled.

Let the world move its own way. In his time, Berrigan worked for good. Let that be the legacy we celebrate.

With an effort, Gordon rises from the pavement, shuffles back into the garage and closes the overhead door, then walks up to his apartment and takes off his weights. He drifts up and makes his way across the ceiling to the mattress suspended there, where he curls into a ball. Soon he is asleep.

"Fourteen thousand dollars," Berrigan chuckled. "That's what I had to my name when I inherited this operation. What a rattle trap it was! I

thought for sure we'd be out of business in the first year, with me running it. But we figured it out. What you realize in time is that you always figure it out, one way or another."

Gordon sat across the table, quietly chewing his burger and waiting for Berrigan to continue. His backpack rested at his feet, so jammed with textbooks that it stood upright on its own. It would be a long night for him, with finals looming. He dreaded returning to the empty old house, full of Emily and George and all of the moments he wished he could remember more clearly. He had managed to gather and donate most of the family's belongings, things to which he had ascribed little value and for which he had even less use. He treasured just a few items, two really: the stone necklace and the motorcycle. Everything else could go, so it pretty much did.

"How are you, son?" Berrigan asked. "There's a lot going on in your life right now, I know. But don't let that distract you from the grieving. You need to let yourself grieve."

Gordon stopped chewing and nodded.

"I miss her. I miss them both."

"Martín said there's a large loft space above the garage that'd make a fantastic apartment. I know he'd like to have you closer, to help out if need be."

"Yes sir, I've been using it as a workshop for Shiva. Gets a little drafty this time of year, but I have an old potbelly stove that'd fix that."

"Christmas is coming soon," Berrigan observed.

"And finals."

"What are your plans for the holiday?"

"Haven't given it much thought. Martín is after me to come to church."

"He's a good man, Gordon. He'd have been a good priest if he stayed with it. He lives his faith."

Gordon nodded.

"Sir? I have a question for you. How do you know what to do first? I mean, with this business we're setting up. Where do you even start?"

Berrigan smiled and leaned back in his chair.

"Well now, that's the million dollar question, isn't it? And I'll tell you, a lot of really smart people have managed to answer it wrong, again and again. But there's only one answer and it's very simple. You *start with your customer. You figure out who he is, how he thinks, what he wants and how you can serve him best. And son, you never stop thinking about him. As soon as you do, you're done. There will never be anyone in your operation who is more important than your customer. If there is, well, you're just plain doing it wrong."*

Gordon jolts awake. He feels an urgent shiver across his skin, despite the bright sun streaming in. With practiced movements, he pushes down to the floor and puts his vest on, then his other weights and his boots. Scooping up his phone and wallet from the island, he hurries downstairs and out the alley to the street. He takes the block in one bound, then makes it to Broad Street in another. He takes a few more aggressive jumps down Thomas Street to get to the Lab before he remembers that he is not allowed to go in. He calls Stan and asks him to come outside, and they walk back across the street and into the main campus.

"Did you hear?" Gordon asks Stan.

"Yeah. Damn shame. He was a nice guy."

"Strangest thing..."

Gordon stops walking and looks at Stan with the intense focus that always precedes the announcement of some kind of insane idea.

"I think Mr. Berrigan just came to me in a dream."

"You were sleeping? At lunchtime?"

"Napping, I guess. Patrick came by and dropped that bomb on me, and all I could do was lay down."

"Understandable. So what did Dan say to you in this highly non-rational conversation?"

"I think he just told me how to move forward with transparent titanium."

Stan's face is a mask of doubt. Gordon explains that he has been hijacked by the limitless number of transparent titanium products that Shiva could produce, and unable to bring any single design to fruition. As he speaks, Stan notices the flask in his back pocket.

"Do you think maybe there are other reasons for your lack of focus?"

Gordon follows Stan's eyes and feels the flask.

"That? Oh, no. I'm okay."

"Sure, pal."

"Listen, this is important. The most expensive thing in all of business is to create a new market for a new product. It's a company killer. We never had to do that with Shiva. Berrigan just used it to make more of his existing tools faster and cheaper and basically printed money. But we have to do it now."

"Why now?"

"Because that--" Gordon points at the Lab "--will die if we don't."

Stan's expression softens. "They kick you out of the Lab and the first thing you think of is how to keep it alive?"

"We can't let them win!"

"'Them' who?"

"North, Carson... who-the-fuck-ever else is pulling the strings here."

"There's more?"

Gordon finally hears the skepticism in Stan's voice.

"You think I'm crazy, don't you."

Stan folds his arms and looks down.

"No, seriously, you think I'm nuts."

"Look, G, you've been under a ton of stress. I don't blame you--"

"You want me to just give up? Just hand them the Lab?"

Suddenly angry, Stan looks up.

"Listen, Wonder Boy, this Lab was a dream of mine long before you were just a teenage hoodlum banging groupies at Martín's bar. I'm not gonna let anyone take it away."

"You got a plan, then?"

"This lawsuit will go away, you know that."

"I *don't* know that. Some powerful people want to see it bury me."

"Uh, paranoid much? It's one old redneck looking for a payday."

"On national television?"

"*Right-wing* television. They air all kinds of crazy shit."

"What was it you said? 'Those yahoos don't say anything that's not written on the back of a check.' So who would write a check like that for Stainfield?"

"I don't know, North probably? Who cares? Jalen said the lawsuit has no merit."

"But the *idea* of it is enough to keep me out here and North in there." Gordon points at the Lab again.

"North's not in there."

"Oh no? Well who's paying the electric bill now that Mr. Berrigan is dead?"

Stan stares at Gordon for a long moment.

"So what'd Dan tell you to do?"

"Think about the customer."

"And that would be...?"

"Every single company in the plate glass supply chain on planet Earth."

For a moment, Stan stops breathing.

"We don't have to invent one new thing," Gordon concludes. "We just have to start printing money."

At six o'clock in the morning on the day of the Reverend Espada Band's debut at the Georgia Theatre, Gordon and Stan visit Jalen's office. They huddle there for hours over coffee and egg sandwiches and stacks of legal pads. At one point, Gordon sets George's flask down in the middle of the table and waits for his friends to ask him about it. They do not. By lunchtime, they have settled on a list of target companies to approach as partners in the transformation of the world's plate glass market. They have determined their cost of entry in year one, their growth plans for years two to five, and a rough estimate of their ten year upside. Weeks earlier, Jalen used the limited liability partnership they formed to hold the Shiva patent to file US and international applications on the formula and production process for transparent titanium. The LLP now owns that exclusive patent in one hundred and fifty-three countries. The three men agree to make equal seed investments in a new company that will acquire and build out the world's first Titanglass production location. They have analyzed ground, rail and sea transport routes and agreed that Northeast Georgia will be their hunting ground. Jalen offers to run point on the project, with his first task being the procurement of a trademark on the product name. He will also serve as the CEO of the newly-formed company. They agree to fly under the radar for as long as they can before pitching a larger partner if they need to.

Gordon picks up the untouched flask and puts it back in his pocket. He clears away the sandwich wrappers and empty coffee cups and erases the whiteboard -- after Jalen takes several pictures of it. He shakes his partners' hands, walks to the tall window and leaps away.

"We just created the most revolutionary company in American history, and the first thing our partner does is jump out the window," Stan observes.

"Actually, the first thing he did was clean up after us."

Stan smiles and shakes Jalen's hand, then leaves by the door.

That afternoon, Gordon sits at the bar with Martín, settling his pre-show jitters with a plate of tacos. When Caroline walks in, Gordon asks for a drink from the private bottle of bourbon that Martín has begun to keep for him. He drains it in two swigs and taps the rim for a refill. Caroline sits down.

"Big night," she says. "You ready?"

"Better be." He doesn't look at her.

"Will you actually get to meet them? Hood and Cooley?"

"Mmmnh."

"Okay, fuck you, Gordon. You get one fancy gig and now you won't even look at me?"

"And you make one booty call and then don't talk to me for a week?"

"I was busy. That kid Wendell is pretty messed up, and it's not like the other ones go away just because he needs more help."

"I heard he's living with his grandparents now. How's he handling not being at the Lab?"

"Better than you're handling not being in my bed."

Gordon cocks his head back and gives her a little nod, then

drains his second glass. He pats the bar to get Martín's attention and waves his thanks, then gets up and walks to the door without another word. Caroline pantomimes a scream at his back, then sits down and pretends to pull her hair out. Martín laughs.

"You love him, Cariña?" he asks.

"Of course I do," Caroline smiles.

"I mean the quarterback."

She freezes, then slumps a little as she looks down. When she looks up at Martín again there are tears in her eyes.

"It was like a different world," she whispers. "California. Stanford. It's so beautiful, such incredible things happening there. It's like the world is being invented--"

"I wasn't asking about Stanford," Martín presses gently.

Caroline stares at Martín for a long time before answering.

"Maybe I shouldn't have come back here," she says at last. "I do love David, but it's easier out there. When we met... he was larger than life. He was this famous guy, from being on television every week winning football games. But with me he was so thoughtful. He took the time to find out about me, what I liked. He listened. It was so easy to talk to him, we just clicked."

Martín nods, leaning on one elbow, his chin cupped in his hand.

"But now... Maybe we're just older, maybe life is more complicated. He's there and I'm here. His business takes so much time... so much... everything. It seems like when I'm with him now he's not even there anymore. And Gordon... well, you know. He's not always present either, but he just knows me. It's like he's in my mind or something, right when I need him to be."

"He pays attention," Martín says. "He don't let on, but he's always listening."

"When you and Julia got married..."

"We didn't have no choice," Martín jumps in.

"What do you mean?"

"I mean, she was it for me, and she says the same thing. We were either gonna get married or spend the rest of our lives wondering why we didn't."

"No doubt?"

"Never." Martín presses his palms to the surface of the bar and leans closer to her. "You know, Cariña. In your heart, you already know."

"That's just it," she sighs. "I don't know, Martín. It's very confusing."

"The heart is not always logical, Cariña. But we have to follow it anyway."

Walking to the theater, Gordon spots Pastor Ken and his small entourage standing in the planter across from the venue. Ken climbs up on the bench in the middle of the small square of earth and points at Gordon.

"Ain't y'all a little early?" Gordon calls out. "Nobody's here yet. We haven't even done a sound check."

"You!" Ken intones.

"Me!" Gordon confirms.

"How dare you disrespect the Lord Jesus with your cheap photographic fakery!"

Gordon crosses the street and walks up to the bench. He motions for Ken to come down and talk and Ken obliges. They take a few steps away from the group.

"Listen, I'm not your enemy," Gordon says quietly. "I got nothin' against Christianity, or preachers even. Heck, one of my best friends was a priest."

"Do you accept Christ Jesus as your lord and savior?" Ken asks, a bit too loudly.

"We don't gotta get into all that now, do we? I'm still workin' out the whole God thing. But I'm doin' it honestly, and I'm askin' myself the hard questions. So I would say, are you willin' to ask yourself some hard questions too?"

"I do not question. I believe."

"Well, do you ever wonder why a country preacher got asked to be on the national news?"

"I was called to bear witness."

"Who by?"

"One of my parishioners."

"That'd be Stainfield? And how'd ya reckon he came to be callin' on behalf of a cable news channel?"

"He is in business with a very influential man."

"Oh yeah, David North. That make any sense to you? Big-time California arms dealer hiring little ol' Stainfield to be his man on the ground for major real estate deals?"

Pastor Ken frowns and squints through his glasses at Gordon.

"Or does it maybe make more sense that North wants to own what I built, without me agreeing to it, and he's using Stainfield's son to get it? Listen, I spend my days helping kids like Stainfield's, great young people who wanna learn. They dream up some amazing inventions and every single one of 'em wants to make 'em right here in Georgia. They're on your side. Heck, *I'm* on your side. The only ones makin' trouble around here are Stainfield and that fancy Californian he's pallin' around with."

Ken puckers up like he's preparing to spit a lemon seed.

"Same two who are askin' you to go on the teevee and lie for 'em."

Gordon turns away to shield his face, knowing the spittle will fly when Ken launches into his tirade. As the pastor hurls epithets and commands Gordon to "get thee behind me, Satan," Gordon chuckles and walks away. He takes out his flask and raises a toast to Ken and his group, then tips it back for a long pull. When one of the group flashes a picture of him, Gordon spreads his arms and hops twenty or so feet in the air to provoke more photos. Then he puts his flask away, blows them all a kiss and walks into the theater.

"Can't you just leave those freaks alone?" Martín asks. "You ain't gonna change them."

"No, but I might learn from them."

Gordon picks up his guitar.

"How you feelin', Tío?"

"Like I ate a bees' nest."

"Yeah, me too."

Onstage, the larger drum set for the main act is covered and

Martín's drums are set up in front of it. One of his friends has painted the band's name on the front of his kick drum in wildly colorful, psychedelic bubble letters. Gordon admires it for a long time as the rest of the band gathers round. They barely have time to sound-check their gear and play a brief warmup, so they hop right into it. Gordon scans the spotlights and rigging directly above the stage. The ceiling is fairly high, but beyond the lights are three massive fans and a few more hanging fixtures. The wireless pickup he mounted to his guitar will allow him to move freely, and seeing all of this with the house lights up gives him a sense of his boundaries. He takes a small jump to test the effect on his sound; there is none. Feeling bolder, he does a high front flip out onto the general admission floor. His foot whacks one of the ceiling fans and starts it turning, but he lands safely.

"Dude!" one the stage crew hollers. "Cut the shit."

"Sorry man." Gordon flashes him a shaka. "Rock 'n roll."

"Yeah, whatever."

Backstage, Martín sits on the floor for a brief meditation. As the crowd filters in and gets louder, Gordon closes his eyes and lets the darkness calm him. Soon, it is time to go.

The first few minutes of the show are a blur of adrenaline and overly careful playing. Gordon relies on Martin's drumming to keep him tethered to the beat of each song. Gradually, he relaxes and begins to engage the crowd, which he cannot see as well as usual through the glare of the stage lights. When they finish a new song called 'Gunning for Jesus,' which Gordon wrote with North's hypocrisy in mind, he wishes he could see Caroline's face. He knows she is out there somewhere.

The crowd is jammed into the standing room areas, nearly back to the bars at the rear of the house. Most hold up their phones to capture Gordon in flight, and he does not disappoint. In addition to his usual hops and flips, at one point he manages to slip out of his vest offstage and float across the audience on his back for the entire last song. When it ends, he kicks away from the facade of the upper mezzanine and awkwardly makes his way down to the stage, where Martín catches him and pulls him in. Martín is ebullient as the audience reacts to the show. Gordon is distracted, but hides it behind a veneer of intoxication and enthusiasm. The highlight for him is a brief hand slap with the main act as they make their way through to the dressing room.

"You were right, vato. They loved the new stuff!"

Gordon grins and tries to share Martín's excitement. They sit and slowly come down as the crew hauls their gear offstage. Gordon helps Martín pack up his kit and load it into the bed of the pickup, and lays his guitar in after it. Julia walks up and gives each of them a hug, but when Gordon asks about Caroline she merely shrugs and says she's in the theater somewhere. Gordon watches the Espadas drive away and turns back toward the door.

Inside, he slips around to the back of the house and hugs the wall as he moves closer to the stage, counting on Caroline to remember their usual spot. She is standing about halfway down, and they see each other at the same time.

"What'd ya think?" Gordon asks.

"I did get a nice shot of your butt as you floated by."

Gordon sees that she's already holding a drink, so he opens the flask and takes a deep draft. He sways slightly as he tucks it away.

"Easy, sailor," she murmurs. "We need you in good shape tonight."

"We?"

"Me, myself and I."

"Ahh, the holy trinity."

Gordon leans closer and pecks her on the cheek. She pulls away slightly.

"How drunk are you?"

"Not very."

She gives him a dubious look. He leans down and asks if she wants to leave.

"I don't wanna miss them again," she protests.

"I got all their records." He loops an arm around her shoulders and they start for the exit. "Play you anything you want."

"Will you float around with your guitar?"

"Sure, darlin'."

"Naked?"

"If that turns you on."

As they hit the cool air outside, she pulls him closer and breathes into his ear. "Oh, it does, Mr. Rock Star, it truly does."

Gordon takes the skillet down from the cupboard above the island and skates over to the stove. Wearing only his unfastened vest and one leg weight, he has to concentrate to remain upright enough to cook. From the bed, Caroline watches him struggle for a while. She laughs and picks up his other leg weight and walks over. Gordon watches her bare breasts bounce and loses track of what he's doing. Despite just having made love, his body quickly responds to the sight of her sleek curves. She presses close and slowly lowers to one knee to attach his other leg weight, but she does not stand back up. Her hair brushes his abdomen, his thighs. Her lips are warm on him. Gordon begins to groan and arch his back, his legs feeling rubbery and weak. As his eyes close, he drops the skillet and she bites down on him. Laughing, she rises again and kisses his chest, then his lips. Eyes wide, he realizes that he has ruined the moment. She slips off his vest and pulls him over to the bed, then forces him down on his back. When she straddles him, he relaxes and closes his eyes again. Soon they are both panting, limp in each other's arms.

"I didn't really want eggs anyway," Caroline whispers.

"Me neither," Gordon mumbles, eyes closed.

"You said you'd play something for me tonight. I liked that new song, the Jesus one."

"Sss about David," Gordon slurs, already half asleep.

Caroline's eyes narrow but she says nothing. Still laying on top of him, she feels his breathing deepen into a steady rhythm. She leans close and whispers into his ear.

"You know he wants to weaponize your Shiva machines. Turn them into massive ray guns or something."

Gordon's barely conscious laugh is really just a series of shorter breaths.

"Is that funny?"

"Caaaan't... Ffffckng idiot."

"He seems very sure of himself."

"Caaan't..."

When Caroline realizes that Gordon is fast asleep, she takes off his leg weights and lets him drift up to the mattress on the ceiling. Then, she grabs her phone and lays back on his bed to check her texts. One is from David, with a link to a video file. She clicks the link and sees the familiar split screen of a cable news program. David is on one side and Stainfield is on the other. A third panel appears briefly to allow the blonde anchor to tee up a question.

"Mr. Stainfield, the university professor who founded the Maker's Lab has unequivocally declared your lawsuit to be without any merit whatsoever."

"That fa--? That homosexual? He's Longmeier's best friend. Heck, maybe that Longmeier is a fag too."

"Mr. Stainfield, please. Mr. Longmeier's counsel has provided documentation to the court that proves your son holds all patents to his invention, with no other filers. The trust that controls the product is set up in the boy's name, funded at arm's length with a no-interest loan. What would you like to say to our viewers who believe you have slandered a fine university program and one of its teachers?"

"I'd say F--."

After a long beep, Stainfield is once again audible.

"Here's a video of him dancin' around in the street like a loon, drinkin' whiskey."

Stainfield holds up his phone. Gordon's encounter with Pastor Ken from earlier that night is already on the web.

"We can't be sure of what's in that container, Mr. Stainfield," the host continues. "And dancing is perfectly legal, even with a device that lets you do it twenty feet in the air."

"I think what we have here is a pattern of deception," David interjects smoothly. "Starting with the mythological idea that this guy invented the Shiva machine when he was only nineteen years old. I mean, who really believes that? He charmed an old man, Dan Berrigan, and made a ton of money off of that technology. Heck, we just paid... uh, right, anyway, how can we be sure it was really his idea? Come on, a college kid building that? He was probably drinking and dancing in the streets back then too. He plays in a rock band, for pete's sake!"

"Sir, those patents were also filed legally, in Mr. Longmeier's name."

"Well, I'd like to see them. We could ask Berrigan, but sadly he just passed away. Maybe ownership of those patents should go to his company, where it really belongs."

"There is a legal basis with which to determine ownership of a patent, Mr.--"

"Why don't you speak with Dr. Carson at the university," David says, his patrician drawl taking on an almost Southern tone. "I'm sure he'll help enlighten our viewers about Mr. Longmeier's past."

"Unfortunately, we have to go to commercial. We'll be back with David North of North Industries after this short break..."

Caroline closes the app and types a text back to David. Within seconds, the phone rings.

"Hi, hon..." Caroline whispers. "How's L.A.? Yeah, long day here. In bed now... Yeah, I saw it. So you went ahead with it anyway... Of course you looked great, but... Yeah, but you know that Gordon... I know, but... Yeah, okay. Talk tomorrow. You too. Goodnight."

Caroline turns off her screen and lets the phone fall onto the rug. She pulls the covers over her shoulder and snuggles them to her cheek, then sighs and closes her eyes.

High above, wide awake, Gordon opens his.

Chapter 29

Farewell

Two motorcycle cops turn on their flashing lights and lead the heavy hearse out of the driveway. The cathedral bells ring high above. At the end of a long line of cars with their lights on, Gordon pulls on his helmet and fires up the Yamaha. Restored to its matte gray tank color and stripped of the drug dealer's adornments, it feels solid and familiar once again. In his suit and tie, the neck of Gordon's shirt strains against the top of his weight vest, but despite this, the morning sun on his face makes him smile. Mr. Berrigan would have approved of the service.

As he idles, waiting for the cars to make their way onto the wide avenue, Gordon thinks about all that he and Dan Berrigan have accomplished. Together, they mapped out the conversion of ten massive production sites across Eastern Georgia; facilities capable of producing thousands of tools each day with nearly no waste at all. Using fifty Shiva installations, they turn steel, iron and other materials into components that often need no further handling, or very little. The process from raw material to assembly line to trucks for transport became so streamlined that Stan had to reprogram Catonsville's inventory management system just to keep up. And now all of it has been handed over to David North. That Gordon, Jalen and Stan have been paid so much money is cold comfort. By the time Gordon toes the bike into gear, his mood is somber.

Gordon feels under the tank for his flask, but looks around and decides that it is not necessary at the moment. He rolls slowly through town and out into the hills that lead to the small private cemetery where Dan Berrigan will be interred. There is no formal parking, just a long grassy hill leading up to a fenced-in plot. Berrigan's wife was laid to rest there years earlier and his new headstone stands beside hers. Around them, the broad sweep of lawn falls away to wooded valleys on three sides and a small farmhouse across the street. The family has owned the land for nearly a hundred years, as the weathered stones within the wall attest. Gordon walks through the crowd to join Frank's sons and nephews as a pallbearer and sees Martín and Julia off to one side. David North and Caroline stand with her parents further up the hill. Nearly everyone wears sunglasses to shield against the Georgia glare and hide teary eyes.

Gordon shakes each man's hand with a grim nod or a brief greeting. Together, they lift the bulky casket and shoulder it for the walk. In his motorcycle boots, Gordon is the only one whose feet don't slip on the way up the hill. A rectangular frame with heavy green straps sits atop the astroturf laid around the grave. Off to one side stands a tall mound of red clay. The bearers set the coffin down on the straps and move to their respective spots as the Episcopal priest steps forward to take control. Rather than join the family with the other pallbearers, Gordon walks to the back of the gathering and stands alone. As he bows his head and looks down at his boots, he feels a hand squeeze his shoulder. It is Jalen. Angelique, Stan and Ravi are behind him.

The priest speaks clearly, but the breeze makes it hard to hear every word. Gordon can imagine what he's saying, however, and finds peace in the idea that while few people depart this world with more integrity than they had entering it, Daniel Berrigan was one. After the brief service, the crowd begins to disperse. Gordon sees Ravi's new Cuban heel boots and smiles; at least the sale of Catonsville Tool & Die made one person happy. They gather in a loose circle and wait to pay their respects to the Berrigan sons as Gordon takes his flask out of his chest pocket, drinks deeply and puts it away.

Walking alongside Congressman Highsmith, David North approaches Gordon and pats his arm.

"Still enjoying the breakfast of champions?"

Gordon smiles thinly.

"Well, you have enough money now to stay drunk for the rest of your life. How does it feel?"

"Disrespectful."

Gordon watches Patrick Berrigan as he navigates the crowd.

"Oh, don't look at it that way," North continues. "Dan would be proud of our commitment to this region. We've already begun to sell most of our other plants, and we're completely remodeling our operation. We're moving it all here to Georgia. Your machines are going to revolutionize everything for us."

Gordon closes one eye and sways a little as he holds up his thumb. He looks like he's taking aim at David.

"Let me know how that goes," he slurs.

Stan chortles. North looks momentarily confused, but shakes it off.

"Listen," North presses, looking over Gordon's shoulder, "no hard feelings about the cable news thing. It's just a little spin, nothing personal."

His own expression impassive, Gordon studies North's face as if the explanation for man's inhumanity were written on it.

"Patrick!" Congressman Highsmith exclaims, loudly enough to draw glances. "Congratulations on the deal with North Industries. What y'all will be doing for North Georgia, well, it's *inspiring*. Just fan*tastic*."

Relieved, North brushes past Gordon and strides over to join the congressman. He clasps Patrick's hand in both of his.

"Such a beautiful ceremony," North brays. "Dan would be proud. Truly, our deepest condolences to you and your family."

With a look of disgust, Gordon turns away and runs directly into Caroline.

"'Scuse me," he mumbles.

He pulls back but she puts a hand on his hip to keep him

close.

"Gordon, I'm so sorry..."

"Are you, now?"

"I know how you felt about him."

She leans closer and he stiffens.

"We're... I'm... a little worried about you," she says quietly.

"Why is that?"

"You're drinking a lot."

When he turns to walk away, she catches his hand.

"Please, Gordon. Talk to me."

He looks down, his eyes beginning to fill with tears. He shakes his head, pulls his hand free and walks down the hill toward his motorcycle. She catches up to him.

"Gordon. Gordon!"

He stops. "What do you want from me?"

"I... Nothing. I just want to know you're okay."

"I'm fine."

Behind him, the sounds of conversation move closer. He pictures the faces, the forced smiles. North, with the Berrigan sons. Family and friends, well-heeled and polite, duly somber. Suddenly claustrophobic, he rocks forward and jumps nearly all the way to the Yamaha in one leap. The voices on the hill grow louder, but he does not look back. He does not want to see Caroline standing in shocked silence or explaining his eccentricity to her fiancée.

Her fiancée.

Ignoring his helmet, Gordon swings on, kicks the starter and roars away.

Chapter 30

Beasts

For weeks, Gordon does not leave his apartment, except to have lunch at the bar each day. When Caroline stops by, Gordon barely makes eye contact with her and she walks out frustrated and confused. For weeks, Gordon does not shave, showers rarely and speaks only to Jalen, Stan and Martín. Nearly everyone in town believes he has lost his mind. Stinking of bourbon, he hardly seems to notice the families that switch lunch tables to keep their children away from him. Each day at noon, Martín places his private bottle next to his plate and allows him to pour his own drinks, which he does liberally. Social media is rife with pictures of his demise. Even Stainfield has mocked his unkempt appearance.

One day a letter arrives on university stationery; Gordon is invited to a meeting of the board of trustees. He texts Stan, who gets to Gordon's apartment fifteen minutes later. They talk it over for a while, then conference Jalen in and talk some more. They agree that they will ride together in Jalen's Audi to the hotel where the meeting will take place.

"Can you get it together by then?" Stan asks Gordon.

"Yeah, man, all good."

On the morning of the meeting, Gordon comes down in his work shirt, oily jeans and motorcycle boots. He has showered and shaved, but his only concession to formality is the rumpled, grass-stained suit jacket he picked up off his floor. Stan notes that he still reeks of booze. When Gordon walks into the conference room, several of the board members sneer as if they expected nothing less from him. Gordon looks at no one, shambles to a seat in the rear corner and drops his backpack onto the floor. Jalen smiles and makes a gracious pass through the crowd, chatting about Georgia football and life after the NFL. Stan sees a few familiar faces and greets them warmly. At last, the session is called to order. The chairman reads out the agenda and calls Dr. Carson forward to address the first item: funding and future planning for the Maker's Lab.

"As I am sure most of you know," Carson begins, "we have had an unfortunate series of events concerning one of the students at the Lab, Wendell Stainfield. He comes from a rather challenging home environment. His mother recently passed away from a drug overdose, and his father has been only nominally employed for the past several years."

"Actually, that's not true," Gordon says, his clear, authoritative tone not at all in keeping with his unkempt appearance. He stands and takes a manila folder from his backpack. "Mr. Stainfield is currently in the employ of North Industries and has been for thirteen weeks and four days. To date, he has been paid a total of seventy-four thousand, eight hundred sixty five dollars. I will circulate copies of his cancelled checks after the meeting."

Gordon sits down and folds his hands politely. Startled, Carson clears his throat and gathers himself.

"Mr. Stainfield has filed a lawsuit against one of our lab assistants, Gordon Longmeier, whose acquaintance you have just been fortunate enough to make."

Gordon smiles and waves at everyone.

"Mr. Stainfield's complaint alleges that Mr. Longmeier manipulated his son Wendell into signing over to a shell corporation, owned by Mr. Longmeier, the intellectual property rights to an invention that Wendell created in the Maker's Lab."

"If I may," Gordon interjects. He rises again and takes another folder from his bag. "I have here the notarized copies of Wendell Stainfield's original U.S. Patent Office application and filing. He filed it in his own name, as was his legal right even as a minor. There are no other names on the filing, save for his attorney's name as required by the form. No other contracts can supersede this legal filing or modify its ownership without an amendment. I will circulate it after the meeting."

As Gordon sits again, several of the trustees look back at Carson with raised eyebrows. Carson continues.

"The lawsuit also alleges that Mr. Longmeier, Professor Stanley Malkovich and Jalen Woods, attorney, formed a limited liability partnership with the intention of coercing Wendell Stainfield to take funding from it in exchange for control of his invention."

Before Gordon can stand again, most of the eyes in the room turn back to him. He reaches into his backpack and holds up another manila folder.

"The original incorporation papers of our limited liability partnership were filed six years ago by myself and Mr. Malkovich, when Wendell was eight years old. We formed it to create a business entity to own and manage my Shiva technology and its related patents. Mr. Woods joined the partnership upon his retirement from professional football. As to the current purpose of this entity, in addition to administering our own intellectual property filings, it is indeed to fund the startup ventures of students such as Wendell. However, we do not take any ownership stake in these ventures and provide only interest-free loans between our partnership and their companies, which are usually owned in part by a trusted adult. In Wendell's case, the adult signatory is his maternal grandfather, Gerald Cobb. Wendell did not trust his father to represent his interests fairly."

There is a titter of reaction as Gordon sits down. At the lectern, Carson shuffles his papers before speaking again.

"Due to the controversy surrounding this legal matter,"

Carson intones, "the Lab's main benefactor, Catonsville Tool & Die, has decided to revisit its funding commitments for the next five years. Since the university cannot afford to fund the Lab as part of its overall operating budget, unless Catonsville's concerns can be allayed, the existence of the Lab will be endangered. In order to protect the Lab and ensure its continued operation, we propose to permanently sever the university's relationship with Mr. Longmeier."

Gordon stands again.

"With permission, a question?"

"Yes, Mr. Longmeier?"

"Who is 'we?'"

Carson's face flushes crimson.

"Is it, perhaps, you and David North?" Gordon asks. "The same David North who recently acquired Catonsville Tool & Die against the wishes of its founder, Dan Berrigan? Is it the same David North from whom these seven wire transfers were made into your own investment account, totaling three hundred forty-two thousand dollars?"

Gordon holds up yet another folder.

"The same David North who sent you a total of fifty-six emails discussing myself and Professor Malkovich, and our stubborn insistence on protecting the intellectual property of our students from rapacious investors like, for example, David North?"

Another folder.

"Or the same David North with whom you had this conversation--"

Gordon holds up a thumb drive.

"--in the atrium of the Maker's Lab, in front of the security guard, Mr. Leonard Williams, whose sworn, notarized testimony is here."

Another folder.

"A conversation in which you discussed the initiation of Mr. Stainfield's lawsuit as a means of removing me from the Lab and isolating Stan Malkovich, a non-tenured, homosexual professor, over whom you believed the university would have powerful leverage to force access to our students' inventions? Or more to the point, my own?"

Gordon gathers all of his materials and walks to the front of the room.

"I think, ladies and gentlemen, that if there is a controversy here it is that a corrupt administrator has placed his own financial self-interest over the well-being of the students entrusted to the care of this university."

He places the materials down on the lectern, directly under Carson's nose.

"Thanks to Mr. Stainfield's lawsuit," Gordon continues, "the discovery process allowed us access to all of this lovely evidence, since it was material to the case. The audio recordings were made by our security system, which was installed to protect our students' work from people like this man right here. The court has indicated that it will rule with us, that Mr. Stainfield's lawsuit is baseless. Oh, and a sealed copy of everything has been sent to Sue Eisenstern at the Banner-Herald, to be unsealed and published unless the immediate termination of the university's relationship with Dr. Carson is announced today."

Carson's knuckles whiten as he grips the podium. Gordon turns and walks back to his seat.

"Uh, Mr. Longmeier," one of the trustees says. "If we sever relations with Dr. Carson publicly, even if it exonerates you, it only adds more controversy to the story. Catonsville will surely not want that."

"No sir, they won't," Gordon confirms. "And since Catonsville is David North now, if you fire Dr. Carson they will almost certainly terminate their funding commitments to us."

The trustees begin to buzz with conversation. Gordon stands and walks to the front of the room again. This time he is holding a single large white envelope.

"When North acquired Catonsville, part of the agreement involved paying out its minority partners. In other words, Stan, Jalen and me. Each of us received seventy-five million dollars for our shares in the company."

Gordon places the new envelope down in front of Carson.

"Enclosed is our letter of commitment, along with a check for fifteen million dollars -- the next five years' operating budget for the Lab. Provided Dr. Carson is terminated, we will fund one hundred percent of the Lab's expenses from this moment forward."

The degree to which an august institution might bend its standards to accommodate a request usually corresponds to the power of the person making it. So, two weeks later when Gordon walks up to the clubhouse of the famous old golf course and sees several massive tents set up on the ninth hole, he realizes how much sway Congressman Highsmith now has in this region. Gordon will not be able to bluff his way into Caroline's wedding. Instead, he walks around the perimeter fence to scout for another way onto the property. He saunters casually to a stand of trees and peers through to the fairway beyond, where most of the wedding guests seem to be occupied with cocktail hour in the tent closest to the green. A larger tent shelters rows of chairs that face a small floral archway. Glancing around, Gordon takes a few steps back to move out from under the trees and quickly jumps over them to the fairway. With his hands in his pockets, he ambles into the cocktail tent and joins the party.

"Gordon?"

Patrick Berrigan looks at him with disbelief. Regaining his composure, he introduces Gordon to his wife, whose empty wine glass explains the hunger with which she admires the dashing figure Gordon cuts in his tuxedo.

"Could I get you another?" Gordon offers, pointing at her glass. "I'm going for one myself. And you, Patrick?"

They thank him as he retreats to the bar for three glasses of wine, scouting as he goes. Spotting David and Caroline, he also sees her father near them. Highsmith's campaign for the U.S. Senate has been buying ads all over Georgia; Gordon has even seen them during the baseball broadcasts at Martín's. Flanking Highsmith are his bodyguard and a small man who holds a camera identical to the one that Martín took from the photographer-spy. The man exactly matches the description Martín gave, except that the front of his pants now appears to be dry. Congressman Highsmith turns and looks directly at Gordon, who turns away, scoops up the three wine glasses and winds through the crowd toward the Berrigans.

"Hoping to break this up?"

The familiar voice is directly behind Gordon. He turns to face the congressman and apologizes for not being able to shake hands. Highsmith's hair is graying at the temples but his face has not changed much from the days when he lived across the street from Gordon. His pupils are pinpricks, his eyes electric with anger.

"I said, are you hoping to break this up?"

"No, sir."

"Then why the fuck are you here?"

"Daddy, play nice."

Caroline sweeps in and gives Gordon a theatrical kiss on the cheek. Her whisper is a hiss.

"Yes, why the fuck are you here?"

"Business," Gordon mumbles, mesmerized by her beauty.

The textured white silk of Caroline's dress makes the velvet of her tanned décolletage even more captivating to Gordon. She notices the Berrigans staring at the wine glasses in Gordon's hands. Removing two, she walks the drinks over to them. When she returns, she plucks the third from Gordon's hand.

"You're really more of a whiskey guy anyway, aren't you?"

"You look... beautiful," Gordon stammers.

"Yes, she does," says the congressman, his tone laced with disdain. "I don't recall seeing you on the guest list."

"Late addition, Daddy."

"You're too old for toys, Caroline."

Still distracted by Caroline's beauty, Gordon misses the slight. When David North walks over and extends a hand to Gordon, the social gravity of their cluster proves too strong for Patrick to resist. He drifts in and joins the circle, then raises his glass.

"To the happy couple!"

Gordon is the only one without a beverage so he takes out his flask and raises it to general laughter, but puts it away unopened. The congressman's face is stone.

"How's the conversion going?" Patrick asks David.

"Conversion?" Caroline asks.

"Oh, yes sweetheart," David replies. "You've been busy with wedding details, so I didn't want to bother you with it. We're converting all of Catonsville's manufacturing facilities to produce our inventory."

"Literally turning plowshares into swords," crows Congressman Highsmith.

Gordon laughs loudly at this comment, for an uncomfortably long time.

"Do I amuse you?" asks Highsmith.

"No sir, but *he* does." Gordon nods at David.

"*He* is the man who is about to expose the second side of your glorious god Shiva," the congressman declares. "Shiva the creator, and now Shiva the destroyer."

"Is he now?" Gordon smiles.

"That much energy, focused and contained and directed with such precision..." David's eyes widen. "What a weapon!"

Gordon laughs again. "You'd have better luck converting a potter's wheel into a trebuchet. Tell me, how *is* the conversion going?"

David's smile fades. "We're experiencing a few software glitches, but nothing we can't overcome. Our best people are on it."

"Let me guess, in the security interface?"

"Yes, how--?"

"Something about a failed biometric confirmation?"

David stares at Gordon, who raises one thumb again.

"Missing one of these? There are only two in the world that will work, and I'm still using this one. Stan's got the other one. What you bought were machines that were specifically created to produce Catonsville's line of products and nothing else. It's in the contracts--"

Gordon turns to Patrick.

"--that I worked out with the adult in the room, your father. Contracts that will 'survive any acquisition or sale' as your man Porter said. Mr. Berrigan agreed with Stan and me, that no Shiva should ever be able to produce anything that we did not personally approve of. So we added the biometric clause to the contract, which must have looked a little odd to your lawyers, and built that security feature into every machine."

Gordon turns back to David.

"So basically, you're in the plowshare business after all."

Highsmith's eyes bore into Gordon, who does not blink. The congressman looks at David.

"So these fucking things can't be used as super weapons after all?"

David's mouth opens, but makes no sound.

"They can't even be used to make water pistols," Gordon says. "But relax. I have a solution."

Gordon reaches into his chest pocket and pulls out a folded document.

"This is a contract proposal to buy all ten of your Catonsville locations for exactly the same price that you paid for them. Unless of course you'd rather operate them as Mr. Berrigan intended?"

Gordon looks at Patrick, who shrugs and watches David's reaction. David snatches the document from Gordon and quickly scans the pages.

"Titanglass? Never heard of it. What is this, a joke?"

"No, it's not a joke," Gordon says quietly. "It's a lifeline. Take it."

"How can a company we've never heard of afford a contract worth more than a billion dollars?" asks Highsmith.

"My partners and I have launched a new company, Titanglass, Inc. We have a conservative initial valuation of roughly two billion dollars. I say conservative because there is no way to realistically project the total value of an entire industry. We are likely to control one hundred percent of the plate glass market within five to ten years."

Now it is Congressman Highsmith's turn to laugh long and

loud.

"How the fuck do you plan to control an entire industry in five years?"

"We have a product that will transform the world. Transparent, bulletproof titanium."

Highsmith's jaw drops. David looks down at the document in his hands, stricken. Caroline looks at him and then at Gordon, who smiles and flicks the edge of David's wine glass. It dings and echoes around their silent circle.

"It's enough money to keep you drunk for the rest of your life," Gordon says, then turns and walks away.

Chapter 31

Rising

In the lobby of the grand old clubhouse, Gordon is surprised to hear shouting. He turns and sees Congressman Highsmith barreling at him and yelling something that Gordon can't quite understand, eyes wild with hatred, hands curved into claws. Gordon braces himself for the impact and feels the man's weight smash into him. Highsmith grabs Gordon's lapels and drives him down into the ground.

"Goddamn you, Longmeier! You ruined my daughter's wedding day!"

When Highsmith's hands close around Gordon's neck, Gordon feels electricity surge through and around his body. The sensation is similar to what he felt with Caroline, but far more painful. Highsmith's eyes open wide as his mouth twists with pain.

He feels it too.

That is the last thought Gordon has before he loses consciousness.

Gordon opens his eyes and sees Joe crouched over him, one hand cupped behind his head, wearing a look of grave concern. The lobby is nearly empty, but the room beyond is filled with people straining to see what's happening. Two policemen hold the crowd back. Slumped in an armchair, Highsmith stares groggily at the floor as his bodyguard takes his pulse.

"Sir, is your son okay?" one of the officers asks Joe.

"He's fine. I'll take him home now."

Joe works his arms under Gordon's body and lifts him off the floor.

"We'd like to get a statement from him about the assault," the officer says.

"Ain't no need for all that. He's fine."

Joe walks out to the old Bronco parked at the top of the circular driveway, lays Gordon into the front seat and walks around to sit behind the wheel.

"The lightning..." Gordon murmurs. "It happened again when he choked me, but it hurt worse this time."

Joe looks at Gordon with concern, then nods. As he starts the engine, Caroline bursts through the front door and runs toward the Bronco. She arrives just as Joe is beginning to pull away and slaps at the window.

"Gordon! Gordon, wait!"

Joe stops the truck and turns off the engine. Caroline opens the door.

"Are you okay?" She holds Gordon's face in her hands, her bridal makeup streaked with tears. "What happened?"

"Your father..." Gordon mumbles, beginning to come around. Slowly, he sits up. "The lightning."

"The what?"

"That electric thing when you touched me. Remember when we were singing back in college? And then that night when it snowed, on the bus? Your dad grabbed me and it happened again. But Jesus, it was strong."

"Why?" She steps back from Gordon. "Why today? Why here? Why'd you do all this?"

Joe bows his head, looking mournful. Gordon steps out of the Bronco and stands in front of Caroline. Fully awake now, his eyes are clear and peaceful.

"I guess I just wanted to see if you'd really marry him," he says softly. "If I really had to let you go."

He shrugs out of his jacket and begins to unbutton his shirt. He reaches down, lifts his pant legs and takes off the weights, then takes off his shirt and does the same with the ones on his arms.

"Gordon, no," Caroline says.

Gordon opens the velcro on his vest and lets it slip down into his left hand. With his other hand, he takes hers and presses something into it, then kisses her on the lips and whispers, "I love you."

Caroline looks down and sees the rough steel lightning bolt, the first object Shiva had ever produced. Gordon smiles and lets go of the vest. As he rises into the sky, too late she grabs at him and falls to her knees. Floating through the treetops, he can hear her wail.

Gordon closes his eyes, overcome with an emotion he cannot name. The knowledge that he must let Caroline go had come to him in an instant, but not in the way he might have imagined. It felt, it feels, mostly like love. Like saving a life more precious than his own, or giving his own to save hers. It is not about her wedding, he knows. Or maybe it is to her, but to him the event does not matter at all. The vows of possession, of permanence... Mere words. What he thinks of now is the soul within her, the life force that feels and moves with its own will, a force that to him is beyond possession. He feels connected to it and even as he moves further away from her, he feels his own animating energy mingle with hers and grow stronger.

He feels the power of her father's connection to her too, focused in the instant of the attack only on her well-being. Despite his scheming and his cynical use of her marriage for political gain, at the moment his hands touched Gordon's neck, Highsmith was nothing but a father, one of the two people who had given Caroline life; a life which was more precious to Highsmith than his own. In Highsmith's instinct to protect his daughter, Gordon sees a reflection of his own love for her, and understands that his own presence in her life will only ever be meaningful to him if it gives her soul the same joy that hers gives him.

The air grows thin and cold, and Gordon feels as if his ribcage is shrinking. Each breath is shorter, faster, not from panic but simply from the machine of his body responding to its needs. Yet even in his distress, Gordon feels serene. The emotion that had overcome him begins to clarify as he thinks of his love for Caroline; it is joy. His heart brims with gratitude for the time he has spent with her, for all that they have shared, for moments warmed and enriched, for a lifetime given and received. He sees her face sleeping peacefully across the pillow, waking with a slow smile, her scent enveloping him as the vision of her whispers to him with one word, again and again: Home.

His eyes swim with tears, first of happiness and then of regret. An animal fear begins to rise in him, a panic that wants to claw its way back to her, to rip and destroy anything standing between them. The love that had buoyed his serenity now yields to a desperate need for her, for more time, for more...

Caroline.

When he looks down, he is shocked at how high he has risen.

Across his skin, he feels a chill that begins to sharpen. It grows stronger, harder, more painful. His muscles constrict, involuntarily bending and contorting his body. He looks around at the sky, the patchwork of houses and farms, the curving horizon. The pain grows more intense, tearing away his peace and filling it with terror. Suddenly, urgently aware of the distance between them, one thought floods his fading consciousness, one idea, screaming in his brain until he cries out loud.

"Caroline!"

The electrical torture tightens around his skin like barbed wire, like a serpent of broken glass. It is not a sign or a clue or a benevolent connection. It is pain, raw and pure, physical pain intertwined with the torment of knowing what it is to love someone so much that you will take on their suffering; to love them so much that you crave their agonies as well as their ecstasies. To a love like that, the only hell is disconnection, and he has cast himself into it.

Ropes of fire constrict around his chest, squeezing off air, shearing his skin. His mind roars for her, knowing that she is the one thing he cannot live without, and that she has chosen to live her life without him.

The coils of lightning finally grip him so tightly that he cannot hold a coherent thought. He closes his eyes and stares into the darkness, begging for death, craving deliverance from this pain. With what feels like it will be his last breath, Gordon cries out to the God who has put this horrible burden of love upon him, because he knows with certainty that it came from the Eternal, and that there can be no harmony for him in this life or the next if this love is not served. He cries out because he knows now that his voice will be heard by that God, but the cry he releases is not one of hope or even pleading. It is submission, acceptance of the awful gift of a love that will never end, and that will never be returned. As his body empties of air and his voice trails off, he feels a stillness settle over his mind. His limbs relax and he feels the chains of flame begin to release, and he understands that the bindings were not so much around him as inside of him, and that the very power that had caused him so much pain is now beginning to surge within him as strength. As this sensation grows, the physical boundaries of his body seem to fade as they do when he sleeps in his weightlessness. His heart surges with love, not only for Caroline but for the spirit within her that is also within him, and that is flowing through him now and gathering him back to Itself. In his last moment of consciousness he smiles, small and knowing, and thinks to himself that the answer was right there all along.

And then he begins to descend.

Chapter 32

Home

Still in her wedding dress, Caroline sits at Martín's bar wearing Gordon's tuxedo jacket. She feels a weight in the vest pocket and pulls out his flask, then opens it and takes a drink. Martín chuckles at her surprised reaction. He reaches down into the well and comes up with Gordon's private bottle.

"Unsweet tea," Martín explains.

"He used to scrub his hairline with bourbon so it smelled like real hooch," Stan adds. "Had you all pretty well fooled."

"He stumbled around like a drunk for two months, but he was drinking iced tea?" Caroline wonders. "Why?"

"Said he was 'harmonizing with the beast,'" Jalen answers. "Whatever that means. He said he couldn't tell anyone but us, me and Stan. And Martín. He felt bad about that."

Caroline's eyes are filled with sadness, but not regret.

"It does sound a little loco," Martín admits. "But when he made his move, none of them seen it coming."

Gordon's motorcycle helmet sits on the bar in front of Caroline. She pulls it close and hugs it tight, then leans her face against it and begins to cry.

"Oh, sweet girl." Julia rests her hand on Caroline's back. "You know you are the only one he ever loved."

Caroline sniffles and nods.

"Joe said it had to be this way," Martín says.

Caroline looks up. "Why does Joe get to be the final authority on this?"

"He been through it, Cariña. The flying thing. He survived it."

The door jingles and Ravi steps in from the dark sidewalk and looks around.

"Why's everyone so glum?"

"Gordon's gone," Stan answers quietly.

"Gone...?" Ravi's eyes widen. "Like, dead?"

When Joe finds Gordon he is rigid with cold, lying in a field between two small farmhouses. Joe cradles his son, trying to warm the ashen skin with his breath. Gordon's pulse is thready, his breathing faint. Joe lifts Gordon's necklace, closes the stone in his palm and thinks of Emily as he begins to squeeze his own heat into it. Part of him holds back, understanding the mercy that death might bring, and knowing from his own experience the sentence of loneliness and isolation that Gordon is likely to serve if he survives his Rising. Still, he cannot help smiling when Gordon's eyes open. He stands and carries Gordon to the Bronco. Blasting the heat, Joe drives as fast as he can toward Athens but it is after midnight when the door jingles and he walks in supporting Gordon's weak shuffle.

Caroline rushes to them and hugs Gordon, sobbing into his chest. He puts his arms around her. She hugs him more tightly and notices that he is no longer wearing his body weights. She looks at Joe.

"It's over," Joe confirms. "He made it through."

Gordon kisses the top of her head. So far from the apex of his torment, safe and warm on the ground with her, his heart still races with fear of the next words she will say, and of the existence to which those words will condemn him. He braces himself, anticipating her kind concern, her polite exit, her return to the life that hours earlier she had vowed to begin with someone else.

"Don't ever leave me again," she whispers.

Gordon pulls back, astonished. He takes her left hand and sees... no ring.

"We never got to the ceremony part." She smiles. "Some joker busted everything up, and after that the bride got cold feet."

Later that summer, high above the trees and buildings of Athens, Gordon holds Caroline tightly as the sun begins to set. She nestles her face into his shoulder as he kisses her hair. When he spots a familiar figure far below, he nudges her, and she looks down to watch Wendell kick the starter and gun the Yamaha away from the Lab. She smiles and rests her head against Gordon's cheek.

"I hope the crazy little bastard doesn't make me regret giving it to him," Gordon murmurs. "But we got better ways to get around now."

Acknowledgements

This story finally crystallized one July in Ann Arbor, Michigan, on a college visit with my wife, Julie, and our daughter, Emma. With the energy and diversity of that town as a backdrop, Gordon began to take on three dimensions, and his narrative began to flow. But as the demand for authentic detail increased, I had to look closer to home for another college town in which to set the story. There was only ever one choice: Athens, Georgia.

I want to acknowledge the people who live on the margins of the majority here in Georgia, men and women of talent, color and conscience who have lent their blood and sweat to the work of civil rights, fair treatment and basic kindness. Often people of deep faith, and always people of boundless empathy, they quietly raise a candle of hope against gales of intolerance. Many of them find a home in places like Athens. Their numbers and their power grow every day, as people from all walks of political life join their ranks. To the Georgians who place love and liberty ahead of anger and repression, this book is for you.

It is also for my wife, Julie Demilio, whose love and constant support fuel everything I do. If there is a north star in my sky, you are it. Thank you for always guiding me back to the light. I love you.

I am grateful for the insight and gentle correction shared by patient readers, including Julie and our daughter, Emma Demilio, my mother, Renata Bouterse, and my friends Matt Tarkenton, Beth Sterne, Tess McKenna, Luis Castro, Cecilia De la Rosa and Tom Shamy. To Beth, and to Chris Morocco, I am grateful for a perspective on Athens that only a UGA grad or a native could provide.

A special thank you to Michael Romeo for lending his professional editor's pen and his avuncular good humor to the process of helping me correct my many grammatical mistakes. Any errors on this page are not his fault; he has not seen it yet.

I'd also like to thank Julie, Emma and our other daughter, Lila Demilio, for their help with the book cover design. Your keen eyes and honest feedback were greatly appreciated.

In addition, I appreciate the moral support of readers who expressed interest in the book, but who could not finish it in time to contribute to the editing process: Ryan McLoughlin, Laura Fenn, Scott Pioli, Mark Shapiro, Josh Chambers, Matt Whalen, Chris Schubert, Meghan McGuinness and Bill O'Connor. Knowing each of you were reading the book made the writing process feel a little less isolated.

To my parents, Renata Bouterse and Al D'Emilio, a big thank you for a lifetime of love and encouragement.

Last, but certainly not least, I'd like to thank Sandra Sobieraj Westfall for taking time away from her conversations with President Obama and President-elect Biden to read my book. You are the undisputed champion of blurb writing.

Author's note: If you enjoyed *Lightfoot Rising*, please take a moment to post a positive review on Amazon.com. Many thanks! Mike

Made in the USA
Columbia, SC
20 October 2022

69766775R00169